D1037757

THE JEALOUS SON

MICHELE CHYNOWETH

THE JEALOUS SON

A NOVEL

MICHELE CHYNOWETH

MANTLE ROCK
PUBLISHING LLC
MantleRockPublishingLLC.com

©2018 by Michele Chynoweth

Published by Mantle Rock Publishing LLC
2879 Palma Road
Benton, KY 42025
http://mantlerockpublishingllc.com

Printed in the United States of America

All rights reserved. No part of this publication may be reproduced, stored in a retrieval system, or transmitted in any form or by any means—for example, electronic, photocopy and recording— without the prior written permission of the publisher. The only exception is a brief quotation in printed reviews.

ISBN 978-1-945094-89-7

Cover by Diane Turpin at dianeturpindesigns.com

All characters are fictional, and any resemblance to real people, either factional or historical, is purely coincidental.

Published in association with Cyle Young of Hartline Literary Agency, Pittsburgh, PA.

ALSO BY MICHELE CHYNOWETH:

The Faithful One
The Peace Maker
The Runaway Prophet

PRAISE FOR MICHELE CHYNOWETH'S NOVELS:

The Faithful One

"…an exploration of what a contemporary Job might look like, Chynoweth's tale should more than satisfy."

—KIRKUS REVIEWS

"Understanding faith can be perplexing for some of us but the story Michele tells in this profound book is worth reading by all of us. She lets us know that faith is not only a mystery, it is a progression of our lives and a product of God Almighty for us to live by day after day."

—DR. THELMA WELLS, (AKA "MAMA T" OF WOMEN OF FAITH CONFERENCES), FOUNDER OF A WOMAN OF GOD MINISTRIES AND GENERATION LOVE-DIVINE EXPLOSION, SPEAKER, AUTHOR, TELEVISION HOST, AND PROFESSOR

"It often seems that the great characters of the Bible are so far removed from us. We sanitize them and dehumanize them. *The Faithful One* puts the character of Job into a whole new contemporary light. The story makes his struggles so much more tangible and relatable to today's audience. Kudos to Michele Chynoweth for helping us get a better handle on what Job may have gone through. It certainly makes my struggles seem much smaller!"

—GUS LLOYD, AUTHOR OF *MAGNETIC CHRISTIANITY* AND *A MINUTE IN THE CHURCH* AND HOST OF "SEIZE THE DAY" ON THE CATHOLIC CHANNEL

≫→

The Peace Maker

"In this contemporary retelling of the Bible's First Book of Samuel, the story of David and Abigail stands the test of time."

—KENTUCKY MONTHLY MAGAZINE

"*The Peace Maker* by Michele Chynoweth is the type of story that many young women have lived in one way or another. Many of us have been like Chessa, caught between the one we love and doing what's right…"

—5-STAR REVIEW BY SAMANTHA RIVERA FOR READERS' FAVORITE INTERNATIONAL BOOK AWARDS

≫→

The Runaway Prophet

"With another novel that will put you on the edge of your seat, author Michele Chynoweth delights again with *The Runaway Prophet*. Prepare to be swept up inside this page-turner…through one heart-stopping event after another, Rory and a team of investigators battle against the clock to remove the mafia and the dangerous bomb they've planted somewhere underground. *The Runaway Prophet* will keep you riveted."

—ALEXANDRA KARLESSAS FOR *DELAWARE TODAY MAGAZINE*

"*The Runaway Prophet* was hard to put down. The author has done a great job of taking the Book of Jonah and making it come to life in the modern era. It's a great book—now it needs to be made into a movie!"

—PASTOR CHRIS WHALEY, AUTHOR OF *THE MASKED SAINT*, A MEMOIR AND MAJOR MOTION PICTURE (WINNER OF BEST PICTURE, 2015 INTERNATIONAL CHRISTIAN FILM FESTIVAL)

AUTHOR'S NOTE

The Jealous Son is based on the story of Cain and Abel in the Book of Genesis in the Bible. It is the latest of my contemporary suspense/romance novels that re-imagine Old Testament stories, written so people today can better relate to the Bible story and understand God's message. While certain elements of the original book have obviously been changed to modernize the story for today's readers, I have, through research and consultation with religious leaders and clergy, made every attempt to stay as true to the original storyline as possible. Whether or not you're familiar with the story of Cain and Abel, I hope you enjoy *The Jealous Son* and it inspires you to have a little more faith in God's plan, no matter what you may be going through in your own life, and know that you "can do all this through Him who gives you strength."

—Michele Chynoweth

For any parent who has ever lost a child…may you find the Peace that is not of this world.

And for my grandchildren, Marley and Liam, thank you for the joy you bring into my world.

ACKNOWLEDGMENTS

I am extremely grateful to the following people who made this novel the best it could be: for his theological and Biblical perspective and authentication, Reverend James Yeakel, OSFS, pastor of Immaculate Conception Roman Catholic Church in Elkton, Md., MA in Theology and PhD in Clinical Social Work, former college professor and licensed clinical therapist; for his historical research and current knowledge regarding the Navajo people and traditions portrayed in this book, Bernhardt Dotson, MA, former journalist and current public relations director of Diné College, a four-year, tribally controlled college serving the 27,000-square-mile Navajo Nation with campuses in Arizona and New Mexico; for their help in authenticating characters, storylines and settings in the book: Eileen Thompson, BS, CRPS, CSCAD, assistant program director and licensed addiction counselor at Harbor of Grace Enhanced Recovery Center in Havre de Grace, Md.; Patricia Lake, MA, adjunct professor and teacher; Teri Repetsky Speck, RN, BSN; Jennifer Coulter, RN, BSN; and Tonya Schulte, a business owner in Phoenix, Az. I would also like to thank my editor, Pam Harris at Mantle Rock Publishing, my literary agent Cyle Young of Hartline Literary Agency, and for his unwavering support and undying love, my husband Bill Chynoweth

"For where you have envy and selfish ambition, there you find disorder and every evil practice."
–James, 3:16

PROLOGUE

SO MUCH DANGER could lie in so much beauty. Cameron Trellis marveled at the phenomenal landscape sprawling before him.

The sun was slipping into its late afternoon yawn, slanting light onto the rocky cliffs of the Grand Canyon, turning coral into garnet, jade into emerald, slate into onyx, and would soon send shadows into night.

Like the depths of the ocean which swallowed ships whole, Cameron mused further. The jagged, icy peaks of Mount Everest which beckoned unceasingly to risk takers who sometimes didn't make it to the top and back. A conniving woman who played you and then left your heart shattered in tiny pieces.

"There is an average of thirty deaths each year here at the Grand Canyon, mostly people acting foolishly and ending up in accidental falls." Cameron had overheard the canyon ranger's remark to one of the many tour groups passing through.

If he didn't act soon, he would run out of light and out of time. He bent over and picked up a small stone. He straightened and hurled it off the cliff, listening for the pinging sound that never came.

He had been to the canyon's south rim trails enough times to know precisely the spot he and his little brother Austin needed to reach in time to carry out their plan to grab a bite to eat and find a place to see the legendary Grand Canyon sunset.

My little brother. Cameron smiled as a fond memory of his childhood crept unwillingly into his thoughts. Cameron remembered the day Austin was born. He had been three years old and so excited at the time to have a new playmate.

Even though he was twenty-two now and two inches taller, Austin was still his "little" brother. The one he had protected when a bully in grade school tried to stuff him in a locker; the one he had let tag along with his girlfriend on a double date when they were teenagers; the one he had partied with after so many band performances together.

"Hey, Cameron, come here!" Austin shouted from where he stood a few yards ahead of his brother, closer to the ledge of the canyon, standing still and looking up, staring at the top of a scraggly pine tree.

Cameron was winded as he approached his brother. The last mile of the climb had been uphill, and Austin, who was in much better shape, had easily outdistanced him. *I need to work out more*, he reprimanded himself, noting Austin wasn't out of breath at all as he drew closer.

He walked up behind his brother, who still stood gazing skyward and was now pointing to the treetop. Cameron looked up and saw the object of Austin's attention, a large raven perched on a branch, its head darting this way and that.

"Yeah, that's nice, c'mon, we better move, the sun's going down and we don't want to get stuck here in the dark," Cameron said. "Plus, I remember a good spot to see the sunset that's just up ahead if we hurry."

"Hey, bird," Austin cooed softly, ignoring his older brother, not even glancing in his direction. "Look, Cameron, it's got something in its beak. I think it's a little mouse."

"That's awful, Austin. I don't want to see that. Let's go." Cameron turned to trudge back to the main path that would lead along the canyon's ridge toward the place he had in mind, but in a minute he realized Austin wasn't behind him. Austin remained fixed in his spot, gawking at the bird. "I think there's a nest up there and he, or she, is going to feed that mouse to her babies."

Irritated, Cameron walked back to somehow divert his brother's attention. The sun was slipping faster now. *I'm not going to let him ruin everything.*

But as he once again approached Austin from behind, another thought locked into Cameron's brain. From where he stood a few steps behind his younger brother, he could see out over the canyon ledge, and he caught a glimpse of the sea-green Colorado River snaking below, looking like a tiny serpent from this height. *We must be closer than I thought.* His selected destination also hovered above the river, which could only be seen from a few of the canyon walls.

Then he turned his attention to the back of his brother's curly mop of black hair. *Perhaps now would be a good time. Perhaps this is the destination.*

Cameron looked right and left, making sure no one was in sight, then strained to listen for any nearby sounds. He heard nothing, save for the distant cry of a hawk.

It would be over in a second. Drawing a deep breath of resolve, Cameron slowly inched toward his little brother until he was within arm's length and reached out his hand.

I

ELIZA

CHAPTER ONE

IT WAS the best Christmas ever, Eliza recalled now, humming the holiday tune, "It's Beginning to Look a Lot Like Christmas" in her head.

Of course, some of the lyrics seemed a bit ludicrous in Phoenix, where the temperature had reached seventy-three degrees that early December afternoon.

Still, Eliza and Alex Trellis had never failed to erect their artificial Christmas tree with the fake snow on the bough tips or to decorate with all the frivolity of folks in Rockefeller Center.

As she trimmed the five-foot-tall cactus that also stood in their family room with red and green miniature lights, she allowed her thoughts to drift back twenty-two years. Austin was just a month old and Cameron a little over three when their new family of four celebrated that first Christmas.

Eliza remembered clearly what Cameron had said after opening his last present, when she had asked her older son what gift he had liked best.

"My baby brover," he said, grinning, sitting cross-legged in his pajamas.

Eliza had cried, sitting on the sofa in her pink, terry-cloth bathrobe. Tears of joy in hearing her son's words, and tears of sadness that she couldn't be a better mom at the time.

AUSTIN'S difficult birth zapped all of Eliza's energy and strength, leaving none for her sweet boy Cameron. She had screamed in agony for at least twelve hours, the epidural failing to take, as the ten-pound baby lay breach within her, finally turning in the last few minutes to be born without a Caesarian section or anything to relieve the pain.

As if the birth hadn't been difficult enough, excessive bleeding and a punctured spinal cord almost killed her. Suffering severe migraines for days, Eliza was barely able to nurse baby Austin until the doctor called her back into the hospital to fix the tiny puncture in her spinal cord caused by a botched epidural administered when she was writhing in pain.

Nothing went right, including the fact that she had postpartum blues for weeks.

"Mommy, will you play with me?" Cameron would ask over and over.

"Mommy can't play, honey, I have a bad headache," she would say, turning on the Disney Channel for him to watch, sometimes for hours, as she lay back on the couch, a cold compress on her forehead.

And Daddy was no help at all.

Alex worked late nearly every night at the ABC Oil Company in Phoenix. He was the fleet manager for the wholesale oil company, a leading distributor of petroleum products on the West Coast. He had just been promoted to the position right before Austin was born.

Often Alex was the last one to leave the offices on Grand Street, making sure all of his drivers were accounted for and the oil trucks had safely arrived with their deliveries. If there were problems—a client calling to complain about a late delivery, a driver stuck in a bad thunderstorm, an accident blocking traffic—he was always the liaison, on the phone with drivers and clients, making sure both were safe and satisfied. It fell on him to stay and help make it right. It got old, being a single parent. Eliza harbored resentments that just turned into numbness over time.

But they needed Alex's paycheck, especially the overtime, since she was only working part-time from home doing data entry for a local accounting firm, and they had two little ones to raise.

Sometimes it all nearly felt unbearable. Until one day Eliza finally found relief.

THE NEXT CHRISTMAS, her friend Marsha Lake asked her to go to the local mall to get a new holiday dress.

Somehow Eliza had mustered up the courage to ask her husband for money to pay a babysitter for several hours. Cameron was five and Austin two, and Eliza desperately needed a break.

Alex put up a little bit of a fight but finally acquiesced, and always the resourceful friend, Marsha had given her a few names of sitters she had used in the past. She didn't need them anymore since her children were old enough to stay home alone.

Eliza felt a little guilty as she kissed her two boys and then waved goodbye to Patty, the sitter, a sixteen-year-old sprite with freckles and loads of energy.

"We'll be fine, Mrs. T, just go have fun," Patty said cheerfully, bouncing a smiling Austin from her hip as little Cameron woefully stared up at her from the floor with his questioning, big brown eyes.

"Okay, we'll be back in a few hours." Eliza heaved a sigh, turning from Cameron, holding back tears as she heard her little boy sniffle as she headed out the door.

Her confident, redheaded friend had to practically drag her by the hand into the various mall stores, urging her to try on dresses she couldn't afford, until she finally splurged on an outfit she couldn't resist. It was a white silk pantsuit with a floral print that somehow made her look thin, voluptuous, and sexy all at the same time. Eliza beamed at her reflection in the dressing room mirror. In this outfit she didn't look or feel like the frumpy, frazzled, bedraggled twenty-four-old she thought she had become. Sure, her long, black hair needed a trim, her skin could use a bit of bronzing in the sun, and her waist could stand to lose an inch or two. But in this outfit, she could see beyond all of that to the young, beautiful girl she had been before the children came along.

"You have to buy that outfit, you look amazing!" Marsha squealed with delight. Eliza did, charging the ninety-nine dollars to her credit card, once again ignoring the twinge of guilt that crept unwelcome into her psyche.

Her mood improved over drinks with Marsha to celebrate the "new" her. Marsha treated her to three large margaritas during happy hour at the Mexican tapas bar.

She felt so much better that Patty's news didn't phase her much, that Cameron had smacked his baby brother on the cheek, leaving behind a small, red splotch. "I sat him in time out and after that he was much better behaved," Patty chirped. "Still, I feel terrible, but …"

"It's okay, ish not your fault." Eliza heard herself slur and wanted to laugh but was rational enough to know better. She scolded herself mentally and handed Patty two twenties from her wallet. "Thank you, Patty."

"Oh, this is too much, Mrs. Trellis," Patty objected.

"No, that's okay, keep it, I hope we can get you to babysit again soon," Eliza replied, her fog starting to lift a bit. *If I pay her well this time, she'll come back. And maybe she'll overlook the fact that I'm drunk.*

"Okay, if you're sure, thanks, Mrs. T, see you again soon."

It must have worked, Eliza congratulated herself.

It was eight o'clock when she arrived home, so the kids were both fast asleep. Eliza had just enough time to slip into the outfit she had bought, sober up with a strong cup of coffee, and brush her teeth before Alex came through the front door, as always loosening his tie, looking exhausted.

But his face perked up when he saw his wife decked out, wearing red lipstick and jewelry. Usually she didn't even greet him, worn out herself from the kids, and was usually reading or fast asleep in the recliner, dressed in her worn, pink robe and slippers.

Without a word, she kissed him hungrily then pulled him by the tie into their bedroom, leaving him little time or inclination to ask questions or protest.

THE MORNING after was a different story.

"What is that red mark on Austin's cheek?" Alex sat at the breakfast table eating his bowl of cereal as Eliza simultaneously handed Cameron his milk and wiped some strained bananas from the baby's chin.

"Oh, that?" Eliza feigned indifference. "Patty said she thought Cameron may have accidentally hit his brother while they were playing."

"That doesn't look like an accident to me. Cameron, what did you do?" Alex addressed their older son, who looked at his father, his eyes welling with tears.

"Sorry, Daddy," Cameron said in his little boy voice.

"Why did you hit your brother?" Alex asked, his voice rising.

"I was mad he was touching my things," Cameron responded shyly.

"You meant to hit him?"

"Yes, but I didn't mean to hurt him."

"Well, it looks like you did hurt him, so you need to be punished for that." Alex stood, pulled Cameron by the arm out of his chair, spun him around, and spanked his backside twice, hard.

Eliza's heart leaped into her throat as her older son started to cry and then ran to hide in his bedroom.

"Why did you have to do that?" She turned to face her husband.

"Because he needs to know that wasn't okay," Alex said evenly. "And you should be teaching him that, not relying on some babysitter to do it."

Eliza sat silently, turning to finish feeding Austin, her heart pounding.

"By the way, how much was that new outfit you were wearing last night?"

"I'm not sure. I threw the price tag away."

"Now that's a lie, and you know it." Alex was straightening his tie in the hallway mirror as he talked, his tone tinged with anger, his face turning red. "You know we can't afford things like that. If it was more than fifty bucks, you'll have to take it back."

"You know I can't do that," Eliza retorted, wiping Austin's chin again and standing to face her husband, who was now grabbing his suit jacket and briefcase from the adjoining living room. He headed towards the front door. "Besides, you didn't seem to mind the price last night when you took it off me."

Alex wheeled around. "Why, you little…" He bit back his words, his mouth a grimace, turning his normally handsome face into an ugly mask of fury. Saying nothing more, he stomped away, slamming the front door closed behind him.

Eliza sat back down at the kitchen table, put her head in her hands, and wept.

"MY HUSBAND IS A GOOD MAN, he really is, it's just that, well, it's my fault he's doing the things he does now."

Eliza blew her nose into a tissue as she sat with Marsha in the mall's food court, her uneaten hamburger sitting cold before her. Marsha had gone with her friend to return the outfit. It was Saturday, and Alex had stayed home with the boys. It was a good thing she didn't get any makeup or food stains on it.

Walking past storefronts all decked out for the Christmas holidays just made Eliza feel more miserable. Knowing she couldn't spend much money, she told Marsha she had a headache and went home right after lunch. She had already done some of her Christmas shopping for the kids and her husband online, and even though she wanted to buy them more, her heart just wasn't into it.

When she got home, Alex and the boys were napping. Eliza

cheered up a bit knowing she would have a little quiet time to herself.

She sat down in the spare room that they had set up as an office and opened her laptop to check her emails. Eliza had applied for several part-time jobs and saw a few responses in her inbox. She hadn't told Alex about it, knowing he would object to her spending any time away from the kids. "We just have to make sacrifices, and besides, any job that means we have to pay for day care won't be worth it," he had said. While she was barely able to fit in the data entry work she was already doing during the kids' nap times, bed time, and "quiet" or TV time, Eliza figured perhaps she could find a way. Anything so she could have a little spending money and things didn't feel quite so tight. Besides, it wouldn't hurt to look for something better out there.

While scrolling through her emails, her breath caught in her throat. There was an email from their bank, and the subject line read, "Bank alert, past due credit card payment."

Alex handled all of their banking, checkbook balancing, budgeting, and bill paying. This was the first time she had ever received an email from their bank, even though all of their accounts were joint. Eliza had never questioned Alex's ability to handle their financial matters, nor did she want anything to do with it all.

Her fingers trembled as she hesitantly opened the email.

"Your credit card account xxx-x-x0254 is past due. The current balance is $5,523." Eliza blinked, not believing the figure before her eyes. How could that be? Even given her Christmas shopping online and even if her return had not gone through yet, she had spent nowhere near that much money in the past few months, not to mention the past few years.

It had to be a mistake. Her heart thumped with fear.

She decided to open up their bank account to take a look, but it had been so long since she had checked it that she couldn't remember the password. *Think!* She knew it was the kids' names coupled with an important date. Their wedding anniversary? Her birthday? She typed in all of the possible combinations she could think of, and still it wouldn't open.

One more try. CameronAustin1225. It worked. Alex must have changed the date. She watched the little circle spin until their bank account opened before her. She scanned the summary of accounts. There was a positive $225 in their checking account, a positive $990 in their savings account, and there it was, $5,523 staring back at her in their credit card account.

She and Alex had had credit issues in the past when they were just starting out in their marriage and at one point decided together to tear up their credit cards and just have one in case of emergency, which she had only used for Christmas and to splurge on the outfit she had bought then returned.

She clicked on the account number and saw several transactions, all labeled "Gila River Casinos." She glanced down the transaction sheet. There were a few payments of $100 or $250, and about a dozen $500 charges.

Her stomach knotted up, and for a moment she thought she was going to throw up the little bit of lunch she had eaten.

And then she heard a stirring, a man's footfalls shuffling in the distant corner of the ranch house, her husband making his way to where she sat. She had closed the door, but it was only a matter of minutes before he'd find her. She quickly closed the account window, shut down the computer, and willed herself to calm down, taking deep breaths like they had taught her in Lamaze class.

"Hey, what are you up to?" The office door swung open, and his words startled her even though she anticipated them.

"Nothing. I mean, just playing around on the computer, but I got bored so I was just going to come in and check on you and the kids." Eliza felt her face flush and turned away to pretend to straighten up a few papers and books on the desk. She stood and stretched, feigning boredom. "I guess I should have crawled in with you to take a nap instead."

"Hmmm…well we could go back to bed, but since I've already had a nap…" Alex playfully winked at her and smiled.

Eliza's stomach lurched, but she fought to control the nausea that resurfaced at his implication.

Mercifully, they heard the sound of Austin talking gibberish on the baby monitor, and then Cameron poked his head in from around his dad's legs. "Hi, Mommy, I'm hungry, can I have a snack?"

Eliza rolled her eyes and shrugged at her husband, trying to be playful. "Sure, honey, let me fix you a snack," she said, taking Cameron's hand to lead him to the kitchen.

"Maybe later," Alex whispered in her ear when she passed him in the doorway.

"I THINK your husband has a gambling addiction." Barbara Paulus, PhD, shifted slightly in her upholstered chair, where she sat facing Eliza who sat nervously fidgeting with a tissue in her hands on the small couch across the room.

Eliza had barely gotten any sleep the night she found out about the credit card debt. She had mulled over calling Marsha in the morning to vent her fears and anger but realized her friend was probably not the best confidante, having a penchant for gossip.

Eliza had done a good job of nearly isolating herself in her post-partum blues. And in her consummation with being a good wife and mother and working her part-time job, her world had shrunk even further. Marsha had become her only friend, and a superficial one at that.

But Eliza wasn't a stranger to loneliness.

CHAPTER TWO

ELIZA HAD ACTUALLY GROWN up as a girl named Anna in the Navajo clan of her mother, Wenona Hosteen, who had married her father, Paco Becenti, or rather, was married off to him by her parents when she was just seventeen.

She lived with her parents and two older sisters, Flo and Dena, within the borders of the Navajo Nation in Arizona. Anna was born with the native Navajo name of Anaba, but it was shortened to Anna by her older sisters, who couldn't quite say her whole name as toddlers.

Anna's father was a highly respected political Navajo leader, while her mother followed the traditions of the women of her clan, making beautiful native jewelry, sculptures, and other hand-made arts and crafts. They sold the items in the Native American Market at the scenic Oak Creek Canyon Vista Overlook off Highway 89-A. The open-air market sat atop the switchback mountains of Oak Creek Canyon at the mouth of the scenic drive that led into the valleys of Sedona.

Her family had been lucky to win the lottery that allowed them to be one of the sixteen vendors who set up daily to sell only the highest quality, authentic arts and crafts as part of the project started by Native Americans for Community Action in partnership with the Coconino National Forest. Anna was adept at beading and hand-painting wooden sculptures, and she enjoyed helping make the crafts when she was a girl. But as she blossomed into a teenager, she grew restless and bored, knowing there was more to the world, wanting only to escape the reservation to see what lay beyond.

One day a white teenage boy strolling through the market with his family caught her eye. He was tall and lanky with blonde hair that fell over his eyes when he bowed down to take a closer look at the carved stone pieces on their table.

It had been a particularly busy Saturday in their high season that May, and as she lugged another batch of jewelry to replenish her mother's table, Anna looked up, and her dark brown eyes met the most beautiful set of blue eyes she had ever seen. They were the blue-green color of the Colorado River at dawn or the turquoise rocks she collected in the mountains for cutting into gemstones.

And when he smiled, she felt her heart melt like warmed brown sugar, turning into syrup, and trickling down to parts of her body she didn't really know existed before that moment in time.

She realized she was staring too long when her mother came up and firmly pushed her aside. "Can I help you?" Wenona politely asked.

"N-n-no, I was just looking, thanks," the boy clumsily muttered and turned to go, probably to look for his parents. But he briefly glanced over his shoulder back toward their table. Anna met his gaze as he flashed her a mischievous grin.

She tried to forget about him, but several hours later as dusk approached, when she was helping pack up their wares, her head bent as she collected all of the jewelry into a satchel, a hand lightly touched her forearm. She looked up, and there he was, his eyes piercing hers. He deftly opened her hand and put a small piece of paper in it, then smiled, winked at her, and waved goodbye, not saying a word. She watched him as he joined what looked to be his parents and his younger brother who were walking toward the parking lot. She waited for her mom to be out of eyesight before she discreetly unfolded the tiny paper. "Meet me back here at the entrance tonight after nine. I will wait for you, Jack."

Jack. She liked his name and bit her lip to keep from saying it out loud.

SHE FOUND a way to sneak out of their house that night, past where Flo and Dena lay sleeping in the room they all shared, out through the back kitchen door, across the back yard, through the woods that adjoined their lot to the thick woods of the Coconino National Forest, and out onto the entrance of the Oak Creek Canyon Vista where hundreds of tourists pulled over each day to view the breathtaking forested canyon that lay beneath.

This is crazy, she told herself, panting, breathless from the steep climb. *I should turn back, I don't even know him, what if someone sees me, what if I die out here?* Although she carried a sharp wood carving knife in her pocket and was no stranger to the wildlife in the canyon, she felt anxious. She had been told by her mother and father to never wander alone through the woods, especially at night. They had warned her that if she did, she could be attacked by stray campers breaking the laws that forbade non-members of the Navajo Nation to abide within its territory, not to mention wolves and bears she might stumble upon.

She nearly screamed when the beam of her flashlight lit up the tips of Jack's boots. He was sitting on an old tree stump a few yards off the entrance. He stood and approached her, his heels crunching on the gravel. She stood and waited for him, her breath still caught in her throat.

"You're trembling," he said gently as he ran his hands down her shoulders. Even though it was an unseasonably warm evening, she had hiked for at least a mile, and she was wearing a bulky knit sweater her grandmother had made that would keep an Eskimo warm, she was still shivering.

"I guess I'm a little chilly," she lied, feeling a drop of sweat trickle down her back.

"You know, I don't even know your name."

"It's Anna," she replied shyly. "Anna Becenti."

Jack shook her hand. "Nice to officially meet you, Anna Becenti. I'm Jack Foreman. And why don't we go get warm?"

He motioned to the tree stump where he had been sitting, and Anna noticed a folded blanket and a big, brown paper bag. Jack also had a flashlight, and he shone it ahead and guided Anna by the arm to the spot.

"How did you get here?" Anna knew the Coconino National Park rangers were usually scarce at night, but still she worried. *What if we get caught?*

"I drove, silly, but I parked my car up ahead off the highway. I had to hike two miles to get here." He spread the blanket in a little alcove under a large pine tree that was a few yards away, motioned for her to sit down next to him, and opened the bag, pulling out a bottle of wine and two plastic wine glasses.

Anna felt her mouth drop open. "Alcohol isn't allowed here," she whispered fiercely. She had never had as much as a sip of wine or beer in her entire seventeen years on earth. Prohibition had always been the law of the Navajo Nation ever since it formed its own sovereign government, laws, and judicial system in the 1920s.

"Relax, I'll hide it if we see any cop cars or rangers drive by," he said with a cavalier flair, twisting the cap off the cheap white wine, then pouring it into the plastic glasses until they were full.

"But…" Anna started to protest as he handed her the glass but stopped, taking it. *He won't believe me if I tell him I've never had anything alcoholic to drink before. I guess it won't hurt to try it and when he's not looking dump it out.* After he tipped his glass to hers in a mock toast, she put it to her lips and sipped. *Yuck.* It tasted like the vinegar her mother sometimes added to tone down the gaminess of some meats like goat and rabbit. But she did like the radiating warm glow it seemed to spread to her insides, so she took a few more sips and then a gulp, realizing it wasn't so bad after all. Besides, she was thirsty.

"Whoa, slow down a little," Jack said, grinning. "We walked a long way to get here, so we need to make this last." He took her hand in his and looked into her eyes as they sat next to each other on the blanket under the night sky. Suddenly his face loomed close, he closed his eyes, and his lips were touching hers, kissing her. Anna had read about kissing, heard her older sisters and friends talk about what it was like, but had never experienced the sensation before. It was her very first kiss, and at first, she hoped she was doing it right, then she just closed her own eyes and experienced the warm wonderful sensation of it.

They talked, laughed, kissed, and cuddled for almost an hour until the wine ran out and Jack said he better get back to the hotel where his family was staying before they sent someone out looking for him. He had told them he was merely making a store run.

On her way back home, Anna mulled over all of the things she had learned about Jack Foreman, smiling dreamily and almost tripping over an old tree root she had stepped over a thousand times in her travels.

She stopped and pulled a few mint and lemon balm leaves from the herb garden in their yard and chewed them quickly, trying to cover the taste and smell of the wine in her mouth. Then quietly as she could, she let herself in through the back door. She opened the refrigerator and helped herself to a glass of cold milk. *That way if someone gets up, I'll just tell them I couldn't sleep.* Milk always put her back to sleep.

But no one woke up. It was just before midnight when Anna finally fell asleep, dreaming of Jack's kiss.

THE FOREMAN FAMILY was staying for three weeks in Arizona, where Jack's father worked at a manufacturing plant while he, his mother, and two younger brothers toured Flagstaff, the Grand Canyon, and Sedona. Then they would head back to their home in Gary, Indiana.

Jack and Anna stole away to their favorite spot a few more times, sharing bottles of wine, making out under the stars.

Anna thought she was in love, so much so that she invited Jack to sneak back with her one night into their family hogan.

The tent-shaped log structure, situated on the Becenti property by the woods about a half-acre away from their more contemporary house, was a traditional sacred space her family used for occasional sweat lodges and other ceremonies her father hosted for family and friends.

The mountain weather had grown chilly with the approach of fall, especially in the evenings. Anna figured the hogan would provide shelter from the cold wind as well as privacy, despite her misgivings that she was somehow being sacrilegious to her ancestors.

She led Jack by the hand through the blanket-covered entrance to what appeared on the outside as a large, clay-covered hut. Once inside, Jack let go of Anna's hand and looked around him in awe. Three ten-foot cedar logs intersected from the ground up to form the foundation of the tent-like structure, with a huge wooden pole rising up in the center for support. The walls were also made of vertical cedar logs.

"This is so cool," he whispered, staring almost reverently at the wooden structure around him as his eyes adjusted to the shadowy interior. "What do you do in here?"

"It's called a hogan." Anna ran her hand along the smooth amber-colored wood of one of the support beams, feeling ambivalent now about her decision to bring Jack into her family's sacred space. "It's a Navajo word meaning 'the place home.' My people lived in hogans for many years up until the early nineteen-hundreds when the government forced the Navajos to buy HUD houses with more modern bathrooms and kitchens. But my dad was one of several Navajo leaders—elders, medicine men, business men—who decided our people needed to remember their heritage and bring the hogan back.

"In 2001, a partnership formed between the Navajo Nation, Northern Arizona University, the US Forest Service, and a Navajo-owned log home factory to start building log hogans from surplus wood out of the local forests. It's like there's been a hogan revival on the Navajo Nation. They're built like this one or in hexagon or octagon shapes, and some are even used as homes if they meet government regulations. Ours is just used for ceremonial purposes."

Jack walked over to a charred, round space toward the center. "Can we somehow build a fire?"

"No!" Anna whispered. "My family might see the smoke. But there are some blankets we can cover up with to keep us warm." She pulled down two Native American wool blankets her mother had made from pegs where they hung in the hogan.

They sat on two of the dozen mats scattered about, huddled under the blankets.

"Too bad we drank all the wine earlier." Jack fished in his pocket and held out a rolled joint. "Good thing I brought my emergency stash." His pout about the cold turned into an eager grin.

"Jack!" Anna pushed his hand away.

"You people are so strict," Jack said, frowning. "No drinking, no smoking." He sat moping until his face brightened with a new idea. "You know, I read some history where Indians used to smoke peace pipes. I'm sure they were filled with opium or something. Plus, marijuana is legal in almost every state now."

"That doesn't matter because our laws govern our land." Anna suddenly felt bad that she sounded so defensive. *It might be nice to try it now that the wine has worn off,* she thought, feeling amorous and adventurous. "I guess we could smoke it real fast."

She watched Jack inhale on the end of the tiny homemade cigarette, hold his breath for a few moments, then exhale. It smelled like the sage they used for their ceremonies, which was a comforting thought. When he passed the joint to her, she tried to mimic Jack but ended up having a coughing spasm, which sent him into a fit of laughter.

They passed the marijuana cigarette back and forth a few times until it became a tiny stub too small to hold. Jack snuffed it out on the hard-packed dirt floor and crawled under Anna's blanket. Then, wordlessly, he took his jacket off, made it into a pillow for both of them, and lay back on it, pulling her down with him. He rolled toward her, the length of his body warm and hard against hers, and started to kiss her. Then she felt his hand go up under her sweater.

"Jack, I don't think…I don't know if…" but she really didn't want him to stop, passion flooding through her, ignited by the pot smoke and her teenage desires, and she let him touch her in places she had never been touched.

She sat up and was about to remove her sweater altogether when she heard the loud crunch of approaching footsteps. Anna sat frozen with fear.

"Hey, come back here," Jack whispered loudly, grabbing her shoulder, his hearing not as attuned as hers.

"Shhh." She put a finger to her lips and held her other hand over his mouth. "Someone's coming."

Jack sat up abruptly, listening. He turned to her, his face turning pale as he heard the sound, too, getting louder and closer.

Anna slunk down and pulled the blanket up over her head, motioning for Jack to do the same.

The footsteps suddenly stopped.

"Phew," Jack sighed.

"Who's in there?" A deep man's voice boomed as the door cover was thrown open, and a gust of cold air and the bright beam of a flashlight intruded on the hogan's interior.

"Papa, it's me." Anna sat up uncovering herself and saw her father's shape filling the entrance.

The flashlight beam shone into her eyes.

"What are you doing in here? I smell marijuana! And what… who is under that blanket?"

Jack threw off the blanket and stood.

"I'm sorry, sir, my name is Jack and—"

"Enough!" In one swift motion, the hulking figure in the doorway loomed over them, a giant hand swooped in like an eagle's claw and grabbed Jack's arm, and the teenage boy was hurled through the doorway out into the night. Paco Becenti growled as he turned and exited the hogan. "Get out of here, you filthy piece of white trash," he snarled, and Anna could hear Jack's racing footsteps receding.

She sat shaking with fear, hot tears of shame streaming down her face.

But her father never re-entered, silently retreating back to their home.

CHAPTER THREE

DESPITE HER PLEADINGS, Paco Becenti forbade his daughter to ever see Jack again.

"He's a snake," her father said, crossing his arms, his back turned toward her as he faced the massive fireplace in their living room. A fire built earlier had burned down to a pile of embers, which deceptively reflected a warm radiance on her father's stern features. He leaned wearily onto his hands, resting against the amber-colored mantel, which he had lovingly carved and finished out of an old oak beam.

In addition to being a former president of the Navajo Nation Council, Paco was a master woodcarver and had made a lot of the furniture that decorated their home, from the huge, oak dining room table and chairs to the cherry wood kitchen cabinets. He had also carved many of the elaborate decorative statues and figurines that his wife sold at the market at prices fetching hundreds, and sometimes thousands, of dollars.

"Papa, you don't know him." Anna stood meekly at the other end of the large, high-ceilinged room. Cedar beams crossed overhead in an A-line frame, and stone covered the fireplace. A large couch and two recliners rested on a homemade rug, which covered a golden wood-planked floor. The room was much like the rest of the Becenti home, grand yet comfortable and homey.

"I know his kind," Paco said, turning now to face her, a tall, formidable, handsome man who had aged well, his black hair graying at the temples, his dark brown eyes flickering with emotion. Anna knew she saw love in them but also sadness and a fierce, father-like determination to protect her. He uncrossed his arms and thrust his hands into the pockets of his jeans. "I know he's up to no good and that you need to stay away from him. How dare he come into our sacred hogan and offer you drugs? How dare he try to take advantage of you? It's a good thing I showed up when I did!"

Anna felt her cheeks flush red, not finding any words to say.

Paco crossed the room and looked into his daughter's eyes, grasping her shoulders firmly, his tone somber and deep. "You are forbidden to ever see him again. Do you understand me?"

Anna nodded meekly, unable to defend herself as she looked up into those piercing dark eyes, her father's figure towering over her petite five-foot-six frame.

His grip softened, and he wrapped his large arms around his daughter, giving her a bear hug, enveloping her, making her feel safe and loved.

"I love you, Anna," he whispered into her hair and kissed her on the cheek. She could see tears of love filling his eyes, and her own tears spilled over onto her cheeks.

"I love you too, Papa."

BUT, as water finds a way to cut through rock, Anna's love and desire for Jack found a way.

Since her parents had taken away her phone privileges, she waited until one night when she was alone in the house to call Jack. Flo had just left for a weekend teenaged spiritual retreat, and her parents had taken Dena out shopping to get new school shoes. Anna complained of having a stomach ache, saying she really didn't want to go shopping.

She called Jack to tell him she was thinking of him.

"I miss you too, Anna." She heard Jack's irresistible voice and smiled. "I really want to see you, to be with you. I think I'm falling in love with you."

Anna's heart pounded. "I am falling in love with you too," she whispered, sighing. "But my father has forbidden me to see you."

"It will be our last chance to be together since we're leaving to go home in two more days. Can we meet tomorrow night at our old meeting space at the entrance to the Coconino National Park? Please, Anna. I need to feel you next to me. I want to make love to you."

Now her whole body ached with desire. *I have to see him one last time, say goodbye to him in person and together we can figure out a way to see each other in the future.* She wanted to make love to him. What did her father know of young love? Her parents' marriage had been arranged like so many Native American marriages in the past. *But I'm in a new generation. And I've been sheltered way too long. I'm old enough to make my own choices, to live my life, to experience love.*

"Yes, oh yes, Jack, I'll meet you. Tomorrow night then."

Her heart felt like it would fly out of her chest, and she danced around the room after hanging up.

Fortunately, Anna knew that her parents planned to dine out with friends the next night, and her older sister Dena had to work.

She waited anxiously for the designated meeting time and then snuck out the door, through the forest, and up the hill. Jack arrived a few minutes after.

But instead of looking happy to see her, the lanky teenager seemed nervous and agitated, giving her a perfunctory hug.

"Jack, what's wrong, I thought you'd be happy to see me." Anna tried unsuccessfully to hide her disappointment. "I took a big risk coming here, but I knew it would be worth it."

"I know, so did I," Jack said tersely. He dug his hands in his pockets, fidgeting from side to side on his feet.

"I thought we were going to talk about when we would...you

know, see each other once you leave here to go back home. And I thought tonight would be the night…"

"Look Anna, I do really like you and all, but there's something you gotta know. I'm in big trouble—"

"We can find a way around my dad, I'm sure he'll cool off eventually and—"

"No, much bigger trouble." The color drained from Jack's face and in the moonlight, he looked haggard, older. "I'm in trouble with one of your people. I helped smuggle some marijuana into Navajo land a week ago to sell to this guy named Frankie who said he wanted it for medicinal purposes. I know, it was dumb, but I really needed the money to get me out of another jam I'm in back home.

"Anyway, I was supposed to deliver more to Frankie tomorrow night, but I couldn't get any from this source I originally found down in Sedona. Frankie said if I didn't show up and bring the stuff he would rat me out and the Indians would come after me and probably skin me alive or hang me. I don't know what to do. I know you can't talk to your dad, but…do you have a friend or cousin who can help me out? Maybe they'll know Frankie and can tell him you and I are friends and—"

"Friends?" Anna raised her voice in indignation. "I thought we were a lot more than friends, Jack Foreman. I was starting to fall in love with you. Maybe Papa was right. Maybe I—"

"I'm sorry, Anna." Jack instantly enveloped her into his arms. "You're right. I was being selfish. We are more than friends. Forgive me?" He stepped back and smiled, and her insides melted all over again. He tilted up her chin with his thumb and forefinger and kissed her on the lips, gently and then fervently until she felt her whole body pressing against his, wanting to feel his hands on her like she did in the hogan.

He backed away suddenly, breathing hard. "Anna, I lose all control when it comes to you. We don't have much time though. Do you think you can talk to someone to help me?"

Achak Yazzie. Her friend's name somehow found its way into her swooning mind. He once told her he would do anything for her.

They had made a blood pact when they were kids, cutting the palms of their hands and shaking on it. Anna and Achak had grown up on the reservation together, and when Achak's father had died of a heart attack when his two children were still under the age of ten, Anna's father had virtually adopted the boy and his younger sister as his own, helping widow Yazzie by providing the children and their mother with anything they needed.

Achak and Anna had practically grown up as siblings. He was a year older than she and had attended the same well-to-do Christian Academy on the reservation since money wasn't an issue for the Becenti family.

"DO you know a Frankie who lives on the reservation?" Anna asked Achak over the phone after she returned home, thankfully beating her parents by a few hours.

"I've heard of him, why?" Achak sounded reserved.

"I need a favor." Anna knew Achak would probably do whatever she asked of him and felt a little guilty since she also knew Achak had lately developed his own romantic feelings for her. She had known his feelings for her had changed ever since they'd gone to the high school prom together. Just as friends, she'd thought. But it became apparent to her that night that he had thought differently. When they danced for the first time, she had seen the gleam of longing in his eyes, feel the charge between him.

She could feel Achak's desire for her that night, just like she felt for Jack now, which is why she had to forge ahead, she told herself. She took a deep breath. "A friend of mine is being threatened by this guy from the reservation named Frankie. My friend isn't Navajo, he's white in fact, and he was hoping I knew someone who could stand by him when he goes to meet with Frankie, so that he doesn't get roughed up or anything. Would you be able to get a few guys and show up tomorrow night at a meeting they've arranged, sort of like protection, just in case?"

She was met with silence at first. Finally, Achak replied. "I don't know, I guess so," he said hesitantly. "I think I know who Frankie is and from what I've heard, he can be pretty mean. I'll round up a few others. Not that I couldn't handle him myself."

Anna smiled to herself. She could picture Achak's chest puffing out with pride. "Of course."

"And who is this friend, and why should I help him?" Achak asked defiantly.

"His name is Jack." Anna hoped Achak couldn't sense somehow over the phone the hotness she could feel creeping into her face. "And I was hoping you would help him for me."

"Well, okay, but you'll owe me," Achak teased.

"Owe you what?"

"I'll have to think about it and let you know."

Anna dismissed his playful banter. She had to let Jack know she had friends who could help him.

THEY GATHERED under a majestic oak tree that marked the entrance of an old sacred Native American gathering place, marked by a circle of rocks on a cleared dirt floor in the northeast woods of Oak Creek Canyon.

Anna had been there as a child, but it was dark that night. She was glad to ride with Achak and his two friends.

Jack was waiting for them when they arrived. They had agreed to meet a half hour ahead of when Frankie was due to show up.

Anna ran up to Jack, who was leaning back against the tree's massive trunk, and hugged him. She introduced the young men to each other, and they peremptorily shook hands.

"Why should we defend this guy?" Achak asked Anna then turned to Jack. "What have you done that Frankie is coming after you and you need me to defend you?"

"I don't need anyone defending me." Jack sneered. "It's none of your business what I did."

"Well then, maybe we should just go," Achak said.

Anna was dressed in jeans and a sweatshirt, the hood of her

windbreaker pulled up over her hair that was tied back in a ponytail. An onlooker might have thought she was one of the boys as she walked over to the tree and stood beside Jack in alliance with him.

"Achak, you promised you would stay," she said. "For me."

"Well, I'm not defending this guy until I know what he's done. Maybe he doesn't deserve defending. You know I'll do what you ask, Anna, but I have to say this goes against my better judgment."

"His name is Jack and—"

"That's okay, Anna, I can speak for myself." Jack disengaged from her side, distancing himself from her.

She looked at him and for the first time, doubt about her feelings for Jack crept into her. He looked small and skinny, especially next to Achak who was lean but muscular, and his face looked pinched and pale. *Like he's afraid or hiding something.*

"I sold some drugs, you know, marijuana for medicinal purposes to Frankie, and he wanted more, and I promised I'd get it but then my source came up dry." Jack shrugged his shoulders. "The big jerk threatened me, telling me he'd rat me out and have his thugs come after me and skin me alive or something ridiculous. You Indians, I swear."

Anna looked at Jack in shock that he had uttered the racial slur.

Just then an old, beat-up Pontiac pulled up in the distance, shining its bright lights directly on the gathering at the tree, rap music blaring from the stereo.

A hulking six-foot tall Native American man who looked to be in his thirties strode toward them. From the light of the full moon Anna could see he was wearing a black leather jacket, black boots, and a baseball cap on backwards over his black dreadlocks. When he came close she also noticed he had a tattooed lightning bolt across his right cheek.

"Well, look at the posse we have gathered here tonight." Frankie grinned, showing huge smoke-stained teeth in his leathery face. "You had to bring your girlfriend and boyfriends with you, huh, Jackie boy? I shoulda known a white punk like you wouldn't have the guts to meet me here on your own."

Achak and his buddies stepped a pace toward Frankie, leaving Anna and Jack standing a few steps behind.

"Relax, I'm on your side." Frankie grinned at Achak, holding his hands up in mock surrender.

"How's that, Frankie?" Achak asked evenly.

"Well, first, the obvious reason; I can't believe you're actually defending this white trash against me, one of your own. Second, because this piece of scum laced the stuff I was selling for medicinal reasons with fentanyl. I found out after one old Navajo dude almost died of a heart attack after smoking his pipe. Turns out his doctor tested the stuff good ole Jackie here sold me. I'm not sure what kind of stunt this dog is trying to pull, but I'd say he's trying to get our people addicted to this junk. I not only want my money back, I want him to pay for what he's done to our people."

"Hey, I didn't know, I was just the middle man," Jack said weakly, not bothering to step forward.

"Shut up, stupid," Achak said, not moving from his stance blocking Anna and Jack from Frankie.

Frankie crossed his arms and scowled. "C'mon, Achak, you aren't actually going to stand in my way now, are you? This guy not only owes me clean drugs, he owes me a refund. I just came to make him pay."

Achak stepped forward directly in front of Frankie, nose to nose with him, his friends a few inches behind.

"That's not gonna happen tonight," Achak answered tightly.

Anna saw Frankie's huge hand ball up in a fist of rage, but just as he was about to take a swing, his eyes grew large and his arm stopped in mid-air. At the same moment, she heard rustling behind her and turned to see Jack disappearing beyond the oak tree into the black shadows of the thick forest.

Achak didn't see Jack fleeing and used Frankie's pause to hurl his fist into the older native's face in self-defense. His two friends stood on guard, ready to back him up if needed.

Frankie fell backward, stunned, onto the ground. As he was struggling to his feet, the older native reached his hand into his leather jacket and pulled out a jagged hunting knife. But Achak was younger and quicker. As soon as he saw the glint of the blade, he lunged like a panther, delivering a solid kick to Frankie's stomach, causing him to drop the knife, which flew through the air and landed a few yards away. Frankie doubled over, grunting in pain, holding his ribs.

Achak grabbed Anna's hand and yanked her behind him, and the four of them ran toward their car in the distance, realizing Frankie was probably calling for back up.

"You're gonna pay for this!" Frankie yelled after them, spitting blood as he slowly stood, clutching his side, and hobbled back toward the old Pontiac.

It was the last time Anna saw Jack and the last time she ever wanted to.

"I TOLD you I forbade you to see him!" Paco Becenti's voice boomed this time, filling the entire house. Anna thought she saw the overhead lighting fixture in the living room shake, just like her legs were doing.

"And you, what were you thinking?" Her father turned next to Achak, who stood by her side.

"I'm very sorry, sir," Achak said meekly.

He could blame me if he wanted to, Anna thought, proud for a moment of her good friend. *I asked him to do it. He didn't know what he was getting into. But I knew.* Anna realized just then that deep down in a tiny part of her gut, she had felt like Jack wasn't the good guy she had originally believed him to be. But she had foolishly ignored her instincts.

"You both have no idea how much trouble you're in now, do you?" Paco's icy anger thawed, melting into sadness.

The two teens stole a sideways glance at each other, and then they looked down, shaking their heads.

"Some members of the Council did some digging into Jack Foreman and his family. It turns out his father works for a pharmaceutical manufacturer. Jack used some Fentanyl that he stole from a shipment at the plant to mix into the marijuana he bought from his dealer in Sedona. The whole time he's been out here in Arizona, he's been mixing and selling bags of drugs to anybody that will buy them but mostly to various people on the reservation, including to young kids."

Paco motioned his daughter and adopted son to come over to the dining room table in the adjoining room, where a manila folder lay. He opened it and laid out four photos of Native Americans, two older, two younger. "Besides the old man who had a heart attack, there was an elderly lady who had a partial stroke after using the marijuana for pain, one twelve-year-old who wound up in jail after hallucinating and torturing and killing someone's pet dog, and one eleven-year-old who is now in a coma."

Anna bit her lip, holding back tears for these innocent victims among her own people. Achak stood, showing no external emotion, but Anna knew if she looked into his eyes, she would see her grief mirrored there.

Paco gathered the photos and put them back into the folder and closed it. He turned and crossed his arms, letting the full impact of what he had shared sink in for several moments. Then he spoke in a firm, even voice, although Anna could tell he was having difficulty holding his emotions in check with what he was about to say.

"Jack is on the run from his family and the law right now, and the FBI has joined our police to hunt him down, but when they catch him, he will be at the mercy of the court.

"The Navajo Nation Council expressed that both of you should also be brought to trial," Paco said, his eyelids drooping a minute fraction with weariness, and suddenly Anna could see the pain she had caused her father. She wanted to wail, throw her arms around him, and beg his forgiveness like she had when she was a little girl, but she knew it would look undignified and disgraceful. It would only make the situation worse for both of them.

As if he could no longer look at her, Paco turned to Achak. "You, son, for assault against one of your brothers." Achak nodded in acceptance. Then he turned to Anna with a blank stare, as if he could no longer see her. "And you, daughter, for drug and alcohol possession. And both of you for aiding and abetting a known criminal who may be wanted for murder should one of these victims die," he added. "Because of my standing in the Navajo Nation as a medicine man, I was able to ask that, instead of you both being brought to trial and bringing shame to your mother and me, you be allowed instead to leave the reservation, never to return."

"We're being…shunned?" Anna's words came out choked with disbelief.

The proud, noble elder silently nodded as he uncrossed his arms then turned his back to them and walked from the room.

"I'd rather go to trial, Papa," she cried after him, but she knew it was too late. Once her father made a decision, it was final.

Anna crumpled to the bear rug at her feet, sobbing, and Achak bent down on one knee to try in vain to comfort her.

CHAPTER FOUR

ELIZA CAME HOME from her waitress job, sweaty and exhausted, that night to their cramped first floor tenement building just outside downtown Phoenix.

Randy's Tex-Mex Diner had been crowded all day, offering air-conditioned refuge from the hundred-degree heat that plagued Phoenix for several days that October. Many customers had lingered for hours over a cup of coffee or soda, not even leaving her a tip.

She quietly unlocked the apartment door and stood a minute until her eyes adjusted from the hallway lights to their dimly lit living room.

Alex lay sprawled, shirtless and sleeping, on the couch, his brown skin glistening with perspiration, wearing only a pair of jogging shorts. Eliza noticed two empty beer bottles and a McDonald's burger carton on the end table. *I feel bad I never cook for him*, she thought dismally, hearing the clanking whir of the air condition unit in the window coming to life. *He looks so skinny.*

But after working day after day at the diner, she couldn't bring herself to even look at food when she got home. Most of the time he grabbed some cheap fast food or made himself a peanut butter and jelly or tuna sandwich for dinner since he always got off a few hours earlier than she did.

Eliza felt sorry for herself and even more sorry for him. Alex had gotten a job with a roofing company, showing up at six a.m. each morning to sling tar and lay down shingles in the scorching sun. Yet they were barely paying their bills, much less eating enough.

She quietly set her purse down on the worn armchair next to the couch and went to take a shower in their joint bathroom. The blast of cold water gave her hot skin a little relief. But it did little to cool her anger over the lack of money she had made for all of her hard work the past fourteen hours delivering plates of greasy tacos, hauling dirty dishes caked with dried-up crusty refried beans, and waiting on even greasier, crustier truck drivers who sometimes tried to grab a quick feel when she wasn't looking.

She towel-dried her hair, put on an oversized tee-shirt and denim shorts, and lay across her bed. She was almost asleep when she was startled by the sound of her name.

"Acha...Alex!" Eliza often had to correct herself, still getting used to their new names. She sat up, blinking, her bedroom light still on. "You scared me."

Both of them were ordered by the Council to change their given names when they were banned from their homeland a month earlier, although to Eliza it already seemed a lifetime ago. Alex Trellis and Eliza Smith had set off together to face life off the reservation and had found jobs and an apartment together that they could barely afford in the busy, dusty, hot city of Phoenix.

"Sorry, I woke up and noticed you were home and thought I'd check on you." He stood leaning against the door frame to her bedroom, which was adjacent to his. While they shared the rest of the apartment, they were lucky to find a two-bedroom unit they could afford together.

Eliza smiled inwardly. *Still the same old Achak, always looking out for me.*

"Well, thanks, but I was almost asleep."

"With the light on."

"You could have just turned it off."

"True, but then I wouldn't have gotten to talk to you and share such wonderful conversation." His sarcastic tone normally wouldn't have bothered her, but she was grouchy now that he had woken her.

"I noticed you had a few beers without me," she said snippily.

"You could have woken me and had one too."

"Um, there were none left." She wished she didn't sound so irritated but couldn't help herself.

"Well, excuse me for wanting to relax a little after a day spent frying like a chicken." He stood tall, his eyes now glinting with resentment.

"And what, you don't think I work equally hard at the diner?" Eliza climbed off her bed and stood to challenge him. She was just a foot away and could smell his familiar musky man-scent.

He remained in the doorway. "And whose fault do you think that is?"

"Get out!" she screamed and pushed his chest as hard as she could, but he was muscular and strong and didn't budge. She started to push again, but he backed up two steps out of the doorway.

"I'm sorry. I…don't know what got into me." His face blushed with embarrassment. "It was a long day. I'm really sorry."

Eliza was still furious, but her energy faded, and her voice sounded like a little girl's in her ears. "It's okay, I had a hard day too. Just go, I'm really tired."

"Okay, good night." His expression was dejected as he looked down, not meeting her eyes as she shut the door on him.

"ACHAK!" She sat upright in her bed, waking from a bad dream in a cold sweat, her tee-shirt nearly soaked. Pulling it off over her head, she fought to remember, not knowing she had screamed his name.

They were in a forest. A white man, scarred and ugly, was lunging for her friend with a huge, dagger-like knife, plunging it into his abdomen. But she was tied to a tree and couldn't free herself to help him.

She heard a soft knock on her door and pulled the bedsheet up to cover her nakedness.

"Come in," she said.

Alex gently opened the door a few inches and peered in. "Are you okay? You called my name. Well, my old name. It sounded like you were in trouble."

"Sorry to wake you, I was having a bad dream."

"Oh, okay, well I just wanted to make sure." He went to close the door behind him.

"Stay." Eliza whispered it so softly she wasn't sure she said the word out loud.

Alex opened the door a little wider and stood in the doorway, dressed only in boxer shorts, looking baffled. "Did you say stay?"

"Yes, please, sit." She motioned for him to sit with her on the end of her twin-sized bed, which, together with a dresser they had bought at the thrift shop down the road, nearly filled the little bedroom. "Sorry I woke you."

"That's okay, you sounded scared to death." He didn't bother turning on the light since the full moon was enough to illuminate his way enough to sit on the edge of her bed. "What was your dream about?"

When Eliza was done relaying her nightmare, she noticed Alex's eyes shimmering with tears in the soft moonlit glow. She reached out and covered his hand with her own, being careful to hold the sheet around her. "Hey, it was just a dream."

"I know." Alex blinked, obviously embarrassed for her to see him like this. He cleared his throat. "It's just that I felt really bad for what I said earlier. You're all I have, Eliza. You're my best friend, and I would never hurt you. I know I've never said this to you before, but, well, I love you."

Eliza was stunned, unable to speak, but her heart filled her chest until it felt like it would explode. Not thinking, only feeling, she reached her arms toward him, and he moved toward her, and they embraced, the sheet falling away between them.

He kissed her, and she felt lightheaded tasting the sweet saltiness of his mouth on hers. Suddenly they were lying together under the sheets, their bodies blending into one.

➡—→

THEY NEVER SPOKE AGAIN of that night together until several moons later, just after her nineteenth birthday, when Eliza realized she had missed her menstrual cycle.

The two had fallen in love with each other that night but decided to honor their heritage and upbringing by staying chaste thereafter. Still, it was impossible for them to be platonic, so they spent many nights kissing and touching, going to bed restless and aching for each other. Not talking about their intimate night was one thing but trying not to think about it was like un-lighting a fire. You could douse it with water to put it out, but you couldn't pretend it had never been lit in the first place nor take away the heat it had already cast upon you.

Alex had surprised Eliza the night of her birthday with a candlelit dinner for two. He had cooked her favorite meal, roasted Cornish game hen with potatoes, and had set their small dinette with folded napkins, the Corelle plates, and silverware they had bought on sale at Walmart. He had even decorated with balloons and fresh flowers. And after dinner he brought her a small chocolate frosted cake topped with nineteen candles and sang "happy birthday" to her.

She cried happy and sad tears at the same time, loving him and missing her family.

During dinner they had actually talked about getting married to put an end to their torture.

"But I don't want to get married for just that reason," she had told him shyly.

"Of course not, me neither." He had quickly added, "I love you, you know that. I want to make you my wife."

"I love you too, but I think we might want to wait until we have a little bit of money saved up, you know, maybe I can buy a nice dress and we can invite a few people, maybe have our wedding at a nice restaurant and even take a little honeymoon." *Not exactly the way I pictured my wedding, with hundreds of friends*

*and family at a traditional Navajo ceremony, but at least it would be
something.*

"Okay, I'll surprise you when the time is right," he said, winking
at her and grinning.

THE NEXT MORNING at Randy's she had cried all over again
recounting the birthday dinner to one of her waitress friends. *I'm so
emotional lately,* she realized, sipping a cup of coffee during her ten-
minute break. *And tired. Oh well, it's probably the lack of sleep I'm
getting from longing to lie next to Alex every single night.*

Because she worked the breakfast and lunch shifts, Eliza got off
before Alex that day. She came home and plopped, exhausted, onto
the couch, her back aching. *Just my period coming,* she thought, but
then realized it was late. At least a week late, and for a girl whose
menses was normally on time each month, Eliza suddenly panicked.

She drove to Walmart, got a pregnancy test kit, went home, and
waited.

And it was positive. It all became clear to her now—why she'd
been feeling weepy and tired and, come to think of it, more
nauseous than usual over Randy's greasy beef barbecue lately.

A baby! She couldn't believe it. It was the only time they…well,
she wasn't so sure about him…she had made love—ever! *It's impossible, I'm too young.* She looked in the mirror and hardly recognized
the thin young woman staring back at her with well-defined cheekbones, a slim, long neck, and slight circles under her huge brown
eyes.

She suddenly noticed how she had lost a lot of weight. But she
couldn't think about that now. She had a whole lot more to worry
about. *Oh my gosh, what will Alex say, what will we do?*

Fortunately, she didn't have much time to fret about how to tell
him the news. He burst in the door two minutes later, whistling
"You Are My Sunshine." "Hey sweetheart, where are you, I have
some news!" he shouted good-naturedly from the living room.

Boy, so do I. Eliza wrapped the pregnancy stick in some tissue and tucked it into the pocket of her black skirt, noting absent-mind-edly that she hadn't even changed from her work uniform. She looked in the mirror again, forced a big smile, and came out to give him a hug.

"How's my girl?" he asked, kissing her neck, tickling her.

"Fine and dandy." It was a saying her mom used to use. Some-times she couldn't help herself, she realized, putting her parents out of her mind. "Why don't you sit down? I have some news for you too." She took his hand to lead him to sit down but he broke free and stood, looking triumphant.

"I bet my news is bigger than yours!"

"Oh, I highly doubt that," Eliza said, slightly annoyed and tickled at the same time over the irony of his statement.

"Okay, then, you go first, smarty-pants." Alex finally followed Eliza's prompting for him to be seated during her news.

She sat next to him on the couch, nervously running her hands over her skirt. "Okay, but don't say I didn't warn you it was big. Um, I'm not sure how to say this, so I'll just say it. I'm pregnant."

Eliza watched as the huge smile beaming across Alex's face slowly faded, the color left his face, and his eyes grew wide with shock.

"You're...preg...pregnant?"

Eliza could only nod, worried that Alex was upset.

"I can't believe...well...okay then..."

"I know, I can't believe that it only took that one time, with me being a virgin..."

"I was a virgin too."

Eliza's mouth hung open and then she felt her heart sing with the news.

Alex sat on the couch, still looking incredulous, his thick, black eyebrows knit in concentration for a minute. And then he unexpect-edly smiled at her.

"Why are you smiling?" she asked, still nervous.

"Because I love you, Eliza, and this means there's only one thing left for us to do."

"What's that?"

"Get married!" He suddenly was kneeling on the threadbare living room carpet in front of her. "Eliza Smith, will you marry me? I'm sorry I don't have a ring and all but—"

"Yes!" Eliza's heart soared, and she threw both arms around her best friend's neck, breathing in his earthy smell. She looked teary-eyed at him, making sure he was of sound mind, but all she saw was love in his eyes. "I don't need a ring. All I need is you."

LIFE GOT EVEN HARDER for the newlyweds. They were married the following Friday by a justice of the peace in the courthouse in downtown Phoenix, each asking a co-worker to stand in as a witness. That way they could at least have Saturday and Sunday off to celebrate, even though it was in their tiny apartment. Eliza had found a tea-length white dress in the Goodwill store, and Alex, dressed in the only pair of khaki slacks he owned with a white polo shirt he had found on sale at Walmart, told her she looked beautiful as she took his hand and they said their vows.

But soon after the wedding, both Eliza and Alex picked up more hours at work whenever they could to save a few extra dollars to put toward the baby fund, both coming home every night exhausted.

Eliza was fortunate not to have morning sickness, at least during the third trimester of her pregnancy.

But Cameron's birth was not easy.

"THIS REALLY, REALLY HURTS!" Eliza gasped between labor pains, lying in the delivery room hospital bed, her head swimming with fear.

"Isn't there something you can give her for the pain?" Alex asked the attending obstetrician, an intern at Saint Joseph Hospital. Eliza's regular doctor was involved in a complicated surgery at the moment.

"No, not yet, she's not far enough along," the young doctor said, checking a clipboard.

I'd like to take that clipboard and whack him over the head, Eliza thought, clenching her teeth as the next wave of pain slammed her abdomen and lower back simultaneously, nearly rendering her unable to catch her breath. *I don't know if I can take this.* Eliza panicked. She had only been in labor for an hour. Sweat dripped from her forehead, but she felt like she was freezing.

"Alex, you've got to do something," Eliza said, gripping her husband's hand until it was nearly white. "Something doesn't feel right."

"Doc, no offense, but can we get a real...I mean, you know, a doctor in here?" Alex flinched as Eliza groaned in agony. "How long is it gonna be until she gets something for the pain?"

The young Hispanic doctor, who looked to be only a few years older than they were, finally took his eyes from the chart and glanced at Eliza as if she were a peculiar animal under observation, not hiding the fact that he was offended by Alex's question. "Is this your first child?" he inquired with authority, his tone tinged with disdain.

"Yes, but this just doesn't feel normal."

"Well, I assure you it is. But let me tell you what, I'll be back in an hour to check on you, and we'll see if your cervix has dilated any further. Then perhaps we can give you a little something for the pain." The young doctor hurriedly jotted something on the clip-board chart and, without saying anything further, turned and stepped out of the room, closing the door behind him.

An hour! Eliza seethed with anger. But then another labor pain took so much energy from her that her words tumbled out in a hoarse whisper between ragged breaths. "Alex, I just don't think I can do this." She started to cry, feeling like a helpless, small child being bullied. Only her enemy, the one who kept kicking and punching her in the gut, was unseen, making it impossible to fight back. She could see the helplessness on her husband's face too, as he wrung his hands, pacing back and forth across the little room.

Another pain cramped her midsection, knifing its way into her back, and Eliza screamed out loud this time, writhing on the bed until the crashing wave subsided, leaving her limp, lifeless form in its wake. She shut her eyes, talking softly. "I feel like I just want to die," she said and started to weep.

But the next pain, hitting her just two minutes later, made her shriek so loud that a redheaded nurse who looked like she was barely a teenager popped her head through the door. "Is everything all right?" she asked timidly.

"No, everything is not all right." Alex jumped to his feet from where he had been sitting on the side of his wife's bed and grabbed the nurse's forearm before she could escape. "You need to get the doctor, a real doctor. Now."

The nurse's blue eyes widened in alarm, her freckled face paling. She wordlessly nodded, and as soon as Alex loosened his grip on her arm, she fled the room, returning two minutes later with Eliza's ob-gyn. Dr. Manning, a kind, graying man with spectacles, had delivered thousands of babies in his lifetime.

In seconds, Dr. Manning checked Eliza, and in a calm voice which apparently masked his concern, he delivered the news to the young couple. "Eliza, you were right, your pains aren't normal. We have to do an emergency C-section to get the baby out as soon as possible. He is pushing against the umbilical cord. We have a matter of minutes to get him out."

Eliza's whole body started to shake uncontrollably. She looked over at Alex, who was standing against the wall, and saw his face turn nearly gray with fear. A nurse covered her with a warm blanket and suddenly she was being wheeled on a gurney into the operating room, counting down. *Thirteen, twelve, eleven, ten, eight...*

CHAPTER FIVE

BABY CAMERON WAS BEAUTIFUL, his skin flawless from the C-section delivery that hot August night.

Eliza and Alex had said prayers of gratitude every night for weeks that their baby boy had made it through. That gratitude sustained them for a few months, even when Cameron developed colic, but soon started to fade into sleepless nights and long days with Alex working constantly, many times on jobs throughout the weekends, to get overtime to pay their bills while Eliza healed from her surgery, nursed the baby, and fought postpartum blues.

Eliza had to eventually go back to work at the diner so they wouldn't lose the apartment and resentfully placed nine-month-old Cameron into a day care. She hated leaving him but knew the alternative would be that they would be living in a shelter or on the streets.

Some light finally shed on the little family when Alex received a well-deserved promotion to team leader of his roofing crew. Eliza had discovered that his hopes for getting the leadership position based on stellar reviews from his superiors had been the good news her husband had never managed to share the day she told him she was pregnant.

Managing a bunch of roofers was tough work, and he often

came home even more surly than he used to be, but the pay was nearly double what he had been making.

Eliza could finally quit her waitress job and work from home part-time doing data entry, which meant she could spend a little more time with baby Cameron. But it turned out that the accounting job started taking up so much of her time that she had to put her one-year-old son back into day care.

When Cameron was almost three, Alex and Eliza had finally saved up enough money to move from their dingy two-bedroom apartment into a little ranch house in the suburbs of Glendale just outside of Phoenix.

And one month later, Eliza announced she was pregnant again.

AUSTIN TRELLIS WAS BORN on Father's Day, a fact that, in years to come, would delight Alex who would always fondly say it was his best Fathers' Day gift ever.

Eliza thought since Cameron's birth was difficult, and since she was also fortunate to have a shorter stint of morning sickness during her pregnancy with her second son, that Austin's birth would be easier.

But she was wrong.

Eliza still had narrow hips for child birthing, but she was determined to have a natural delivery after her C-section. She ended up experiencing twenty-four hours of excruciating labor pains, the last half in agony when the epidural didn't take. Eliza felt like her bottom was being ripped open when the doctor pulled ten-pound baby Austin from her, and it took her weeks to heal from the episiotomy, and months for the postpartum blues to slip away.

Cameron was a big help to her with the baby. Too tired and depressed to get up off the couch most mornings, she would ask him to fetch a bottle from the fridge or the baby's pacifier when he cried or sometimes some cereal or crackers for himself when he wanted a snack.

She knew she relied too heavily on her older son when he was practically still a baby himself, but Eliza couldn't help the over-whelming depression and anxiety that flooded her.

Eliza usually waited until both Cameron and Austin were napping to go to her little desk set up in a spare nook of the house, which doubled as the laundry room. She had to make sure the washer and dryer weren't on when she was talking to clients, though inevitably sometimes, she'd be on an important call and she'd hear the baby cry on the monitor, or Cameron would get up early from his nap and forget what she had warned him not to do and come bounding into her makeshift office yelling "Mommy!"

Sometimes she lost her temper then asked the client if she could call him or her back and yelled at Cameron. "Don't you remember Mommy told you never to come in here talking or yelling, to always walk into Mommy's office quietly and to wait until I was off the phone to speak?"

Cameron always told her he was sorry, then she felt exasperated and guilty.

Alex typically didn't get home in time for dinner, and some nights he rolled right into bed around ten p.m., too exhausted to do much more than say goodnight if she was even awake.

When they did manage to talk for a few minutes, she often lied to him about her day, cheerfully telling him as he started falling asleep that she and Cameron had played for hours.

BUT THE NIGHT he walked in after she had discovered his gambling debt, all of the lies both of them had harbored were revealed in all of their ugly truth.

Eliza was in the living room, bank statement in hand, ready to confront him as soon as he laid down his briefcase and loosened his tie.

"I've found out where you've been going, and that you've charged more than five thousand dollars gambling," she said, her voice and hands trembling. "I cannot believe you've not only been spending time away from me and the kids for who knows how long each week, but you've been wasting our money. Making payments on a gambling debt, money I could have spent on clothes and shoes for the kids, or even maybe going out with you once in a while."

Alex had removed his jacket during her rant and then put his hands on his hips defensively. "Well, if you could work more hours at a real job and make a little more money, and wouldn't spend what we have so carelessly, like ninety-nine dollars on a pantsuit, maybe I wouldn't have to try to go to desperate measures to try to get more income."

"That's just an excuse, and you know it!" Eliza waved the paper statement in front of her husband's reddening face. "You just don't want to be with us, you don't even care about us anymore! Do you think it's easy raising two boys on my own? Did you ever think maybe I would like to go out and play slot machines or whatever it is you're throwing money at?"

Alex practically ignored her, walking past her to go into the kitchen and grab a beer from the refrigerator. He popped open the can, stood leaning against the counter, and started to guzzle the contents.

Eliza followed him, her fury mounting. She couldn't stop the words from slashing out of her mouth, didn't want to. "You know what, Alex Trellis? You're a terrible husband and a terrible father!"

"Well, you're just a hypocrite!" He slammed the half empty beer can onto the countertop, sending beer suds spilling out. "You sit home pretending to work while you practically have our older son babysitting or watching TV all day."

Eliza felt her face flush with shame. How did he know that?

As if to answer her unspoken question, Alex continued. "I know the truth. I've talked to a neighbor or two who say their wives have tried to stop in but you're always busy, and that they always catch you lying on the couch in front of the television." He was spying on her! And here he was in the wrong, accusing her!

"Me, a terrible father? You're a worse mother!" he thundered. He guzzled down the remainder of the beer and was opening another when they heard the whispering shush of little feet on the vinyl floor.

Eliza turned around to see Cameron standing there, gazing at both of them with a worried look on his face, his cheeks red, his hair tousled, wiping sleep out of his eyes.

"That's not true, Daddy, she's a good mommy," he whined.

Alex had apparently been drinking before he arrived home, because he staggered toward them, losing his footing for a moment. His voice was soft at first. "Cameron, go to your room, this is none of your business." But when their son stood, crossing his arms, refusing to budge, his father's voice rose in anger. "Cameron, do what I say!"

"No!"

Eliza came to her son's rescue. "Cut it out, Alex, he's just a little boy defending his mom." *And I'm really proud of him*, she thought smugly.

Alex took one stride closing the gap between them and reached out to smack Cameron with his open hand, but Eliza grabbed his wrist, and Cameron ducked fast enough to escape his father's wrath and ran wailing from the room.

"How dare you..." Eliza couldn't finish her statement and ran after her little boy. The baby started crying with all the noise and Eliza heard the front door slam, the house shuddering from its impact.

ELIZA BEGGED Alex until he finally agreed to go with her to see Dr. Paulus for couples' marriage counseling, not letting on her friend Marcia had originally referred her after admitting she had seen the counselor when she had been stuck in an abusive relationship in her thirties.

A tall, slender blonde in her fifties with a PhD in psychology, Dr. Paulus greeted the couple, warmly shaking their hands and motioning them into her office to have a seat on the couch across from her chair.

This lady seemed to have her life right where she wanted it. Eliza couldn't help but feel a little bit of envy, noticing the framed photo on the desk in the corner. It was a picture of the counselor with a handsome, middle-aged man, obviously her husband, two beautiful, young blonde-haired girls in their teens, and a younger boy who looked like a younger version of the man.

They all looked joyful, sitting on a beach with a sunset sky behind them. Some people had all the luck. This woman could never understand what she was going through.

Alex and Eliza sat at opposite ends of the couch, not looking at one another as they took turns telling their story to Dr. Paulus. Alex complained his wife was overly protective and soft with the boys and that she tended to drink and shop excessively. He explained that his anger would build up because he worked so hard and had no outlet, so he gave in to his addiction and turned to the casinos to numb his feelings. Tears fell down his cheeks as he admitted his regrets. "I guess I've changed since that young man who left the reservation," he said, a tear slipping down his cheek. "Working so hard has made me really hard." He turned to look at his wife, regret and sorrow welling in his eyes. "I'm sorry," he said, taking her hand in his. "I love you, and I'll do whatever you want me to do to change."

"I'm sorry too." Eliza took one of the tissues from the box the doctor handed her, her cheeks wet with grief. "I guess I felt trapped and gave into my own addictions and should have been more supportive." Dr. Paulus smiled as Alex took Eliza in his arms.

At the end of the session, after their emotions subsided, Dr. Paulus suggested Alex attend Gamblers Anonymous, a gambling addiction recovery twelve-step program, and that Eliza attend Gam-Anon, a recovery program for friends and family members of those addicted to gambling.

THE TWO OF them hired Patty to watch the boys the next Thursday night and drove mainly in silence to the Gamblers Anonymous meeting in the basement of the Desert View Bible Church. They got lost, even though they followed their new GPS, and argued until Eliza finally rolled down her car window and asked a stranger walking by for directions.

They walked into the church basement hall a few minutes late, feeling embarrassed and conspicuous, and took seats in the back of the meeting room, which was half full with about twenty people of varying ages and ethnicities.

Listening to some of the stories shared that night, Eliza thought for the first time in a long time that maybe she and Alex had a chance. *Our problems dim in comparison,* she thought, listening to a man named Jimmy T. share his story.

"My wife divorced me after I traded in the last of our welfare stamps for gambling money," Jimmy said, tearing up. "The only food left in the house was a little bit of pancake mix and a few cans of soup, and we had three kids to feed. I just couldn't stop. I kept thinking, 'just one more time and when I win, I can fix everything.' And then I'd be up a couple hundred bucks, and I'd think 'that isn't enough yet,' and before long, after a few drinks and a few more hours, I'd walk out broke again. She got tired of hearing the same old story. Thank God I found you all. I know that won't bring her and my kids back, but it helped get me off the streets before I wound up in jail, or worse, dead at the hands of some crime boss I couldn't pay back."

She heard muted laughter and realized it was coming from another room off the hall that she couldn't see. After all of the people took turns talking, except for Alex who passed, they stood and joined hands and said the Lord's Prayer. Eliza noticed a small group of about a dozen people coming out into a hallway in the distance, chatting and smiling.

The GA meeting had been mostly comprised of men, with only two other women who were much older than Eliza. A few men gathered around Alex to shake his hand and give him their phone numbers. Eliza stood fidgeting idly, trying not to make eye contact with anyone. Just as she was saying a prayer to herself that this whole night be over quickly, a middle-aged Native American woman approached her with a broad smile and, without warning, hugged her.

"Hi, honey, you look a little lost. I'm Sunny, short for Sundance, and I just came from Gam-Anon yonder and was wondering if maybe you didn't belong there tonight?" Her smile revealed a missing tooth, and her skin was well worn.

Eliza was initially flabbergasted at her effrontery and looked around for Alex, who was nowhere to be seen, but then she looked into the woman's kind eyes, which reflected her warm smile, and realized she had nothing to fear. "I think I was supposed to be in Gam-Anon according to my counselor," Eliza meekly replied. "But we were late and I didn't know where to go. Is that where you were just now?"

"Sure was, honey, and you're welcome to come back next Thursday night and join us." The gap-toothed woman grinned again. She fished in her pocket and pulled out a scrap of paper on which she wrote her telephone number. "Call me if you need a ride, I'll be glad to come getcha."

"Thank you, um, Sunny."

Just then Alex walked up to her and put his arm protectively around her. "Ready to go, honey?"

ONCE CAMERON and Austin were both in school, Eliza got a part-time job as an assistant clerk with the local Phoenix Public Library, which helped ease their family's financial burden but kept her too busy to keep seeing Dr. Paulus, whom she had continued to visit for a few sessions on her own when Alex couldn't make it.

Alex and she had gone to a few more counseling sessions, but then he became embroiled in corporate changes at his job that required more of his time and attention.

They had also attended the weekly GA and Gam-Anon program meetings at night for several months, and then slacked off as the boys got involved with after school and weekend activities like soccer and baseball, and her husband's job got even more demanding. Eliza had wanted to keep attending regularly, but Alex had told her he was better and suggested she didn't really need it anymore and really couldn't afford to spend the extra time.

Eventually, as the years passed, Eliza stopped going to see Dr. Paulus and quit attending the twelve-step program meetings altogether. Although it was more hectic, life seemed to be back to "normal," and they vowed on the ride home from their last program meeting to stay strong in their marriage and not let anything come between them.

ELIZA WAS busy filing books on the shelves in the library when she her cell phone rang. Luckily the head librarian was working the counter and nodded to her to go take a break and answer the call.

The number that showed up on her phone was her sons' school. She hurriedly answered, fearing something bad had happened.

"Mrs. Trellis, this is John Dunleavy, principal at Phoenix Elementary," the nasal, monotone, middle-aged man's voice said. Eliza recognized the principal's voice immediately, although she had only met the man twice at back-to-school nights.

"Hi, Mr. Dunleavy, is everything okay with my boys?" she asked, getting quickly to the point.

"Yes, everything is fine, I hope I'm not interrupting you at work?"

"Well, yes, but that's okay, I can talk for a minute or two."

"I just wanted to ask if I could set up an appointment for you to come into the office and speak with myself and the guidance counselor about your son Austin."

Eliza's heart beat hard in her chest. "Austin?" She was surprised to hear the principal call about her younger son, expecting that perhaps he was calling about misbehavior of some sort on Cameron's part.

Cameron was ten-years-old, almost midway through fifth grade, and was starting to come home from school now and then with stories of some of his mischievous antics on the playground, in gym class, or at lunchtime.

Eliza thought her older son was still a good boy, but she could see he had a streak in him that sometimes crossed the fine line between ornery and bad. On the other hand, Austin was sweet, shy, studious, definitely not the kind who got into trouble. He was only in second grade. How could he be in trouble?

"Yes, Mrs. Trellis, Austin," Mr. Dunleavy interrupted Eliza's thoughts. "The guidance counselor would like you and Mr. Trellis to come in to discuss the possibility of placing Austin in a magnet or charter school for the gifted and talented." Eliza could hear a faint trace of pride in the principal's voice, as if his elementary school were promoting one of its own and were thus being recognized for the achievement. "I know the Christmas break is around the corner, but we were hoping to place Austin before the next school semester. If you can possibly come in next week sometime, that would be great."

Eliza sighed with relief. "Well, Mr. Trellis works long hours, but I can ask him. If we can, we would be happy to come in and meet with you." She felt proud herself. She had heard of students who were labeled "gifted and talented," which she believed meant they were unusually smart.

"Great, please hold, and I'll have my secretary make an appointment."

ELIZA HAD to go alone to the school meeting in the principal's office the Monday after Thanksgiving, promising her husband she would fill him in on all of the details. Alex couldn't take off an hour, much less a half day, in his new job. It was too intense.

She wore her best skirt and sweater, which she had gone out and purchased on Black Friday off the clearance rack at the local department store.

Still, she felt out of place, like she was too young and dumb to be a mom, especially of a gifted and talented boy.

While she was sitting in the principal's office waiting for Mr.

Dunleavy to go get the guidance counselor, she was absentmindedly staring through the open office door when she saw Cameron and two other boys, perhaps classmates or friends, walking down the hallway, talking and laughing. Cameron looked up and caught his mother's eye.

Eliza waved to her son, grinning. Not only did he not acknowledge her, Cameron glared at her for a moment with obvious shock and embarrassment, turned without pause in his step or his banter, and ignored her.

Before her hurt could sink in, Mr. Dunleavy was back in the office introducing her to the school's head guidance counselor, Miss Posey, who walked in with Austin in tow. Austin skipped into the office, saw his mom, and gave her a big hug. Tears came to her eyes, but she didn't want to make a scene. She blinked them back before they fell down her cheeks.

Mr. Dunleavy closed the door to the office and sat down behind his desk, the three of them sitting in chairs across from him, Austin between his mom and Miss Posey, who ended up doing most of the talking.

The petite, spritely young redhead explained how Austin had been observed by all of his teachers to be increasingly restless in his classes the past semester. They eventually recommended that Austin go for special testing by the school district's psychologist. The results had come in.

Mr. Dunleavy opened up a manila folder, cleared his throat and shared that the psychologist's findings. Eliza shook her head, still a bit confused by the principal's report.

"It's our opinion that Austin is acting out of boredom and needs to be further challenged in school," Miss Posey said confidently. "I am recommending he be transferred to the Paradise Valley School for the gifted as soon as possible, as long as you and your husband authorize the transfer, of course."

"Of course." Eliza sat uncomfortably in her chair, nervously clasping and unclasping her fingers. *How had Austin gotten so smart?*

"Mommy, I don't want to go to a different school than

Cameron." Austin broke her reverie, looking up at her with his soft brown eyes.

Eliza could feel Miss Posey and Mr. Dunleavy staring at her, waiting for her to answer.

"Well, honey, Cameron will be going to middle school, which is a different school, next year anyway." She could see the young counselor and principal nod in approval out of her peripheral vision, encouraging her to go on. "And this school will be much more fun for you, plus if you go now, you can make new friends right away instead of waiting over the summer."

She watched her son grasp all that she told him, a frown on his face. Then he smiled slowly. "Will it have cool music and art classes?" he asked.

Eliza looked to Miss Posey. "The best!" the young counselor answered enthusiastically.

"Good, because I think music and art are kind of boring here."

Mr. Dunleavy looked disgruntled at the little boy's comment, but Miss Posey interjected. "Well, that's why we want you to go to this new school, Austin. What is good for some students your age is probably boring to you because you have special talents and skills many of them don't have, and…" Miss Posey's confidence waned a bit, so Eliza finished her sentence.

"That's just the way God made you, honey." *Careful what you say. You don't want him thinking he's better than everybody else. You still have another son who's not as gifted and talented.* "It's not that you're any better than the other kids, just maybe a little smarter in one area or another. But each of us has special talents to offer. Mr. Dunleavy, Miss Posey, and your teachers just think you'll be able to grow your special talents better in this new school."

"Okay, Mommy. Can I get back to class now? I think I'm missing gym and we're learning how to play basketball today!"

"You have a great kid there, Mrs. Trellis," Miss Posey said, smiling appreciatively at Eliza, who warmed with pride and smiled back as she hugged her son and watched him scamper off.

"I don't know where he gets it all from," Eliza said half-jokingly.

"Like you said, God," Miss Posey said.

Mr. Dunleavy cleared his throat, signaling the end of the meeting and his displeasure at Miss Posey's last statement. It was a public school, and teachers were not supposed to be voicing any religious commentary. "We will make the transfer beginning next year then, if you and your husband agree."

IT WAS the family tradition that the youngest go first in unwrapping their Christmas presents. Austin beamed with delight, standing in the middle of their small living room in his plaid flannel pajamas as he unwrapped his last gift under the tree. He opened the large cardboard box, pulling out a child-sized acoustic guitar.

"Wow, a guitar!" he exclaimed, pulling it out and strumming the still out-of-tune instrument.

"Santa must have figured you're going to need it for music lessons in your new school," Alex said, winking at his wife.

Eliza turned to Cameron, catching him rolling his eyes at his father's comment. He had announced just days before Christmas that he no longer believed in Santa, that according to his friends it was just a thing parents made up to make sure their kids were good, especially around the hectic holidays. Eliza had made her older son swear to secrecy involving Santa so Austin wouldn't find out.

Cameron had also reached the bottom of his pile of gifts, and he opened his big box, pulling out a huge Matchbox race set with double looped tracks and at least two dozen race cars. He had often watched the Nascar races on TV with his dad, and Eliza had thought it would be the perfect gift for him. But she watched in dismay as her son, looking downcast, sadly put the set back in the box, not bothering to even pretend he wasn't disappointed.

"What's wrong, Cameron? I thought…I mean, I'm sure Santa knew you loved race cars," Eliza said.

"I kind of wanted a drum set," he replied softly.

Eliza looked hopelessly at her husband.

"Ah…that's right, you did mention it once a while back." Alex sat his spiked eggnog down on the end table and leaned forward in his chair. "Well, son, maybe you'll get one next year for your birthday or Christmas. Santa probably didn't have enough money to give a whole drum set out to all the kids who wanted one."

Cameron hunched over cross-legged on the floor by the tree, his elbows resting on his knees, and put his face in his hands, pouting and sullen, not looking at any of them. Eliza realized he was trying not to cry.

Austin walked over and tapped his older brother on the shoulder, extending the guitar toward him. "Hey, Cameron, I'll let you play my guitar," he said cheerfully.

Cameron swatted at the guitar, sending it banging to the floor. "I don't want your stinking guitar, stupid." He uncrossed his legs, stood up, and started to stomp out of the room.

"Cameron, get back here." Alex rose from his chair and grabbed his son by the arm, spinning him around. He looked down at his son and shook him angrily. "You need to apologize to your brother, and to your mother and me. You're being an ungrateful brat, and you should know better than that."

Cameron flinched, and he looked down, unable to meet his father's gaze. "Sorry, Austin," he mumbled, his voice trembling. "Sorry, Mom and Dad. Can I go now?" His lower lip quivered.

"Sure, honey," she said, noticing with agitation that her husband still looked angry. But she held back from saying anymore, wanting to protect her son from further humiliation.

Alex let go of his arm, and Cameron fled from the room.

CHAPTER SIX

THE SLIGHT MARKS on Cameron's arm—impressions from his father's anger that Christmas morning—healed quickly, but the bruises to the ten-year-old boy's ego didn't. Cameron stayed silent for a week, not bothering to talk to the rest of his family.

Several months later, Eliza was called into Mr. Dunleavy's office again, but this time not for good news. Her fear from the first time, that Cameron was in trouble, was now being realized.

She sat once again across the desk from the lanky principal as he relayed the episode.

"I'm afraid Cameron was bullying another student, Mrs. Trellis," he said in his authoritative, nasal tone. "The students were on the playground, and Cameron and another fifth grader, Donny Slade, approached a younger boy who's in fourth grade, Bobby Montrose, and asked him if he had any money to lend them. When Bobby said he did but refused to give it to them, they shoved him into the rock-climbing wall, and his glasses fell to the ground and broke. They pushed him hard enough that he has bruises on his face and shoulder, according to his mother. They also emptied his pockets and took the dollar worth of change he had. I am suspending both Donny and your son for one week for assault and petty theft. Cameron will have to make up the schoolwork on his own time."

Eliza listened somberly, nodding in agreement. She tried to put herself in Bobby's mom's place and felt like the punishment was a little harsh, but fair.

That night when she sat with her two sons at the dinner table, she noticed Cameron picked at his food, only eating about three bites, and then asked to be excused early. *He's probably afraid of what will happen when I tell his father,* she surmised.

She had sent Austin to his room to do his homework and was sitting with Cameron in their small living room talking when her husband finally walked in the front door at eight p.m.

"Sorry I missed dinner," he said, like he did a few times each week. "Hey, Cameron, what are you doing out here with your mom?" Both boys were usually in their rooms doing homework or listening to music when he got home.

"Cameron has something to tell you." Eliza gazed at Cameron, who sat hunched over on the couch.

Alex sat in an armchair, loosening his tie, rubbing his eyes tiredly. "Okay, Cam, shoot."

Cameron told him an abbreviated version of Mr. Dunleavy's story. "But Donny was the one who came up with the idea to take his money in the first place. I didn't want to go along but I was afraid the other kids would call me a chicken."

"What were you thinking, picking on a younger kid? Cameron, I don't know what's going on in that head of yours, but you better straighten it out, or it's going to get straightened out for you." He stood, looking down first at Cameron then on Eliza, contempt in his eyes as if the whole thing was her fault. "What have you done about this?" he asked his wife irritably.

"The school suspended him for a whole week," she answered defensively.

"Well, we have to punish him on top of that if he's going to learn any type of lesson." Alex held his hand out toward his son. "Give me your phone, that's going away for a week too."

"Dad!" Cameron crossed his arms and slumped back on the

couch defiantly, a stray lock of long, black hair falling over his dark eyes.

"I think the school is punishing him enough." Eliza gently put an arm around her son protectively.

"That's his problem, you baby him too much. Hand over the phone, Cameron."

Cameron slowly reached in his pocket and put the phone in his father's outstretched hand.

"And you're grounded this weekend too."

"But, Dad! You can't do that!" Cameron stood, arms crossed.

"Alex, it's the weekend of his best friend's Christmas party. If Cameron is grounded, he'll miss it, and it's a big deal," Eliza interjected.

"That's too bad, he should have thought of that." Alex walked past his wife and son tiredly to head to their bedroom, ignoring Cameron's pleas.

Eliza was too tired to argue, and knew if she started a fight over this, she would be sure to lose in more ways than one.

WHEN AUSTIN GRADUATED from Paradise Valley, his parents were faced with the decision of where to send him for high school.

Unfortunately, they were having money issues again, since ABC Oil was facing financial and political hardship in the wake of newly elected US President Eileen Stewart, the liberal Democrat who had vowed during the race to increase oil imports from Mexico, tear down the US-Mexico border wall, decrease border patrol forces, and loosen the tough immigration enforcement laws put in place during the past president's term in office.

Striving to compete with the other larger oil companies, ABC had been forced to bring in cheaper labor and hire more immigrants from across the border, which put many long-term employees of the company out of a job. Alex hadn't been fired, but his job security was threatened, so he agreed to work even more hours for the same pay. Wage increases were frozen, and his small share of profits from the company's stocks took a nose-dive.

Although Eliza continued to work her part-time job from home, she and her husband crunched the numbers and realized that, short of sinking back into debt, they just couldn't afford a private school for Austin.

And Lord knows I don't want Alex to go back to gambling. Eliza shuddered from the thought.

While Austin wasn't thrilled to switch from his private junior high to the local public high school, his older brother was even less enchanted with the idea.

Cameron instructed Austin to sit at least ten rows away from him on the bus to school the first day and to walk at least twenty paces behind him, so no one would know, at least for a few days, that they knew each other.

But that notion fell apart at lunch in the cafeteria.

Cameron was sitting with his two friends, Charlie and Max, at his usual table reserved for seniors, when he noticed in his peripheral vision that his brother was seated eight tables away. He was trying to ignore that fact when Charlie, seated across from him, started laughing.

"Check it out." Charlie pointed over Cameron's shoulder toward the table where Austin was seated, apparently with one other freshman boy.

Cameron reluctantly turned to see three tall boys, a sophomore and two juniors, walk up and stand over his brother and the other freshman at the table. In seconds, one of the older kids pushed his brother's shoulder and swiped part of his lunch from in front of him.

Austin stood to get his stolen food back when another of the older boys pushed him back down onto the bench.

Cameron rose quickly and strode over to the table to confront them.

"Hey, what do you think you're doing, picking on these measly freshmen?" he asked, standing nose to nose with the guy who had just shoved his brother.

"Who, these geeks?" The gangly, long-haired, tough-looking Hispanic teenager sneered at Austin and his new friend, who looked down, their faces red with embarrassment. "What's it to ya?"

Cameron stood tall, about an inch taller than the Hispanic, and glared down at him. "This 'geek' here," he said, pointing at Austin, who still averted his eyes, "is my brother. I don't know who this other 'geek' is…" Cameron glanced at the chubby white boy with curly blonde hair and glasses, "…but he doesn't deserve to be bullied just because he's younger or smaller or different from you. I used to be a bully once. I learned the hard way it doesn't pay in the end. If you want to learn the hard way…"

The Hispanic boy backed away a few inches, looked side to side at his two cohorts, and turned to walk away, his two friends in tow.

Austin looked up at his big brother with a smile. "Thanks, Cam, I—"

"Shut up," Cameron said between clenched teeth, glancing at Austin and then the other freshman, silencing them with his stony look. And then he walked back to the table where his friends sat, staring open-mouthed at him.

Later that evening at supper, when Eliza asked her sons how their first day at school was, neither boy said a word about the cafeteria incident.

CAMERON HAD EVENTUALLY SAVED up money from side jobs as a busboy and cook at a few local eateries and pizza joints to buy that drum set he never got for Christmas.

He, Charlie, and Max had formed a band in their senior year and practiced in each other's garages until they were finally ready to play a gig for the first time live at the local indie music club and bar, Last Exit Live, just south of downtown Phoenix.

They were second in a lineup of four punk rock and blues bands that Eliza had never heard of. The tickets she had purchased listed the band names: Bare Bones Gully, Cactus Moon, Skull House, and Desert Crawl.

Eliza poked her head into the bathroom the boys shared toward the back of the ranch house, thankful that she and her husband had their own bathroom off their master bedroom. Well, most people wouldn't call it a 'master' bedroom due to its size. Still, it was slightly bigger than the bedroom the boys shared, and she was grateful they at least owned their own home instead of throwing money at monthly rent like they did in their old apartment.

The single vanity in the small bathroom, lined in blue-striped wallpaper Eliza had laid herself, was littered with razors, shaving cream, hair gel and deodorant, and smelled of spicy aftershave and teenage sweat.

She caught Cameron's deep brown eyes gazing back at her from the mirror, where he stood gelling his wavy, short, black hair straight up into some type of punk rock hairdo she'd never seen before. She tried not to smirk and held back a laugh in her throat.

He looked back into the mirror, concentrating, nervous, avoiding conversation.

"What type of music should I tell my friends you play?" She tried to sound casual, as if it were every day her son played on stage at a bar in front of a crowd where she would be front and center.

"Ska punk, ma, you should know that by now." Cameron never took his eyes off his own reflection as he looked at his hair creation apprehensively. "And what 'friends' are coming?"

"Well, I invited my friend Marsha, and of course we know Charlie's and Max's parents. Ska punk. What is that exactly?" Eliza didn't mean to sound condescending, she just wanted to know what to call the music she had heard coming from the shed in the back yard when the boys practiced at their house. They didn't have a garage like Charlie's or Max's families, but the shed seemed to work when it was Cameron's turn to host the band.

Seeing that Cameron was much too busy to answer, Eliza looked it up on the Internet on her phone. Ska punk, a fusion music genre that combines ska and punk rock, Wikipedia said. *Yep, that's what it sounds like. Not bad really.* Eliza actually liked some of the songs they played. She also liked how the band seemed to bring her two sons closer at times. Cameron usually allowed Austin and one of his friends to hang out with them when they practiced. She often overhead Austin singing the songs they played in his bedroom when he thought no one was listening.

Cameron was interrupted from his bathroom routine by the buzzing of his cell phone, which sat precariously perched on the top of the toilet bowl cover. He gave his mom a look that said, *do you mind?* Eliza excused herself, shutting the bathroom door behind her, but in seconds, it banged back open and her son emerged, frantic.

"I can't believe this! Max just texted me that he has strep throat and can't sing tonight! This is our big break. But we can't perform without vocals." Eliza had gone into the kitchen to prepare dinner and looked up to see her son pacing the hallway.

He looks like a young man but he's still so much a boy, she thought, watching his gelled hair limp over into his eyes as he strode back and forth, his hands jammed into the pockets of his jeans. He wore a black tee-shirt that bore the name of the band, Cactus Moon, a logo of a cactus against the backdrop of an orange full moon screen printed on it.

Then she heard Austin call in a muffled voice through the door of the back bedroom, "I can sing." Her eldest son stood straight, as if he was straining to make sure he just heard right.

"That's a great idea," she said softly, trying to concentrate on not burning the chicken enchiladas in the pan in front of her.

"It's a terrible idea." Cameron frowned at her with annoyance for a split second then turned away, ignoring her again. He was on his phone texting, apparently back and forth with his band mates, trying to figure out a solution to their latest dilemma. Then he held the cell phone to his ear. "Man, we can't cancel now, we'll never get a chance with this place again," he pleaded into it. "Are you sure you can't sing?"

Cameron had told her enough about the band for her to know that Charlie was a talented bass guitar player but couldn't hold a tune, and Cameron was a decent backup singer but wasn't good enough to fill in for lead vocals. "Can't you take something...well, I don't know…" Cameron paced with his cell phone, his voice rising with agitation. There was silence for a moment, and then Cameron said softly, almost in a whisper, but Eliza could hear him, "Austin said he would sing. I guess he knows all the songs, and his voice is decent enough. I know he's not as good as you, but at this point we don't have any other options. All right, see you down there in an hour for the sound check."

Eliza quickly looked down into the pan of rice and peppers, stirring, pretending she didn't hear. She looked up to see her son still standing in the hallway, his face contorted with the effort of making an important decision.

"Austin!" He yelled as if his brother was two miles in the distance instead of five feet away. Eliza heard the back bedroom door fling open, and her younger son, face flushed, emerged into the hallway. He stood only a few inches shorter than his brother and looked almost identical to him, with his tanned skin, dark brown eyes, and slim, angular build. His jet black hair, however, bent in haphazard curls unlike Cameron's straight hair, making him look much younger than his fourteen years.

Like Eliza, Austin had obviously been eavesdropping during the entire conversation. "I promise I'll do great, I won't let you guys down." His enthusiasm was met with big brother indifference, and Eliza felt a tug at her heart both because her younger son was so excited and her older son was actually giving his brother a chance despite his apparent misgivings.

"You better not blow it," Cameron said gruffly. "Go change and put on a black tee-shirt, we don't have an extra band shirt but that's okay, nobody will notice."

"Thanks, Cam!" Austin ran from the hallway back into their bedroom to change. Then he quickly turned around, frowning. "Wait, how should I wear my hair?"

Eliza saw Cameron hide a quick grin that almost broke through his scowl. "It's fine the way it is, hurry up, we gotta go."

⇒→

THE SUN BURNED bright orange on the horizon as Alex and Eliza pulled up to Last Exit Live. From the outside the box-like building looked more like an oversized garage or warehouse along a strip of similar gray and tan concrete buildings. As Alex parked in the half empty parking lot, Eliza was suddenly sorry she had asked Marsha to come. She was going to think this was so grungy and low-class. Plus, she'd probably hate their music.

Inside the place was fascinating though. The interior looked nothing like the exterior. The stage was framed by old-time, red theater curtains, huge speakers on either side. Spotlights, dimmed now before the show, softly lit up the stage, filtering the smoky, dusty air with their blue-white beams.

As they walked in, Eliza noticed posters plastered on the walls announcing the evening's band line-up along with the ticket price of twelve bucks and the minimum age of twenty-one. *I hope Austin is going to be okay in this crowd.* She couldn't help but worry. But she was secretly really proud when she saw the name, in smallish letters, second from the bottom: Cactus Moon. *That's my sons' band, there on that poster.*

Alex handed Eliza a mug of beer, and they jostled their way through the growing crowd of twenty-somethings and teenagers who had snuck in, all starting to gather to stake their ground. They finally made their way to the front stage area where Charlie's and Max's parents were waiting for them.

"Hey, great to see you, this is so exciting," Charlie's mom, Rose Marie, yelled over the increasing volume of voices. Eliza nodded, smiling. She suddenly felt self-conscious, dressed in what she thought had been a conservative choice of a tan, short-sleeved knit top and black slacks but now screamed "frumpy mom."

Max's mom, a tall, thin blonde, was dressed in tight black jeans and a red lacy top, and Rose Marie was decked in a black leather skirt and hot pink tee-shirt with silver sparkles that spelled Rock On across the front.

Marsha sauntering up in a low-cut, white blouse, sequin studded jeans, and big hoop earrings didn't help her cause. She was sipping what looked to be a cosmopolitan.

Eliza introduced her spunky, redheaded friend to everyone, and then a screeching microphone interrupted them.

"Sorry, folks, just doing sound checks, we'll be going live in just a little while," a good-looking young black man with a black fedora and blazer announced, obviously the stage or concert manager.

Eliza caught a glimpse off stage of Cameron carrying pieces of his drum set and then Austin carrying a speaker behind him while Max and Charlie tuned their guitars.

"Hey, I hope Max is okay to be up there tonight?" Eliza asked Max's mother, Jane.

"I tried to get him to stay home, but I think he would have trampled my dead body to get here tonight." Jane smiled, tossing her blonde tresses behind her shoulder, her eyes gleaming with pride. "I'm just sorry he can't sing." Then she looked contritely at Eliza and Alex. "Oh, I'm sorry, that didn't come out right. I'm sure your son… it's Austin, right? I'm sure he'll do just fine."

"I'm sure he will," Alex interceded, sounding a little defensive. "He's a great singer, wait 'til you hear him. Of course, I'm sure Max would have done great too."

Eliza fought hard not to roll her eyes at her husband but was secretly proud of him.

Fortunately, cheers from the crowd ended their conversation. The first band was walking onto the stage.

"Let's give it up for Bare Bones Gully!" The stage lights glared onto the three guys on stage, one playing guitar and singing. *If that's what you call it*, Eliza thought. One was on drums, and another was on bass guitar. Eliza had to strain to make out even a few of the words the goth-dressed singer screamed into the mike. He was bald with piercings on his face glinting in the strobe lights, and every inch of his skin that showed around the tank top he wore was covered in tattoos.

Not what I want for my boys. Eliza's mind drifted above the harsh growls and screams and guitar wails.

Mercifully, the first band only played four songs. Eliza was afraid to look at Marsha until after they were finished.

"Well, that was interesting," her friend said. "I need another drink." And with that, she was off.

Eliza didn't have time to search for her in the growing crowd and turned just in time to see Cameron, Austin, Charlie and Max take the stage.

"Ladies and gentlemen, let me introduce for the first time ever, Cactus Moon!"

Austin looked like a baby compared to that last dude. This crowd was going to eat him up and spit him out. Eliza said a prayer, closing her eyes. She couldn't watch.

But then the voice that came out of the microphone made her open them in shocked wonder. *Surely that isn't Austin singing? I mean, I've heard him sing in the shower, but this...he's really good. Maybe I'm biased as his mom. But* Eliza noticed that the audience was captivated, too, by the perfect baritone belting out the lyrics that Cameron had originally written for Max to sing. Austin stood in a single spotlight, his curls lit up like a halo. His voice started out soft and slow and then built to a crescendo at the refrain filled with passion and emotion, the drums and guitars building with each line until all of it exploded together.

You hurt me, Lynette, yeah, hurt me real bad,
It's hard to explain, the way I cried every night,
But I'm through being used, I'm through being sad,
So drive your little car off and get outta my sight,
Yeah outta my sight, outta my sight, outta my sight!

By the end of the song, the whole audience was singing in unison, "outta my sight!" including all of the parents.

IT WAS A LONG NIGHT, but Alex and Eliza walked proudly hand

in hand, filing out of the black and red glow of Last Exit Live into the glare of the parking lot lights.

"Austin did really well. I bet he'll be part of the band now." Alex beamed at his wife as they trudged wearily to their car.

"Both of them, all of them did great, I think they were definitely the best band of the night," Eliza replied, not recognizing her own voice which was hoarse from all of the talking, yelling, and singing.

"Yeah, but…" Alex's words hung unsaid as pot smoke hit the couple from the right, as if someone had sprayed it in the air like a can of hairspray.

They looked in the direction of the smell to see about a dozen kids and young adults standing several yards away in the shadows of the back entrance of the concert building, smoking cigarettes, some drinking from beer bottles and plastic cups, a few apparently taking hits from joints.

They were almost to their car. Eliza let go of her husband's hand, stopped, and squinted her eyes to try to make out faces among the figures. She thought she saw a familiar mop of curls shining in the reflected light of the moon and parking lot.

And then she thought she saw that same curly topped youth laugh and reach out his hand to take a small cigarette. No, it looked more like a joint. A beer bottle dangled at his other side.

"Austin!" She wanted to shout but no sound escaped her. She turned to tell Alex to take a look and see if her vision was correct, but he was already unlocking the passenger door of their car. *I don't want to embarrass Austin. Besides, if I tell Alex he will lose it and ruin the whole night.*

She silently got into the car, her husband shutting the passenger door for her and climbing in the driver's seat.

I will talk to both of them tomorrow.

CHAPTER SEVEN

ELIZA HAD NEVER, in the thirty some years she had known him, seen her husband get this mad.

A pity, too, since the morning had gone so well.

They had gone to church the morning after the concert without the boys, who had come home late after hanging out until the last few people had left Last Exit Live. They were still sleeping, of course.

She and Alex tried to attend St. Augustine Catholic Church every Sunday, but sometimes she went alone if Alex was exhausted from his work week.

But her husband seemed energetic the morning after the concert, once he got two cups of coffee and some bacon and eggs in him.

"That was fun last night, we should do that more often." He smiled, sipping the last of his coffee after cleaning his plate with the last bite of buttered toast.

Eliza noticed the gleam in his soft brown eyes. Was that still love after everything they'd been through lately, the long hours, late nights, arguments over the boys and discipline and money? She smiled back wearily. She was not feeling so energetic, having had a restless, fitful night of sleep, her mind replaying the scene outside the concert hall.

"It was fun, especially to see the boys up there performing," she agreed, taking his plate to the sink. "And it was fun being out with other adults. And with you." Eliza tried to sound sexy and loving but wasn't sure if her tone matched her will. She was so worn out lately and didn't feel the words. *I wonder when I stopped feeling them.*

"Yeah, they were great," Alex said as he got up from his chair to finish getting dressed. He was already wearing his gray slacks and a button-down, white shirt but hadn't put on a tie yet. The top shirt button was undone, and a few black hairs peeked out from his brown chest. *A sight that a few years ago made me swoon with longing.*

"Who knew Austin could sing like that?" he said, his voice filled with admiration.

I knew, she thought, but didn't say it out loud, knowing it might come off to him as if he wasn't around much, wasn't a good father to not know his teenage son could sing. Although he was apparently in a great mood, she knew, given his Gemini personality, that his emotions could flip back and forth like a hooked fish, and she didn't want to risk him getting defensive.

"And Cameron could play the drums like that?" she added, but he was already headed for their bedroom to find a tie.

When they returned home from church, Cameron was up cooking scrambled eggs.

"You guys did great last night," Eliza said, laying her purse on the kitchen table and walking up to the stove to give him a sideways hug. The smell of toast, mingled with the faint scent of cigarette smoke clung to her son's tee-shirt.

Cameron turned the eggs with a spatula as the toast popped up. "Thanks, Mom," he muttered, giving her a weary smile.

Just then they heard the sound of retching down the hall.

Alex frowned at Cameron while Eliza went to the hall bathroom from where the sounds emanated.

She knocked on the closed bathroom door. "Austin, are you okay in there?"

Silence. She knocked again. "I'm fine, Mom," Austin replied in a weak, garbled voice. She heard the retching sound again. "No, you're not fine, open the door."

"I don't think you want me to do that, Mom. Hold on just a sec, I'll be right out."

Eliza waited patiently by the door. Alex sidled up behind her, his hands on his hips. Austin opened the bathroom door and emerged, his face ashen, dressed only in basketball shorts. There was a scrawled tattoo, about an inch in diameter, of a skull and crossbones on his left shoulder.

The smell that wafted out into the hallway from behind him was a strange and sickly mix of lemon room deodorizer spray and vomit.

"Austin Daniel!" Eliza softly exclaimed. "Where did you get that tattoo? And why are you so sick? Are you hung over?"

Alex continued to stare, frowning, hands on hips, standing squarely in the hallway, blocking the way to the kitchen. Austin sheepishly looked up at his mother, not daring to glance in his father's direction.

"Were you drinking and smoking pot last night?" Alex finally asked, his voice rising.

After a few moments of more silence, Eliza said in a voice that belied her anxiety, "Answer your father."

Austin looked into his father's eyes. "Yes." And then he looked at his mother. "And I got the tattoo from one of the members of Skull House. It was part of my initiation."

"Initiation into what?" Eliza couldn't help her voice from rising too.

"Into the local band scene. Everyone gets one. Don't worry, it didn't hurt that bad."

"That's good," Alex boomed. "Because your punishment is gonna hurt a whole lot worse. Get back in that bathroom, clean it up, then go to your room."

Eliza's heart sank. She had wanted to tell Austin how proud she was of his singing the night before and hear all about his first stage experience. He stood there, his dark chest sprouting only a trace of hair. Still a boy. Now she knew he would clam up. But it appeared he wasn't intimidated by his parents' reactions.

"Fine," he said, standing up straight, pride glinting in his eyes. He turned, went into the bathroom, and shut the door behind him.

Eliza and Alex headed into the kitchen where Cameron was obviously doing his best to ignore the rest of them, clanging his breakfast plate loudly into the dishwasher.

He started to wordlessly shuffle by them, but Alex held up his hand to block him.

"Wait a minute, where do you think you're going?"

"To do my homework," Cameron said, feigning innocence.

"Nice try. Come out to the living room and sit with your mother and I and tell us all about last night, how your little brother ended up with a tattoo and getting drunk and smoking weed."

"Hey, it's not my fault," Cameron protested, still standing in the same spot. "Why aren't you grilling him?" He pointed down the hallway to the boys' bedroom where his little brother had already escaped to freedom.

"Because you're his older brother!" Alex barked, his eyes gleaming with anger. "You should have known better than to let him get a tattoo, or drink and smoke pot with your buddies."

"He's a big boy, Dad. I can't believe you're yelling at me instead of him."

Alex balled up his fists, and he looked like he was going to hit his son, his face turning red with rage. "How dare you talk back to me? He's only fourteen. You're seventeen. That's a big difference." Alex turned to Eliza. "Aren't you going to say anything?"

Eliza also wanted to run from the room and hide, escape, from her husband's wrath. "Cameron, you should have known better," she said tiredly. "Do you also have a tattoo from your initiation?"

Cameron took off his tee-shirt, revealing a roughly inked coiled snake of the same size on his left shoulder, his chest and arms bigger and more muscular with age than Austin's. "Everyone gets one," he said proudly.

"Put your shirt back on," Alex said, his voice seething with disgust. He started pacing, taking off his tie and tossing it onto the living room couch. "Both of you are going to be grounded. No money, no phones, no band for at least a month."

"Dad, you can't do that! We have to practice, we're going to have more gigs coming up and—"

"If you keep it up, it's going to be two months!" he yelled. "Do you want to make it two?"

Cameron stood the same height as his father who was only inches away. He stepped an inch closer.

Please don't start a fight, Eliza prayed, although she realized Cameron would probably win since his father was starting to get a bit flaccid with age and a lack of exercise.

Cameron silently shook his head back and forth, putting his hands into his jeans' pockets.

"Then go to your room and don't come out until we say so."

Cameron didn't look at either of them as they stepped apart to let him pass through into the hallway.

Guilt flooded through Eliza. *I should have defended him, he's still a boy too.* Alex could be so unreasonable. Eliza suddenly started to hate her husband.

CAMERON HAD ASKED a girl he had met the night of the concert to his senior prom, which fortunately fell after the month he was grounded.

Eliza helped him pick out his tux, which had a tie that matched the emerald color of his date's gown, captured in a picture on his cell phone.

Her name was Megan McGee. Although Eliza hadn't seen her in person, from photos she thought Megan was very pretty, with a petite frame, shoulder-length, wavy auburn hair, big green eyes framed by long lashes, and a smattering of freckles.

Cameron had told his parents she was of Irish heritage, her parents and two brothers lived in West Encanto just outside Phoenix, and she was a sophomore at the Arizona Academy of Science.

"She's pretty smart, huh?" Eliza asked, straightening her son's tie, stopping him from nervously pacing the living room. He was so much like his father sometimes, with all that energy. She smiled at the comparison.

"I guess," Cameron answered. "Of course, her parents must have loads of money. Her dad is a chemist, and her mom is a nurse at Banner Hospital. You'll see when you drop me off at the McGee estate."

Since they only had two cars and Alex was working late that Friday night, Cameron had asked Eliza to drop him off at Megan's house. A limo, paid for by the McGees, would be taking them to the prom itself.

"Wait until you see where she lives, Mom, it's like a mansion." Cameron had taken Megan on two dates, to dinner and a movie, after he had apparently gained some superstar status at the concert.

"Hmmm, well you should bring her to dinner here some time."

Eliza saw Cameron roll his eyes and felt the heat of shame rise into her cheeks. *He's embarrassed to bring her here. Can't say as I blame him.*

Austin burst through the front door, grimy and sweating in a tee-shirt and shorts. He had been down the road playing basketball with some friends.

"Hey, Cam, look at you." He grinned, taunting his brother. "Don't you look pretty. You cleaned up real nice."

Cameron sneered at his brother. "You're just jealous."

"You're right, Megan has looks and is loaded I heard," Austin said, draining a glass of water in the kitchen, basketball under his arm. "Plus she must be smart going to the science academy. How did she possibly fall for you?"

"Because I'm charming, good looking, and a famous drummer now," Cameron said, smiling.

"Yeah, right, thanks to me."

"Why you little—" Cameron wrestled free from his mom's tinkering to chase after his brother, but Eliza caught him by the arm.

"Cameron, it's time to go," she said, looking at her watch. "Just ignore your brother."

"Yeah, he's too young to realize what women really want," Cameron said haughtily.

Eliza stifled a laugh. He really was like his father. Charming, good looking, and a little full of himself at times.

THEY PULLED up into the long driveway that circled in front of the two-story Spanish-style stucco home, framed by palm trees and colorful landscaping with fiery Arizona poppies and white primroses that hedged the manicured lawn which overlooked a lake and the ninth hole of the championship golf course.

"You look very handsome," Eliza told her son as he rang the doorbell, holding a corsage in his hand.

"Thanks mom, you look pretty too," he said, smiling, standing tall in his black tux, and Eliza's heart melted. She had worn her best summer dress and high heels and had carefully done her hair and nails earlier that day.

Megan answered the door. She was even prettier in person. Eliza liked her immediately. Megan warmly shook Eliza's hand and invited them both inside to introduce her to her parents. She was wearing a jewel green satin gown that shimmered when she walked and brought out the jade green of her eyes. Emerald stones lined the bodice, and an emerald pendant hung from her slender neck with a tiny gemstone that Eliza guessed was probably real. Her auburn, shoulder-length hair was swept up to the side with curls cascading from a silver barrette.

Eliza shook her parents' hands, and they warmly invited her to help herself to the spread of hors d'oeuvres set out on the granite island in the massive kitchen.

The doorbell rang, and another set of parents and another mom bustled in with their sons in tow.

Three more teenage girls dressed for the prom excitedly entered the kitchen and met up with their dates and accompanying parents.

Megan's mom ushered the small crowd into the adjoining living room. A huge stone fireplace adorned the far wall, and leather furniture surrounded a big bear rug and large, glass coffee table, which was also covered with snacks and noshes.

A photo session in front of the fireplace ensued, and then the gathering walked out of a back door onto a sweeping veranda that overlooked a movie-star swimming pool surrounded by Italian marble statues, palm trees, and colorful landscaping.

Wow, was all Eliza could think as she smiled for the cameras beside her son, his date, and her parents.

After some small talk in which the McGees gushed, but in an authentic, not fake way, over Cameron's drumming abilities, making him blush but Eliza feel extremely proud, the limo pulled up and drove the four couples off into the Phoenix sunset.

CAMERON GRADUATED from high school that May and applied, albeit halfheartedly, to the local community college to take courses in business and music production. But he really hoped to make a full-time career out of drumming with the band. Meanwhile he worked as a pizza delivery boy, saving as much money as he could toward his music career.

Cactus Moon had catapulted to a bit of local fame the night of their first concert and was working on producing a CD that summer, which cost each of the band members a few hundred dollars.

Meanwhile they showed up to play at any venue that would have them and still practiced in between gigs.

Eliza actually liked hosting the band in her house, supplying them with homemade cookies, snacks, and soda. But Alex would often be ready to kick them out long before their curfew, saying their music gave him a headache most of the time.

Cameron dated Megan for almost a year, telling his parents he was serious about her, but then they broke up when she started seeing another boy, according to Cameron.

It seemed that their son got over his first love fairly quickly and just weeks after the break-up, moved on to dating a string of other girls. Eliza missed Megan for a while but knew it probably wasn't going to last since they had been so young when they first fell in love.

Eliza had liked when Megan would come over to the house to listen to the band for a while and then join her on the couch in the family room to talk about school and her dreams of becoming a doctor one day and traveling on missions to third world countries.

She will make a fine wife and mother one day, Eliza often thought. *She's smart, funny, warm, and truly a loving, kind soul.*

Ah well, we can't choose our daughters-in-law, Eliza realized sadly when she first heard of the break up.

While Cameron had told his parents that Megan had "ditched" him to date someone else, the real reason surfaced when Eliza overheard her sons arguing in their bedroom one night while she was gathering laundry from the boys' hamper in the bathroom.

"Megan was too good for you," she heard Austin say glumly.

"She was a prude," Cameron said a bit haughtily. "I'm glad she broke up with me. I would have broken up with her anyway."

"Everything's not about sex, you know."

"How would you know since you've never had any?" Cameron snickered.

"Shut up." She heard Austin whisper. At least he didn't defend himself by saying that he had. Eliza exhaled with relief, aware suddenly that she'd been holding her breath the whole time she had stood outside their door eavesdropping. The laundry basket was starting to weigh heavy in her arms, and she turned to go but not without hearing Cameron's last few words.

"At least Ivy isn't like Megan."

Ivy who? Eliza heard the rustling of feet. She quickly hurried back down the hallway toward the laundry room.

CHAPTER EIGHT

ELIZA AND ALEX met Ivy Brown at one of the band's concerts at the American Legion Hall that summer. Cameron had just started at the local community college while Austin was entering his sophomore year of high school. The boys were actually being paid to give a concert for a bar mitzvah party, having advertised their music on social media, much to Cameron's chagrin.

Ivy was tall and wildly beautiful. Stunning, with jet black curly hair that cascaded down to her tiny waist, big, sea blue eyes framed by long, black lashes, and a perfect smile. She was two years older than Cameron and had just graduated from the small two-year college he was attending.

Ivy was quite confident as she shook their hands and introduced herself as Cameron and his bandmates were busy setting up for the party. "It's a pleasure to meet you both," she said, flashing her brilliant, even, white teeth. Her skin was pale but flawless, and she had high cheekbones and perfectly sculpted eyebrows. Eliza noticed she had long, slender hands with manicured nails. "Well, I best be off to see if Cameron and the boys need anything, I hope to see you soon." She smiled again and turned to go, flipping her mane of curls behind her.

"She could definitely be a model," Alex remarked, watching her as she walked away from their table, her long, lean legs meandering off under a very short denim skirt.

Cactus Moon had kept Austin in the band as a backup singer to Max, and he played backup guitar and a few other instruments as needed. The boys in the band had had several arguments about whether Max should continue as lead singer and had taken a vote, with Charlie voting that Austin should take the lead and Cameron siding with Max to continue as main vocals. Since the vote was split down the middle, they decided that, since Austin had a lot less seniority, they would stick with Max.

But Austin's addition had definitely added depth to their sound, and the crowds that came to hear them had started to grow.

The morning after the bar mitzvah gig, a Saturday he would long remember, Austin received a call that would change everything.

Unbeknownst to him, his family or his bandmates, a talent scout attended the party at the Legion hall the night before and had heard Cactus Moon play. More importantly, he listened to Austin sing.

Dexter Poseidon was a friend of the bar mitzvah boy's family and sat off to the side that night, tapping his foot to the music. A single, balding, hefty Jewish man in his sixties, Dexter worked for the record label Stardust and had helped produce several Grammy-winning songs by at least a dozen new punk and rock bands, turning unknown kids into hit recording artists.

But he stayed in the background of the music industry, not dressing all flashy like most. He wore a tired, plain, brown suit and dress shoes, looking like a long-lost uncle who came to the American Legion to eat his share of the buffet and fulfill his obligation to the family, quietly eating at a table next to the wall.

No one noticed him, but Dexter noticed Austin as he sang back up to the song "Leavin' Lynette."

Austin's baritone voice sailed over Max's tenor, "get outta my sight, outta my sight, outta my sight!"

And when the fifteen-year-old crooned the love ballad, "Marie," his only solo of the night with Max playing lead guitar and singing harmony, Dexter sat up straight in his chair and leaned forward, pushing his half-eaten plate of knishes and potato salad aside.

"MOM! Dad! Cam! Come quick, you won't believe this!" Austin shouted, running out of his bedroom into the hallway and then living room, clutching his cell phone to his chest, nearly jumping up and down with excitement.

Cameron and Alex were in the kitchen helping Eliza clean up. The three of them froze as Austin relayed that Dexter wanted him to come in for an audition at the Stardust studios.

"He doesn't want to hear the whole band?" Cameron banged a plate down on the kitchen counter.

"Well, he said he wanted to hear me, but I guess I could call him back and ask if—"

"No, don't bother, moron." Cameron threw down the dish towel he was using, grabbed his car keys, and headed for the front door.

"Cameron, that's terrible, you should be happy for your brother," Eliza called after him but then let him go so she could congratulate her younger son.

"TELL ME ABOUT IVY." Another year had passed and it was almost winter, although in Phoenix it still felt like Indian summer. Eliza was sitting on the couch next to Cameron as he played video games and watched television, sulking.

Austin was out at one of his voice lessons. Eliza and Alex had sat down with Dexter Poseidon and had made it clear that Austin would take the whole music business very slowly and would at least finish high school before signing any contracts with Stardust or anyone else. Austin was a junior and would still have to wait a whole year, but Dexter was a patient man and agreed to work with him part-time, pro bono, until he graduated.

Cactus Moon kept playing gigs without Austin, with Max as the lead singer once again, but band gigs were beginning to wane as the boys, now men, were drifting apart to pursue "real" jobs, college careers, and girls.

Eliza decided to take advantage of the opportunity to talk one-on-one with her oldest son and reached for the TV remote, shutting the screen off.

"Hey, Mom," Cameron weakly protested and then sat in moody silence for a moment before answering her. "I really like her...actually I think I love her. She's beautiful, smart, fun to be with, but I'm not sure we're good for each other." Cameron absentmindedly twirled the shoestring from his sneaker around his finger, lost in thought, his nineteen-year-old, six-foot, lanky frame stuffed crookedly into the couch, his long arms and legs all jutting angular-like out of the soft plushness of the cushions. His hair, black and straight, fell over his eyes, and his pouty lips, which had turned up with his first statement, now straightened into a grim line with the last.

"Why not?" she dared to ask. *He looks so much like a little boy sometimes, lost in his dreams.* Eliza's heart ached with compassion for her son. *And then he's forced to grow up when his dreams get lost. It just seems like nothing ever goes right for him.*

"Well, I know this sounds crazy, but I think she might be narcissistic." Eliza saw in her son's deep, dark eyes a hint of the sadness that comes with growing up and knowing you can't always get what you want. And suddenly it seemed like the little boy in front of her vanished and became a very old soul, hunched over with the burdens of adulthood.

Eliza sat up straighter to listen and was curious now. How did he know that word, narcissistic?

"I know what you're thinking, how do I know what that means? I looked it up. I know I can be self-centered sometimes, but I think she takes it to the extreme once in a while. It's like, she knows what pushes my buttons, and she pushes them on purpose to get her way."

Eliza simply nodded, encouraging him to continue.

"I guess it goes hand in hand with the whole Victoria's Secret modeling thing."

"Oh. Is that what Ivy is planning to do now?"

"That's all she talks about. There's a lot of competition, and it's really tough to break into it, but she thinks she has a good shot."

"Well, I think she does too."

Cameron's face flushed. "But…well, never mind."

"No, tell me." *You can trust me,* Eliza pleaded silently with her eyes. She could tell Cameron was wrestling with whether to tell her what he had apparently kept secret for a long time.

He took a deep breath in and then exhaled. "But she's still doing drugs."

Eliza tried hard not to overreact, her sharp inhale uncontrollably escaping, echoing loud in her own ears. She contemplated asking questions but sat quietly, waiting for him to go on.

"I was doing them, too, for a while, but I didn't feel addicted, so I gave them up. I just didn't have time with the band, work, trying to get into college, and all of that."

"What drugs?" Eliza summoned the courage to ask.

"Marijuana. Cocaine. We tried heroin once, but I was too scared to try it again, and I just stopped doing any of it. But she…she can't seem to stop. I think she might have a problem. I hope I can help her stop and even told her I'd go to some Narcotics Anonymous meetings with her. I don't know, I do love her, maybe if she stops using…"

Eliza wanted to shout "run away and fast" to her son but knew he had to come to his own conclusion. Saying something like that to him would probably not only push him away from her but also push him further into Ivy's clutches.

She is very bad news, Eliza thought dismally. "I know you'll do what's best," was all she could muster to say, knowing anything more would fall on deaf ears. It was so hard being a parent of a young adult.

ALEX'S fortieth birthday was coming up in just a few months, and Eliza was planning a big surprise party for her husband.

She had reserved the Knights of Columbus hall and invited about fifty guests, mostly coworkers and friends, plus her sons and their friends.

After a big debate with herself, Eliza called Alex's little sister Doli, who still lived on the Navajo reservation. Doli had married a Native American who had also grown up there, and they had three children who went to the local schools.

Eliza knew Alex had kept in touch over the years by phone with his sister, while she herself had not had any contact with her own family. She had found out through Doli, however, that her sisters, Flo and Dena, had also stayed in the Navajo Nation, married natives there, and started their own families. When she first heard the news, the pang of remorse and isolation seized her just like it did the day she walked away, banned forever by her father, who, she had also found out, had warned her sisters to never have contact with her or they, too, would be disinherited just like she had been.

She would especially never forget the pain in her mother's eyes as she turned for the last time to go carrying a large duffel bag full of everything she owned at the time: some clothes and shoes, an ornate wooden jewelry box and some jewelry she had received as gifts, and a letter of farewell her mother had written, encouraging her to live her dreams, love with all her heart, and be a good mother if the good Lord were to bless her with children, letting them know their roots and that their grandmother loved them from afar.

Eliza had read that letter so many times it was tattered and torn, the ink worn over time, but she had never talked about her parents to Cameron and Austin. She had cut her family off like a useless limb, an arm that had become dead with gangrene that would have killed her if it seeped into the rest of her bloodstream and poisoned her heart.

When the boys asked about their grandparents and aunts and

uncles over time, they only spoke of Aunty Doli. Alex's mother had also disassociated herself from the young couple.

Eliza's fingers trembled as she held her cell phone to her ear after dialing Doli's number. The younger woman's familiar voice answered "Hello?"

"Hi, Doli, it's me, Eliza," she said, her voice sounding like a timid little girl's in her ears. She took a deep breath, trying to sound older and more confident now. "I'd like to invite you and your mom to a party I'm having for Alex's fortieth birthday. I wasn't sure where I should mail the invitation."

"Mama isn't doing good, so I'm sure she won't be able to come," Doli hurriedly replied. "And I would come but, well, I don't think it's a good idea since I have to be here for her and all. But thank you for asking."

Eliza wasn't sure how to even reply, her sister-in-law's words stinging, opening the wound again. *They have always blamed me for losing their brother, their son,* she reminded herself. *You have no family but Alex and the kids, why would you invite these people? They're not family, only strangers from a distant past that was better left untouched. Why would any of that change? What was I thinking? Still, I had to try…for Alex.*

"Okay, well I just thought I would ask," Eliza said softly.

"Please let him know that we…that I send my love and best wishes," Doli said and hung up.

AT FIRST, she had been a bit annoyed by it, but in the end, Eliza was relieved and extremely grateful for her friend Marsha's help in the weeks leading up to the party. Marsha loved event planning and immediately took over all of the details, from ordering food from the caterer to selecting the decorations and DJ.

She tricked her husband into walking in under the premise that they would be aiding Austin in planning his first solo gig at the Knights of Columbus venue.

When they entered the dimly lit hall, suddenly shouts of "Surprise!" exploded, the lights flooded the room, and the Beatles' "Birthday" song rocked through the giant speakers.

Horns blew and confetti swirled, blowing from two giant fans, mimicking New Year's Eve in Times Square, the theme Marsha had wanted to convey.

Eliza looked at her husband's beaming face and realized all of the anxiety she had felt leading up to the big bash had been worth it.

"Happy birthday, honey." She put her arms around his neck and kissed him on the cheek. He smiled, wrapping his arms around her waist and hugging her, but the moment was quickly lost amid the shouts and backslaps of party guests and well-wishers.

She finally had a chance to feel his arms around her again as they danced to a slow song she had added to the evening's playlist, the band Journey's "Faithfully."

After the cake was cut, it was time for Alex to open the stack of presents that awaited.

At their request, Eliza let her sons go last in presenting their gifts.

Cameron had gotten a job at a local florist shop, working around his college class schedule. It didn't pay much, but the shop had offered to give him a half-price discount on any product in the store. When he started thinking about what type of gift to give his dad for his birthday, albeit a little belatedly just two weeks before the party, he had kept an eye out for plants coming into the back warehouse that were pretty but couldn't be sold due to a flaw such as a torn leaf, browning flower, or slight lean to the right or left.

Finally, one had come in that seemed acceptable to him to give his father.

He pulled out a wagon onto the dance floor where his dad sat surrounded by all of the party guests. In the wagon sat a four-foot-tall, three-foot-wide, paper-wrapped gift topped with an enormous silver bow.

Alex unveiled the wrap to find a beautiful flowering cactus.

"Wow, Cam, this is really neat," Alex said, clearly surprised.

"I thought you could put it in your new office at work, that it could be like a conversation starter," their oldest son, now twenty and a gangly six-feet-tall, said, awkwardly bending down to hug his dad, who sat surrounded by gifts, people and confetti. Cameron had fixed the cactus's flaws, picking off the dying brown flowers and a few dead thorns.

"Thank you, Son," Alex said. He fingered a yellow blossom on the giant cactus with his left hand, which he immediately drew back. A big thorn had pricked his palm. "Ouch!"

Cameron looked embarrassed. "Sorry, Dad, I didn't mean—"

"That's okay," Eliza said, hurrying to see if her husband's hand was okay. Seeing the thorn had only drawn two drops of blood, Eliza worriedly looked at her son, who stood not knowing what to do, his face flushed with embarrassment. "Alex, tell him you're okay."

Alex pressed his right thumb into his left hand to staunch any more blood, wincing. "Yeah, of course, that was my fault, thanks again, Cameron."

"You're welcome." Eliza saw her son's look of enthusiasm and pride fade like the cactus bloom that now drooped a little after having been handled, and she felt sad for him.

Where was their younger son? Eliza looked up desperately for Austin but didn't see him in the crowd.

As if reading her thoughts, Marsha sidled up to her friend and whispered in her ear, "The party is dying here, we need to lighten the mood."

Cameron moved aside, and Alex looked expectantly around the room.

And then Eliza heard her younger son's familiar voice over the microphone up by the DJ's stand.

"Hey, Dad," Austin said, peering at them from under his unruly black curls that he had let grow down to his neckline, a broad grin on his face.

Everyone turned to see the seventeen-year-old standing alone at the mike at the far end of the room, smiling mischievously.

"I got you something kind of weird, I hope you like it."

The DJ, a young guy in his twenties, wheeled out another

wagon-like cart with a package that looked about a foot shorter but a little bigger around than the one Cameron had given.

It was wrapped in paper with a big, gold bow on top.

Austin pulled the cart out to where his dad sat, carrying the wireless mike in his hand. Alex ripped open the paper to reveal a giant birdcage.

In it sat an African grey parrot, a beautiful bird about a foot tall, with medium gray feathers and white circles around his beady, black eyes.

Austin had also been working a side job at a local pet store during his senior year in high school. He had saved for months for his father's fortieth birthday to get him something special before he even knew about the party.

When the parrot had come into the shop, Austin loved it immediately and knew it would make the perfect gift. He asked his boss, the store manager, to hold the bird for him and take automatic debits out of his pay until he could afford the four-hundred-dollar price tag.

Now he gingerly opened the birdcage door and encouraged the parrot to inch onto his dad's arm with his large, leathery talons.

"This is Pete, he's your present." Alex held the microphone up to the parrot's black beak, which opened, his little black tongue sticking out as he spoke.

"Happy birthday, Dad," Pete the parrot said, causing everyone to gasp in awe. "My name's Pete. Happy birthday. Many more. Many more."

"Oh my gosh, Austin, this is the best present ever!" Alex gushed and then laughed as the bird answered back, "Best present ever! Happy birthday. My name's Pete. Best present ever!"

"It's an African grey parrot, and the man at the pet shop said it makes a great pet and it's super easy to care for."

"How did you possibly get him to say all of that?" Alex was truly awestruck.

"I trained him at my friend's house for the past four months, so he better know how to say a few things." Austin grinned with pride.

Alex stood with the bird still firmly clutching his arm and hugged his son with his free arm. Austin held out his arm, and the bird climbed on. "Well, Pete, we'd love to have you entertain all night, but we have some dancing to do," Austin said charmingly into the microphone.

"Wait, let's get a picture of the whole family with the bird," Marsha chirped, running up in her high heels, cell phone in hand.

Eliza looked around and noticed Cameron turning his back and quietly walking away. He had come to the party with Ivy, whom he was dating again after a brief breakup, much to his parents' dismay. As she turned to follow him, Eliza heard her say under her breath, "Your parents have always favored your little brother. It's unfair."

As Marsha positioned herself in front of the birdcage, where Austin and Alex still talked, Cameron shot his mother a look of warning, his face crestfallen, his shoulders still drooping like the flower. He must have known she wanted him in the picture and was about to call out for him to come back, but he shook his head back and forth, his mouth silently forming the word "no." Then he quickly walked out of the room, Ivy in tow.

Eliza let him go, her heart aching for him.

"Eliza, come on, let's get a family photo with the bird." Marsha impatiently waved, urging her over to where Alex and Austin stood with the bird between them.

Some of the guests were already snapping away, taking photos of the two of them with Pete, who still had everyone mesmerized.

Eliza walked over and stood next to her husband, the bird and her younger son, plastering on a smile. Only after Marsha was finished taking the picture did Alex notice his other son was missing.

"Hey, where's Cameron?"

Eliza wanted to scream at him, "You're just now noticing?" but held her tongue. Instead she said, "Oh, he had to leave and take Ivy home. I don't think she was feeling well."

Alex shrugged and went back to watching Austin entertain the crowd, trying to get Pete to make different animal sounds now like he had trained him to do.

"You guys should be on a major talk show with this bird!" one of Alex's work buddies shouted, and everyone laughed. Except Eliza, who couldn't quite bring herself to join in the gaiety.

Marsha whispered in her ear, "Hey, it's time to cut the cake, Mama. This party is going great, don't you think?" Her bright pink lips parted in a self-congratulatory smile.

"Yes, great," Eliza said, trying not to sound sarcastic.

CHAPTER NINE

ELIZA HAD TAKEN a full-time job as an assistant librarian now that her sons were practically grown and was just returning home from work that night, tired but happy they were now paying their bills on time and getting out of debt again.

Austin was at a friend's house, and she figured Cameron was probably out with the band, so she looked forward to some quiet time before Alex came home from work. It was rare she had time to herself anymore.

It was chilly for Phoenix that November evening, and she had worn her jacket. The house was dark except for the corner lamp they usually left lit. She took off her coat and laid it across the living room recliner along with her purse and grocery bag full of items she had picked up on the way home that she planned to somehow whip together for tonight's dinner.

Suddenly Eliza was startled by a strange noise coming from the other end of the ranch house. She slowly and stealthily walked toward the noise. *What if it's a robber?* Then she heard the noise again, only louder, and realized it didn't sound like an intruder. It sounded like a teenage boy moaning in his sleep.

Her pace quickened until she was standing outside the boys' closed bedroom door. The half snoring, half moaning or groaning sound was definitely coming from one of the boys, although she couldn't tell which one.

"Austin? Cameron?" She said it quietly at first, but when no one answered, she raised her voice. "Boys? Is one of you in there? Can I come in?"

No answer. She knocked softly then loudly. No response. Eliza turned the doorknob and gently swung open the door. She had to blink for her eyes to adjust to the darkness. In a moment she could see the usual messiness of her sons' bedroom: worn socks and tee-shirts strewn on the floor, punk rock band posters, sports paraphernalia, and a few model pin-ups plastered on the walls, books and laptops and papers covering every inch of space on both desks.

Again, a snore and a moan came from the lower bunk bed. Her eyes riveted to the sleeping body turned away from her toward the wall. It was Cameron.

She walked over and gently laid her hand on his shoulder. "Cameron?" He lay curled up in a fetal position in his gray sweatshirt and jeans, a blanket rumpled at his feet that he had apparently kicked off while tossing and turning.

When he didn't move, she tried to wake him again. "Cameron, it's me, Mom. You must have dozed off, wake up."

Still, her son didn't budge an inch but merely kept on snoring. She summoned her strength, bent over as she was under the upper bunk, and yanked with both hands on his shoulder to roll him toward her. This was crazy. Why wasn't he waking up?

"Cameron!" she yelled when she saw his face. His skin was red as if he had developed a rash, and there were dark circles under his puffy eyes. His hair and skin were damp with sweat, yet he was shaking like he had chills. She touched his cheek, which felt both clammy and hot at the same time.

She stood up and frantically looked around. She tried to stuff it down but she couldn't deny the suspicion that crept into her mind that her son had over-dosed on something. And then she saw it lying on the floor next to his bed. A bottle of Benadryl. She opened it and saw it was empty. She looked under the bed, reaching under it amidst the dust, dirt, shoes, socks and who knew what else, and her hand clasped around a bottle. She rolled it out. It was an empty vodka bottle.

Eliza shook Cameron hard, and his eyes finally fluttered open. "Cameron, what have you done?" Terror seized her, rendering her numb for a minute. What to do next?

"Mom." The word came out in a muted croak. And then his head lolled over to one side, and he was out of it again. Eliza thanked God her son was at least breathing. She pried open one of his eyelids and saw his pupils looked like pinpoints, even in the dim glow of the bedroom lamp.

"Don't worry, honey, we're going to get you to a doctor."

She rushed to retrieve her cell phone from her purse on the recliner and called Alex but only got his voice mail. It would take him at least thirty minutes with traffic this time of day to get home. She left him a vague message that Cameron was very sick and to meet her in the emergency room at Banner Hospital downtown.

Then she called 911.

WAITING for the ambulance seemed to take forever, but the interval in the ER was even more excruciatingly long.

She used the time to call Austin and leave him a voice mail that Cameron had a high fever and was in the ER, but not to worry, and told him to ask if he could stay overnight at his friend's house since she and his dad might be at the hospital until late. She received a text from him a little while later saying he'd be spending the night at his friend Johnny's and to tell Cameron he hoped he felt better soon.

After about an hour, she looked up as Alex rushed into the ER lobby and approached the front desk. The nurse pointed in Eliza's direction and soon she was in her husband's arms, weeping.

Alex pulled away and held her by the shoulders to settle her. "What happened?" Eliza could tell he was trying to remain calm despite the panic he must be feeling.

"Oh, honey, it was awful. Cameron tried to OD on Benadryl

and vodka, but luckily the ambulance got him here in time, and they pumped his stomach and said he'd be fine and—"

She was interrupted by a young male intern who walked up to them. "Mr. and Mrs. Trellis?" They nodded. "You can come with me. Cameron is awake and ready to see you."

They approached the hospital bed where Cameron sat, propped up by pillows. He recognized his parents but seemed disoriented and instead of being sleepy, was restless and agitated. "Cameron, your parents are here to see you," the intern announced.

"I can see that," Cameron replied testily. "Mom, Dad, how did I get here?" Before Eliza had a chance to answer him, he kept talking, a little too loudly for her comfort. "It doesn't matter, you guys have to get me out of here." His words came out in a desperate order.

Cameron was lying under a blanket, dressed in a hospital gown. He started flicking his hands over his bare arms, as if swatting some unseen bugs swarming him.

"I need to warn you he may be experiencing side effects from the drug overdose like mild hallucinations and extreme irritability," the doctor whispered.

Suddenly Cameron glared at the doctor and then at his parents. "I'm right here," he said loudly, practically yelling. "And I need to get out of here. This place is crawling with bugs."

The doctor walked up to Cameron's bed side. "You'll need to stay overnight," the intern told his patient. "We need to watch for seizures. He'll need to be observed for at least thirty-six hours," he added in Eliza and Alex's direction.

"That ain't happening," Cameron barked and started to get down off the hospital bed, pushing the blanket down and swinging his legs to one side. He tried to pull the IV line out of his right arm, but suddenly a nurse seemed to appear out of nowhere and stopped him, holding down his left arm.

Alex stepped up to the other side of the bed and he, the doctor, and the nurse held Cameron's arms, restraining him. "Son, do as the doctor says." Alex reprimanded his son calmly but firmly.

"If you don't lie still, we will have to put restraints on you, and

I'm sure you don't want that," the middle-aged, heavy-set nurse said in a deadpan tone as she instantly produced a needle and expertly injected a clear fluid into Cameron's forearm before he had a chance to protest. "We are giving him a shot of Ativan to calm him down and help him sleep," she told Eliza and Alex matter-of-factly, like this was an everyday occurrence.

It seemed to Eliza like it took a very long time for Cameron to calm down but finally, around nine p.m., he was resting, and a new doctor poked his head in to let them know he'd be in shortly to speak with them again. He was a tall, older, gray-haired gentleman in a white lab coat and introduced himself as the hospital's chief psychiatrist, Dr. Jay Fulton.

Eliza sat with Alex, nervously fidgeting at Cameron's bedside in the cramped space of the makeshift ER room behind curtained walls. She tried to calm herself by playing games on her cell phone, then when that got tiring, she read a fashion magazine she had mindlessly picked up in the waiting room. *Please God, let him be okay*, she prayed to herself over and over, her heart doing double time. Alex stiffly sat, legs crossed, in his brown suit and shiny brown dress shoes, reading the newspaper from front to back and then back to front. Noticing his wife's agitation, he put down the paper and took her hands in his. "He'll be okay, honey." Eliza looked into her husband's eyes and saw in them that his rigid businesslike manner belied his own worry and despair. *He's trying to be brave as always for me.* She took a deep breath, willing herself to refrain from jumping out of her own skin so the hospital staff wouldn't try to restrain her too.

Mercifully Cameron finally dozed off and after what seemed like an eternity, Dr. Fulton returned to the ER cubicle and asked Alex and Eliza to step out into the hallway, where he told them that Cameron would be transferred later that night into a room in the hospital's psychiatric ward. He would be kept there for at least three days for observance, counseling, and medication. The doctor also informed them that Cameron had a blood alcohol level of nearly

.23, which was extremely dangerous combined with the fact that the teenager had admittedly taken twenty-five Benadryl pills.

Then came the questioning. "Has your son been suffering from depression, or had any negative occurrence recently, or been involved in a relationship that may have just ended or is negatively impacting him?" Dr. Fulton looked down at them, peering over the rims of his glasses. He seemed a little stern but not condescending or judgmental.

Almost fatherly, Eliza thought, reminding herself to be grateful. *My son is alive, and I have to trust he's in good hands.*

"Not that we know of," Alex responded, clearing his throat and sitting up straight, all business-like, sounding both professional and concerned.

"Um, actually he did talk to me recently and told me he and his girlfriend, her name's Ivy, weren't getting along, that he was thinking it may not work out..." Eliza's words quietly trailed off as she saw Alex staring at her.

"You never told me anything," her husband said with a hint of accusation.

"We just talked the other night." Eliza tried not to sound defensive and turned away from Alex to face the elderly psychiatrist. "And he was a little down about his brother leaving the band. He and his friends have this punk rock band that was starting to take off and now I think they're falling apart."

"Well, he shouldn't blame his brother for that," Alex interjected.

"I know that." Eliza huffed. "I'm just answering the question. I think he was a little depressed is all. And come to think of it, he wasn't happy that you raved about Austin's parrot at your birthday party but didn't seem to say much about the cactus plant he gave you. I think he felt like he disappointed you."

"Hey, don't go blaming this all on me."

"Um, this tension isn't helping anything," Dr. Fulton interrupted, breaking up what was about to become a marital argument. "I appreciate your honesty, but let's focus on Cameron. Clearly he was having issues with depression and/or anxiety, and perhaps jealousy, anger, and some resentments, and we will help him address all of that during his stay here. Since he's an adult, he will need to sign an agreement that he will stay voluntarily."

Eliza and Alex simply nodded. *This is all so crazy*, Eliza thought dismally. *How did we get here?*

"Does addiction run in the family?" The doctor looked up from his clipboard, looking first at Alex then Eliza. They glanced at each other and then proceeded to briefly outline their family history.

BEFORE FOLLOWING the doctor back into Cameron's ER room, Eliza looked at Alex and saw his frustration with her and his son melt as he embraced her. Eliza could feel Alex's sadness and pain, and she was grateful that as bad as everything seemed, at least they were in this together. She pulled back from her husband's arms, looking up at him and smiling through her tears.

"It will be okay," her husband whispered, his mouth turning up a bit in a small smile. "He will be okay, and so will we."

The comfort was all too brief, though, as Cameron suddenly awoke and became agitated, starting to fidget and complain again. Although Dr. Fulton had explained this was likely to happen, it was still hard to see him this way.

All three of them spoke soothing, comforting words to Cameron until he calmed down and sat upright in the hospital bed, looking dismal once more.

Dr. Fulton kindly but sternly instructed Eliza and Alex to take a seat in the chairs against the far wall several feet away from their son's bed and to wait quietly while he questioned Cameron. They sat obediently silent, holding each other's hands for support.

"Cameron, I'm sorry you felt the need to overdose." The elderly doctor sat on a stool he had pulled up beside the bed. "What made you feel so down that you got to this state?"

"I was feeling depressed about the band falling apart, angry at my brother Austin and my parents, and upset about my girlfriend

Ivy," Cameron answered, not looking at either his mom or dad, who both remained silent.

Dr. Fulton quietly took notes on his clipboard, nodding for Cameron to continue.

"She had been clean for a while, off drugs, but had relapsed again, and I told her we were through. She cried and begged me to come back to her, to give her another chance. I just felt bad for her, guilty for not sticking by her. And she's the only person I really have right now. I felt like I had lost everybody."

"Oh, honey, that's not true—" Eliza stopped mid-sentence when the doctor darted her a silencing look that said *this isn't about you.*

"Why were you angry at your brother and your parents?" the doctor asked. Eliza wondered as well, and her husband's hand gripped hers a little more tightly. *Alex must be asking himself the same thing.* "Why did you feel so alone?"

"I don't know, I just feel like Austin always gets everything he wants," Cameron said dejectedly with a sigh.

"Like what?" the doctor softly asked.

Cameron shook his head, his eyes welling with tears as he looked first into his mother's eyes, then into his father's. Eliza felt like her heart was shattering, and she held back tears, afraid to say anything either in the way of an apology or in defense as Dr. Fulton gave her the same stern look of warning before turning back to address his patient.

"Cameron, it sounds like you are feeling resentful about several things and that you need to talk about that further, but it will take time to work on everything." Dr. Fulton inched closer and took Cameron's young hand in his own weathered one. "We can help you get started on the process, and you may need some counseling and possibly medication, but a big part of whether or not you stay healthy will be up to you, the work you do to rid yourself of those resentments and the choices you make going forward. Understand?"

Cameron nodded solemnly and laid his head back on the pillow, exhausted and resigned now. The doctor smiled at him then turned to face Eliza and Alex. "Mr. and Mrs. Trellis, I'm going to talk to

Cameron alone now, get him to sign some papers, and then we're going to transfer him to a room upstairs." Dr. Fulton perfunctorily stated the directions, his tone much more stern and commanding than before.

Where did we go wrong? Eliza couldn't help but feel the pangs of helplessness and guilt, hearing her son say he felt alone and abandoned and seeing him lying there, his skin sallow, his hair limp, his eyes vacant with surrender. It took every ounce of energy she had within her to remind herself: *this isn't about me.*

And then a hot rage boiled up inside her against Ivy. *She better stay away from my son.* Eliza needed to shift the blame from herself, her husband, or even Cameron or Austin, onto someone else. Anger felt better than guilt, blame better than shame right now.

This is all her fault.

CAMERON WAS RELEASED from Banner on Monday afternoon after a three-day stay. He had been diagnosed with bipolar disorder and prescribed a low dose of lithium.

Eliza and Alex picked him up from the hospital, talking cheerfully on the way home about college, the news, the weather, everything and anything but Ivy or Austin or the band.

Eliza felt guilty again as she cringed a little when Austin walked into the house shortly after they got home from the hospital and greeted his brother with a warm bear hug. But thankfully, Cameron seemed truly glad to see his kid brother, and the two bounded toward the kitchen, ravenous as usual, to get a snack before dinner.

The four sat around the kitchen table eating dinner for the first time in a long time. Eliza had cooked meatloaf, mashed potatoes and gravy, peas, and apple sauce, one of Cameron's favorite dinners, and watched with glee as both of her sons cleaned their plates and helped themselves to seconds.

She glanced up to find her husband conspiratorially smiling at her as the boys chatted about music, school, the latest rumors in the neighborhood, and the most recent videos that had gone viral. Eliza's heart warmed toward him like a stream thawing in spring, warmth slowly cracking ice that had formed on the surface, allowing a trickle of love to flow that had lain frozen over time.

She smiled back.

"What are you two goofballs smiling about?" Cameron, always the more inquisitive of their sons, noticed the exchange.

"We're just happy," Eliza answered, wiping her mouth with her napkin, unable to wipe the grin off her face.

"Oh brother," Austin said. "Hey, Cam, wanna come with me to a party Friday night?"

Suddenly the mood shifted to an uneasy silence.

"What?" Austin stood, looking at his parents with a challenging stare. "It's just a high school party."

"Yeah, I don't know if I want to hang out with all of you loser kids." Cameron sloughed off his parents' concern, trying to lighten the mood. "I'll have to check my calendar and let you know. I might, but I can't promise you anything."

"There will be girls…" Austin drew the last word out, wadding up his napkin and throwing it teasingly at his brother. "And I invited Charlie and Max too."

"All right, I'll think about it," Cameron said, sounding uneasy. Eliza detected a bit of embarrassment in her oldest son. It was probably too soon for him to feel excited about being around a bunch of people, especially at a party, she thought, shrugging it off.

CHAPTER TEN

AS PROMISED, Austin signed a contract with the Stardust label the summer after he graduated from high school and turned eighteen. He had also received a scholarship to Stanford University where he decided to explore a degree in biology.

Austin's first record, "Front Man," became a hit and eventually climbed the billboard charts to number one. Eliza knew it was only a matter of time before she would lose her younger son, who would probably eventually stay in California working on his music in Los Angeles where his agent Dexter lived. Stardust was located just about a six-hour drive away from Stanford.

Eliza could tell, during their weekly phone conversations, that Austin felt a little homesick for the first month or so of college, but that quickly disappeared when her sociable second son started to find his stride at Stanford. He made a few friends, went to parties and soon joined the school newspaper staff.

She was happy for him, although it had been really hard to say goodbye and watch him leave home.

One night he called her sounding especially thrilled. "Mom, you'll never guess who I saw on campus today." Austin's voice sounded rushed and excited.

With Cameron out seeing Ivy and Alex working late most nights, Eliza was often alone in their house, which sometimes seemed to engulf her in loneliness, so she welcomed his call.

"Who?"

"Megan McGee."

Ah yes, lovely Megan. How could she forget Cameron's prom date and girlfriend for all too short a time? She had been one of her favorites.

"Anyway, I found out she's a student here. She just transferred from Duke. She said she wanted to be out here where it's warmer. She's so smart and rich, I guess she could go anywhere she wants."

The Trellis family had been fortunate that Austin was smart enough to receive a partial scholarship on top of the financial aid they had gotten, since there was no way they could have afforded to send him to Stanford outright.

"How is she doing?" Eliza eagerly sat up in her recliner to listen intently.

"Good. She looks great. I saw her at the library. We decided to meet for dinner tomorrow night at this little Mexican café just off campus. You know, catch up from the 'hood type of thing. Plus I heard they have good tacos. Not better than yours, of course."

Eliza smiled. "Well, tell her I said hello."

"I will, Mom. I gotta run now, some of the guys are getting up a poker game. Don't worry, we're only playing for pennies. Oh, how are you and Dad?"

Sweet Austin. He had always had a very compassionate streak in him. "Good. But we miss you."

"How's Cam and Ivy?"

"They're good too." Eliza sighed wistfully.

"Well, tell them all I said hi."

"I will, honey." She bit her lip and steadied her voice, missing him so much. "Are you enjoying it out there?"

"It's great. I love it." Eliza heard guys' voices in the background and then heard laughter.

"Well, you go. I love you, Austin."

"Love you, too, Mom."

ONE DAY as she was emptying the boys' laundry basket, Eliza noticed Cameron's medicine bottle sitting out on the bathroom vanity counter. Absentmindedly, she looked at the prescription on the bottle. "60 tabs, Lithium 600 mg, twice daily, do not take with alcohol, zero refills."

It had been several months since Cameron's overdose and the prescribing of the pills. As far as she knew, he had kept his monthly appointments with his psychiatrist and had gotten the prescription refilled on a regular basis.

Eliza shook the bottle. It seemed full when it should be nearly empty according to the expiration date. She twisted the medicine bottle cap open and looked inside. It was more than half full.

That was odd. Out of curiosity, she dumped the pills into her left palm and counted. There were forty pills left when there should have only been about ten.

And then it dawned on her. Cameron had stopped taking his medicine, hadn't been taking it for at least two weeks.

Eliza froze in fear, her hand shaking as she slowly let the pills fall from her hand back into the bottle, two of them missing and falling to the floor. She scrambled to find them and put them back into the bottle, concentrating on breathing, trying not to panic, her heart thudding. She remembered what Dr. Fulton had said when he talked to Cameron before he checked out of Banner.

"You need to make sure you take all of your medicine on a daily basis and see me for regular checkups. Going off the medicine can have severe consequences," the doctor warned. "You need to make smart choices, so you don't fall back into your anger and depression. Your bipolar disorder is like a tiger crouching at the door, and it's up to you to master it by taking your medicine."

Cameron had told Eliza that his monthly check ups with the psychiatrist were going well, that Dr. Fulton had told him the medicine appeared to be working, and that he would keep him on it and possibly decrease the dosage. Her son had complained from time to time of feeling bouts of fogginess, when he just felt "out of it," but said the doctor had dismissed this as "normal."

She had offered to take her son to the appointments but he had resisted, saying he was a man now at the age of twenty-one, and was responsible for himself, therefore she hadn't insisted although she had wanted to at the time.

Now she regretted that decision. She knew Cameron had a fiercely independent streak and that he sometimes was defiant or even arrogant when it came to authority figures such as teachers, the police, and even doctors, thinking he knew better than they did, like the time he was stopped for speeding. He ended up with tickets not only for exceeding the speed limit but also for failure to obey a police officer when he argued and refused to sign the ticket or provide his license and registration.

Dr. Fulton had explained that the side effects Cameron could experience if he stopped taking his medicine without being properly weaned off by a physician, especially if he went "cold turkey," could include flu-like symptoms, headaches, irritability, or a severe relapse of the disease, including mania, anxiety, depression, or even suicidal tendencies again.

"I know this all sounds scary, but I believe it's best to be up front with you," the doctor had said, trying to sound stern, turning his gaze from Cameron to Eliza and looking sharply into her eyes for added effect.

Oh no, I should have stayed on top of all of this. The bile of guilt rose up in her. She immediately called Cameron's cell phone and got his voice mail.

"Cameron, call me," she said, willing her voice to remain calm. "It's important."

⇛——▶

CAMERON DIDN'T COME HOME that night, which wasn't out of the ordinary. Sometimes he stayed at Ivy's house.

Lately Eliza had come to accept that Cameron's behavior, like staying out and not letting her know, was out of her control, although she did forbid girls to ever spend the night under the Trellis roof. She knew she was old-fashioned compared to many women her age, probably a throwback to her Navajo upbringing. And even though Alex still thought at times she babied her boys, he supported Eliza, and they tried to be a team in making decisions that erred on the strict side of parental discipline.

A few times over the past year, Eliza considered asking her son to leave since he couldn't obey his parents' simple request to keep them posted on his whereabouts, especially if he wasn't coming home. But Eliza felt like she was walking on a very narrow balance beam. One move the wrong way and her life could fall into disaster if she caused her son to plunge into the darkness of his disease again. *I could never forgive myself if I caused him to overdose and maybe even succeed at killing himself,* she often thought.

Eliza kept her mouth shut, although Alex could be vocal about the situation at times.

When he argued with Cameron, sometimes she and Austin retreated to the farthest corners of the house or left altogether if they started shouting.

"It's like you and Ivy live on another planet!" Alex shouted the last time. "You fall off the face of the earth, like you're both hippies or something. You don't call or even talk to your mother and me unless you need money. Something's got to change, Cam, or you'll be finding another place to live."

"Fine!" Cameron always ended the conversation abruptly and stormed out, aware his father could no longer physically stop him since he was taller and stronger than his dad now.

WHEN TWO DAYS passed and Eliza still hadn't heard anything

from her son, she started feeling frantic and decided to call him for the tenth time.

Her heart leapt into her throat when she saw his number pop up just as she reached for her cell phone.

"Hi, honey, how are you, I've been worried sick."

"Mom, I'm fine, take a breath," Cameron said, calming her.

Eliza didn't even realize she had been holding her breath, and she exhaled, waiting for him to let her know why he was calling, trying not to give in to her motherly instinct to lecture him.

"Are you sitting down?"

Uh oh. This couldn't be good, she thought, pulling out a chair at the kitchen table and quickly sitting in it. "Yes, I am now. What's up?"

"You're going to be a grandmother."

Eliza's breath caught in her throat, and her chest tightened.

Just like that. I'm going to be a grandmother. Wait, that's not possible, I'm too young…is it Ivy's? He hasn't been back with Ivy that long, has he? Her thoughts scurried to and fro like squirrels chasing a nut attached to a string that was pulled this way and that, never quite grasping it in their little paws. *This is exciting, crazy…a baby? A girl? A boy? I'm not ready for this…*

"Mom? You still there?"

"Yes…I, uh, wow, congratulations, Cameron." Eliza forced happiness into her tone. "That's great."

"Yeah, Ivy and I are really happy." It sounded to her like Cameron was also making an effort to sound happy.

Eliza's mind finally wrapped around the nut, but the joy of that didn't quite reach her heart yet.

My baby is having a baby, she thought with a mix of happiness and sorrow. Then questions like needles shot through her brain. Where would they live? How would they live?

And suddenly, a dart of anger pricked her soul. *Ivy tricked my son. She had this planned all along.* They had only been together for about a month. "When are you coming home?" she asked instead, trying not to let her anxiety show through.

"We have a lot to figure out, so probably not until the weekend. But I'll see you then and we can talk more. I gotta run, I'm on a break in between classes. See you soon. Love you."

SHE TOLD Alex the news about the baby over Easter dinner, which she had fixed for just the two of them since Cameron was eating over Ivy's parents' house. Alex froze, his hand hovering mid-air halfway to his mouth, and he slowly lowered his forkful of apple pie. Eliza had baked it for him, knowing she would be telling him about Cameron, Ivy, and their grandchild to be. She thought the pie would sweeten the news going down a little like Mary Poppins' "spoonful of sugar," but she was wrong.

"You have got to be kidding me." Alex's voice was deadpan but started to rise in anger. "That little…I'm sure Ivy had this planned all along. How could Cameron be so stupid? He's an idiot! He never thinks of the consequences of his actions, but this time takes the cake."

It was futile to argue with him, and she knew even if she tried to sound positive and suggest that maybe they'd planned to have a baby, or at least perhaps Ivy hadn't tricked him, her husband would know she was lying.

"Honey, try to calm down," she said soothingly instead, but Eliza's words only seemed to fuel his ire, and he angrily pushed his plate away, scraped his chair back, and stood, balling up his paper napkin and then throwing it down onto his half-eaten piece of pie in disgust.

"How long have you known about this?" he asked her accusingly.

"I just found out two days ago but thought I should tell you in person."

"What did our smart son say they were going to do?"

Surely her husband was not intimating that there was any choice but to keep the baby? She shook the notion out of her head. "What do you mean?"

"I mean where are they going to live? How are they going to afford to raise a baby? I hope her parents can support them because we sure can't."

Eliza was at least relieved to hear her husband wasn't asking whether they were going to keep the child, their grandchild-to-be.

She remained silent and let him pace for a bit and then pour himself a glass of whiskey. He went into the living room, where he turned on TV and began to watch a basketball game on ESPN. *I wish I could divert my attention so easily.*

CAMERON PROPOSED TO IVY, and they decided to get married the second week of May so that Austin would be home from college and attend.

Cameron asked Austin to be his best man, and Ivy asked her only sibling, Linda, to be her maid of honor. It would be a small ceremony at a restaurant in Flagstaff where Ivy's parents lived. Just immediate family members—both sets of parents and siblings—and a few friends including their band mates would be invited. Only fifteen people would be in attendance at the ceremony, including the minister.

Not how I imagined my son's wedding, Eliza thought dismally. She tried to hide her disappointment by forcing a smile on her face as the engaged couple relayed all of the details when they were out to dinner in Scottsdale the following weekend with Ivy's parents, Joan and Kyle Brown. The dinner was arranged to be sure both sets of parents could meet before the wedding. The Browns had driven down to meet them at the fancy local Italian restaurant Ivy had suggested so they could get to know each other.

Cameron must have recognized his mother's disappointment and quickly interjected, "We're going to have something bigger down the line after the baby is born and we can afford it."

"And I'm sure we can help." Kyle Brown winked at his daughter and future son-in-law and then smiled across the table at Alex and Eliza.

"THE BROWNS SEEMED NICE ENOUGH," Eliza said as she sat on their bed, wearily removing her high heels. It had been an exhausting evening trying to keep up with the pleasant banter at the table. Even though she and Alex admittedly wouldn't have picked Ivy as a wife for their son, Eliza was proud of Cameron for doing the right thing and marrying her, and she had really tried to like the Browns and stay positive about the upcoming wedding.

Joan and Kyle were a handsome couple, and Eliza could see where Ivy got her exotic looks—her black hair from her Italian dad and her big, blue eyes and slim figure from her petite, blonde-haired mom.

"Yeah, they're okay, although they seemed a little snooty." Alex sat on the edge of their bed, taking off his jacket, shoes, and tie. "I still don't like Ivy much though. I just think Cameron could have done a lot better. She just seems fake and phony and manipulative. Did you see how she ran the show tonight at dinner?"

"Well, she's young, hopefully she'll grow out of that," Eliza offered, not believing her own words but also not wanting to get into a heated discussion. Her bones ached, she was extremely tired, and she felt talked out for the night. All she wanted to do was crawl under the covers and go to sleep. "I think she was just trying to impress us, and probably her parents too. At least they seemed to like Cameron and are very supportive of them."

"Yeah, they made me feel guilty, saying how they're going to pay for everything including a big wedding down the line, and how they insisted on paying for dinner tonight." Alex grimaced. "I guess they can afford it though. Kyle must make a ton of money at his law practice."

They learned that night that Kyle Brown was an attorney with the Flagstaff law firm Jones, Brown, and Laymon, while Joan worked part-time as a realtor.

Eliza knew her husband was feeling a bit sensitive, so she chose to remain silent. She lay in bed unable to sleep for a long time that night, worrying about her son. She realized that she was more upset about the small, rushed wedding than Cameron seemed to be.

Besides, she remembered, *Alex and I got married in the same way and look where we are now.* Somehow that thought, while causing her to realize she'd be hypocritical and judgmental if she tried to talk her son into waiting and having a bigger, better ceremony, also deepened the sadness in her heart. She didn't regret for one day marrying Alex. She just looked back and wished it could have been different. Bigger and better.

I guess you always wish for more for your kids. And even though you hope they learn from your mistakes and don't make the same ones you did, ultimately, they have to learn from their own.

And at least our son would have his parents at his wedding. The unintended thought sent a sharp pain tearing open the scarred wound in her heart. She looked over at Alex sleeping peacefully, his worn yet still handsome face turned toward her in slumber. *Love finds a way past the pain though*, she thought, finally comforting herself to sleep.

"...FOR better, for worse, for richer, for poorer..." Cameron and Ivy repeated the ancient wedding vows uttered by the minister, a short, stocky, bald man with glasses.

She is pretty, Eliza thought, gazing at Ivy, who stood smiling, her red lipstick matching the roses she held in her hands. The flowers contrasted with the snow-white dress she wore, her long, black hair swept up in a side chignon accented by a single red rose.

Eliza was standing to the left and slightly behind her son during much of the short ceremony, and she couldn't see his face during the vows and exchange of rings to tell how he was feeling. But she could hear the dedication, perhaps even love, in his voice.

And after the minister pronounced them husband and wife and they kissed and the young couple turned to face their siblings and parents, Eliza saw the smile on Cameron's face and could only hope he was happy and would remain content in years to come.

Following the dinner reception, Cameron and Ivy went on a weekend honeymoon stay in the mountains in Flagstaff, given as a wedding gift by the Browns. Then the couple planned to go home to their little apartment in Phoenix to start their new life together and prepare for the baby on the way.

CHAPTER ELEVEN

PUSHED BY HIS AGENT DEXTER, Austin spent a grueling summer following his first year at Stanford cutting his first album and touring several southwestern states in concert, which included a week's stint at Harrah's Resort in Las Vegas.

He had rapidly become known as the newest boy wonder in punk rock.

Going against Dexter's advice, Austin went back to Stanford for his sophomore year and had to cut back on his musical career again, but with the help of a tutor, which he could now afford, he would at least have time in the studio to record on weekends and breaks and would have his summers free to tour.

Eliza heard from her busy youngest son even less that next year in school, so Austin's call one late September evening came as a surprise, but his news was even more shocking.

"Mom, you won't believe this, Dexter is going to submit me and my music to be nominated for the Grammy Awards!"

Austin practically shouted, and Eliza had to hold her phone away from her ear a few inches. "Congratulations, honey!"

"He's asking the Academy of Music to nominate me for five Grammys. Best New Artist, Best Record, Best Song, Best Album,

and Best Rock Performance. Now that doesn't mean I'll be nominated, but I might!"

"When are the awards?" Eliza had only caught snippets of past
awards shows and really wasn't into any particular artist, although if
she did have to name her favorite type of music, she favored country
more than the rest.

"Next February, but I find out the first week in December
whether I'm nominated or not."

"Well, I'll say lots of prayers that you get nominated. That is so
exciting. Your father and I are really proud of you, Austin."

"Thanks, Mom."

THAT SUMMER and fall in Phoenix were particularly hot and dry.
Patches of lawn lay scorched, brown and bristly, and only the
heartiest of cactuses and desert plants survived.

The state of Arizona placed a temporary ban on water usage
for anything other than drinking or bathing, forbidding outdoor
water usage as well as placing a limit on the use of electricity to
prevent power outages from the constant running of air conditioning. The mandate curbed corporations in the major cities and
fined them if they were found in violation of the government
restrictions.

Cameron came home from work every day hot and sweaty, only
to deal with his exhausted wife, who complained often of nausea and
ran to the bathroom at least three times a day to throw up. The first
trimester of Ivy's pregnancy had been rough, and unfortunately,
unlike the experience of most women, the second trimester so far
hadn't been any easier.

He had to drop out of college to get a full-time job to pay their
apartment rent and most of the other bills plus save a little extra for
the baby on the way. He started as a bricklayer, working with a small
residential construction firm in downtown Phoenix. Every day he
had to wake up at five a.m. and be on the job by six, no matter what
the weather, putting in nine-hour days. Cameron had been lucky to

find a job that didn't require a bachelor's degree and paid more than minimum wage.

It was mind numbing and back breaking work, and he hated it, but it paid twenty dollars an hour, and it was the only job offering a steady paycheck that he could find right away.

Ivy had been working as an assistant manager at a Victoria's Secret store at the Paradise Valley Mall but was eventually fired when she took a few too many sick days.

Eliza talked to Cameron even less than she did Austin, even though he lived just ten miles away. She usually only heard from her older son or his wife when they needed to borrow money, but still Eliza hungrily welcomed every text or phone call she received from Cameron.

Now she and Alex were "empty-nesters." As happy as she was for Austin, she was equally sad for Cameron. She worried about him, knowing he seemed discontent with his life.

Cameron had confided in her that he had finally had to quit Cactus Moon because he couldn't make practices much less any gigs they may have lined up, even though they had become few and far between. Max and Charlie eventually gave up on the band without Austin or Cameron.

When her older son called in early September, Eliza was both elated and worried, hoping he had good news.

Instead the news was terrible. "Ivy had a miscarriage," Cameron said softly in a broken voice, and Eliza could tell her son was crying.

She desperately wished she could be there to hold him, comfort him, but all she could do was listen as he wept. After a minute or so, he heaved a sigh and continued, his words coming out in a rush. "Mom, it was awful, she started cramping and bleeding yesterday and we didn't know what to do so I took her to the hospital and we met there with her doctor who did an ultrasound and we didn't hear the heartbeat and he told us he was really sorry but the baby had stopped growing somehow and it wasn't our fault and he would have to do a D and C, which he did last night, and she's home now resting but..." His voice trailed off in another hopeless sigh. "I'm not sure if she's going to be able to handle this, Mom. I don't know if I can."

Eliza said a quick prayer to find the words to say to her son, in the back of her mind doubting if a God could exist that allowed a baby to die before it even had a chance to live outside its mother's womb.

"Honey, I'm so sorry," she said soothingly. "But you're strong, and so is Ivy, and I know you two will get through this together, and if there's anything I can do ... I can come over if you like and be with Ivy."

"No, Ivy really just wants to be left alone," Cameron said firmly, his tone turning instantly from despair to determination.

"Are you sure, honey, because I would think she could use some company, and since her parents live so much farther away, I could come over and make dinner and—"

Cameron cut her off with a tone that had turned biting.

"Mom, you need to listen, I said that's okay, we don't need anything from you and Dad, we'll let you know when we do. I have to go back to work now, my lunch break is over. Goodbye, Mom." And the phone disconnected.

The sting of his rejection hurt, but Eliza told herself to be patient, reminding herself her son's sudden shift in attitude was probably just his bipolar tendencies surfacing.

She found herself wondering if all of the drugs Ivy had done in the past caused the miscarriage. Cameron had told his mother that Ivy had stopped using when she found out she was pregnant. Eliza chose to believe him, although Alex never did.

Eliza had tried to accept her daughter-in-law, but Alex never had liked Ivy. She knew her husband secretly thought Ivy was a high-maintenance shrew who had tricked their son into staying in a relationship with her by getting pregnant. Sometimes Eliza couldn't help but find herself feeling the same way.

But she knew it did not do her any good to allow herself to wonder what Cameron's life could have been like if not for Ivy.

AUSTIN CAME HOME from school the first of December for the Christmas break and was lounging around in his bedroom when the call from Dexter came.

Eliza and Alex were on the couch watching a rerun of "Everybody Loves Raymond" when their son came bursting into the living room, his cheeks flushed with excitement.

"I'm in!" he said, standing before them with his hands on his hips.

Eliza reached for the remote and muted the television. "In what?" she asked with anticipation, sitting up straight.

"I've been nominated for three Grammys!"

Alex stood up and high-fived his son. "Congratulations!"

Eliza's mouth hung open. After the initial shock of his news wore off, she stood and hugged him tight. "Wow, that's fantastic, Austin! We are so proud of you!"

He stood grinning, shaking his tousled mop of black curls back and forth in disbelief. "I still can't believe it! I've been nominated for Best Song, Best Album and Best New Artist!"

"Well, we'll have to go out this weekend to dinner and celebrate!" Alex stood with his chest puffed out proudly.

"I'm going to call Cam and tell him the news." Austin bounded from the room back down the hall to his bedroom to get his cell phone.

Eliza fervently prayed her older son would be equally happy and proud.

CHRISTMAS EVE WAS A JOYFULLY chaotic affair that year with Ivy talking about her plans to try for another baby and Cameron and Austin excitedly talking about the upcoming Grammys. Cameron had seemed to take the news better than Eliza thought he would.

She and Alex had followed their family tradition and lavishly decorated the Christmas tree and the entire house with ornaments, wreaths, and lights, making the unusually warm holiday at least seem festive.

They all went to the four o'clock mass at St. Augustine's and came home to a big ham dinner Eliza had prepared ahead of time.

Austin did most of the talking at dinner, chatting about school, his new record coming out, and the upcoming awards ceremony in between bites of mashed potatoes, sweet potatoes, green bean casserole, and pineapple bread pudding.

"Who's coming with me to the awards?" he asked, mischievously smiling, his dimples deepening and his eyes glittering with delight.

There was a moment of nervous silence before Cameron cut the tension. "Well, dummy, first you have to tell us who's invited."

"You all are, of course," Austin said.

"Are you sure, honey?" Eliza had hoped she would be able to go and had even picked out an aqua sequined dress that she had found on sale at the mall and put on hold, just in case.

"I can invite up to five guests, but one has to be Dexter, of course."

"Well, thanks, but I know I won't be able to get off work. I've already taken all my time off coming to me," Cameron said, biting into a buttered roll. "Some of us have to work to pay the bills."

Eliza caught the look of disappointment that shrouded Austin's face and interjected, "Well, your father and I are definitely going, I already picked out my dress so it's a good thing we're invited!"

"You already picked out a dress? I'm afraid to ask how much that's going to cost me!" Alex playfully said, his eyes twinkling. "Just kidding, but seriously, do I have to wear a tux?"

"Of course you'll wear a tux, dear, we'll rent one in LA." Eliza was elated.

"Hey Ivy, you coming?" Austin asked his sister-in-law. "Just because Cam can't make it, you're still invited."

"Yeah, right." Cameron said sardonically. "I'm not letting her go to some awards show in LA without me. Besides neither one of us can afford it."

"I could pay your way," Austin offered, looking cautiously across the table at his brother. "I'd be glad to help you both out. I've got so much money coming in from record sales that I don't even know what to do with it all. I've been meaning to tell you this for a while now. Let me pay your way to LA, give you some extra money for everything you need, help you pay your bills even."

Eliza winced, not daring to even look in her older son's direction, fervently hoping he wouldn't be offended. She knew Cameron was proud like his father. Sometimes a little bit of that pride went a long way in building a dream, a house, a family. Sometimes too much could make it all fall apart.

Cameron slowly put down the knife with the butter still on it, but Eliza noticed his hand was still clenched around the handle. His words came out in a low, slow monotone, as if he was spitting each word out like it was poison. "That's okay, little bro, we don't need your charity."

Ivy smiled, pretending to be oblivious to her husband's obvious jealousy. "Well, I would love to come but I guess I also need to work." She sighed loudly. "Thanks anyway, Austin."

Austin took a deep breath. "All right, I didn't mean to offend anyone, I was just trying to help. But since you two can't make it, I think I'm going to ask Megan," he said quickly, reaching for the plate of ham.

"Megan who?" Cameron asked, squinting curiously at his brother.

"Oh, Mom didn't tell you? Megan McGee is at Stanford now."

Cameron's face reddened, and his eyes darkened as he stared at his brother.

"Megan McGee? You've been seeing Megan McGee?" Cameron's voice rose an octave as he said her name a second time, and the crimson in his face deepened. Eliza wasn't sure if it was out of shame, anger, jealousy, or all three.

"Well, yeah, nothing serious, we're just friends and all." Austin saw that his brother was clearly agitated by the news and tried to switch the subject. "Mom, dinner was great, let us guys help you clean up." He stood to take his plate to the kitchen.

"Wait a minute." Cameron shoved his chair back from the table and stood, throwing his linen napkin onto his plate. "How could you see her and not tell me?"

"I thought Mom told you. Besides you broke up with her a long time ago, I didn't think you'd care. And like I said, we're not dating, just seeing each other as friends and—"

"Yeah, right. I can't believe this. Mom, how could you not tell me?" Cameron indignantly glared at Eliza. *The mother always takes the fall,* she thought, willing herself to remain calm.

"Tell you what?" Ivy glowered suspiciously in Cameron's direction.

"Nothing." Cameron began to collect his plate and hers to take into the kitchen.

"Well, obviously it's not 'nothing,' You sounded upset." Ivy was clearly not going to let the subject drop.

Cameron's eyes narrowed at his brother with a silent warning, "Don't tell her," but Austin either didn't get the message or was provoking his brother in the way only siblings can do.

"He's just upset I'm asking his ex-girlfriend to the Grammys, even though I told him we're just friends."

"Shut up, I am not." Cameron protested a little bit too loudly.

"What ex-girlfriend?" Ivy's big, blue eyes narrowed into jealous slits.

"Okay, you two, that's enough." Alex also stood, grabbing his plate. "Into the kitchen, time to clean up." When the boys stood still, not budging, he ordered, "Now."

Eliza sat helplessly silent, not knowing what to say. She had wanted to tell Cameron about Austin seeing Megan on campus but had never had the opportunity since her time was limited with work lately. Plus she had figured that Cameron had had enough trauma in his life to upset him even more.

Her husband and sons started carrying dishes and leftovers out to the kitchen.

"We will talk about this later at home," Ivy muttered to Cameron in a soft yet steely tone.

THE FOUR OF THEM—Alex, Eliza, Austin, and Megan—arrived in LA, unpacked their suitcases, and settled into their rooms at the Roosevelt Hotel in Hollywood the day before the Grammy Awards ceremony. They had just enough time and energy to see some sights and have a dip in the pool and have a nice dinner out before heading to bed to try to get a good night's rest before the big night.

They all met in the lobby the next morning, grabbed a quick breakfast and then headed out to go shopping for new outfits to wear.

Austin gave Megan his credit card to treat herself and his mom to anything they wanted. Eliza decided to save the dress she had bought at the mall for another evening and go shopping for a new one. After the guys got fitted for their tuxes she and Megan hit all of the stores on Melrose Avenue, Wilshire, and Sunset Boulevards including big name stores like Neiman Marcus, Nordstrom's, and Saks, and trendier boutiques like Fred Segal, Reformation, American Apparel, Heist's, and Maxfield's.

Megan found a Prada buttercup yellow sleeveless chiffon tea-length dress with a brocade bodice that looked as if it were made to fit her and set off her auburn hair.

Eliza tried on at least a half dozen dresses until she finally discovered the one she felt she had wanted to wear her whole life. It was a warm red satin, floor-length gown by Yves St. Laurent that flowed from a halter top covered in rhinestones. She felt a little guilty when she looked at the price tag, but at least it was on sale.

Since they had saved a little money by getting discounts on their dresses, Eliza and Megan splurged on getting their hair, makeup, and nails done at the popular downtown salon and day spa, The Well.

When Eliza walked into the door of their hotel suite that afternoon all decked out, Alex looked up from the television set, and his mouth literally fell open, his eyes wide with awe. He was sitting on the edge of the bed in just his black pants and white shirt, which was unbuttoned, revealing his tan, muscular upper torso. Alex was lately spending the time he had once used gambling at night working out in his new mini-gym room, which they had had converted from Cameron's old bedroom.

He's just as attractive as he was the first day I met him, Eliza smiled, gazing at her husband. *Maybe even more.*

Alex whistled softly. "You are absolutely breathtakingly gorgeous." He stood and slowly walked around his wife as she turned for him to admire her.

"You like my new dress?" Eliza painfully remembered for an instant the time she had sneakily bought the silk pantsuit years ago that she had had to return due to their gambling debts and poor finances. She forced the memory from her mind and looked teasingly into her husband's glittering dark eyes that smoldered with passion.

He wordlessly approached her and stood facing her, his breath heavy, letting his fingertips trail along every part of her as he named them, caressing each with admiration. "Your hair…your eyes…your lips…your arms…your hands…your body…"

He rested his hands on her satin-covered hips, his head bent, studying her. Then he raised his eyes to hers, and she saw a naked and all-consuming love there, like she had seen in them the very first night he had made love to her.

"Make love to me, Alex."

"With pleasure."

He carefully unzipped her gown, revealing new, matching lacy lingerie which he also gingerly removed, worshipping her body. Careful not to smudge her makeup, he laid her across the king-size bed and covered every inch of her with feathery kisses that made her ache with desire.

➤➤➤

A SHUDDER RAN THROUGH ELIZA, and a small smile played across her lips as she recalled the moment from a few hours ago.

"Are you cold, darling?" Alex asked, helping cover her bare shoulders with the wrap she had laid on the back of her chair, and when their eyes met briefly, she knew he could read her thoughts, and his eyes lit up with a mischievous smile.

"Yes, it must be the air conditioning in this auditorium," she said, mindful that her son and his girlfriend were seated to their right.

Eliza and Alex sat with their son and Megan in the seventh row of the Shrine Auditorium in Los Angeles, eagerly awaiting the start of the show.

Prior to the show, Eliza and Megan had a grand time gawking at all of the stars, but they especially delighted in watching Austin parade down the red carpet,

Austin was dressed in a navy tux with a bright white shirt and a matching navy tie he had picked out when the four of them had gone on a shopping spree in LA.

His father had selected an inky black tux with a starched white shirt and tie to match Eliza's dress.

Suddenly the candelabra lights overhead flickered on and off, signaling it was time for the show to start in a just a few minutes.

Eliza held her breath, excitement like electricity coursing through her. She could hardly believe she was actually sitting here in the Shrine Auditorium in LA with her son who had been nominated and might actually win a Grammy Award!

She looked over at Austin, who was gazing at Megan sitting on the edge of her seat, busy trying to nonchalantly snap photos of the stars all around her with her cell phone.

My son. He has turned into such a handsome, talented young man.

Eliza couldn't believe that her favorite actor, Matthew McConaughey, was hosting the Grammys this year.

He came out onto the stage to thunderous applause, drawling his famous line from his movie *The Lincoln Lawyer*, "All right, all right, all right."

It was a long, star-studded, glitzy night, and finally, the moment they'd been waiting for arrived. Eliza's heart clutched and tightened as the nominations for Best New Artist were announced by superstars Nick Jonas and Selena Gomez.

Nick opened the envelope. "And the winner is…" Selena charmingly declared in her breathy voice into the microphone, "…Austin Trellis!"

It was almost as if she were caught in a dream that was flashing fast-forward and slowed to a stop at the same time. Eliza stood in a daze as Austin embraced his parents, hugged and kissed Megan, and then gallivanted down the aisle, throwing his fist in the air, whooping with delight as he bounded onto the stage to accept his award.

"This is incredible," Austin said, beaming, holding the gold-gilded gramophone trophy in the air. "First, I'd like to thank my mom and dad, who helped me get here. Literally." The audience laughed. "My agent, Dexter Poseidon, who discovered me at an American Legion bar-mitzvah." This drew more laughs. "My label, Stardust Records, my girl Megan, and most of all, my brother Cameron Trellis who wrote the lyrics to the song, 'Front Man,' and who is the best drummer, brother, and friend I could ask for. And thanks to all my fans out there. I'll see you on the road!"

II

CAMERON

CHAPTER TWELVE

THAT SHOULD BE ME. Those are the lyrics I wrote.

Cameron watched his little brother accept his Grammy award on the thirty-two-inch television set he and Ivy had bought each other that Christmas, sitting in the shabby combination living room and family room in their tiny third-floor apartment in the run-down Metro section of Phoenix.

Why am I even watching this freak show anyway? I should just turn it off. Cameron couldn't help himself, though, watching as his brother jumped up once again to receive his third and final award of the evening, Best Song, for "Front Man."

His gut churned with a burning envy that gnawed through his core as he watched Austin this time dip Megan back in his arms and plant a dramatic kiss on her lips, then gallantly lift his mother's hand and bow to kiss it, and then high-five his dad. He felt like he had swallowed a drop of acid a long time ago, and it was now as if someone had lit it on fire, and it boiled within him.

Their dad. Their mom. Their Megan. Well, not anymore. But she was once his. Before that stupid kid brother of his stole her away.

Cameron was convinced, despite all of his brother's denials, that Austin had gone after Megan, at least within his heart, the very moment Cameron didn't want her anymore. But that was the problem, wasn't it? *I never stopped wanting her, she stopped wanting me after I pushed her away.*

Still, his own brother had taken advantage of the situation.

He's always wanted what I wanted, Cameron reflected, feeling his jaw tighten with rage. *And he's always gotten it. And I didn't.*

The guitar. The fancy education. The music lessons. The agent. And now Megan. Oh, and of course Mom and Dad's attention, affection, approval. Over me.

He was choked now by the thick, dark memory of his father's birthday party, and the burning ember of envy inside was fanned into flames.

Cameron had never felt so rejected and humiliated as he had when his father half-heartedly thanked him for his gift and then raved over his brother's.

He admitted to himself that his was a gift half-heartedly given. *I could have done better,* he had realized belatedly. *Still, Dad didn't need to show so much favoritism to Austin. You'd think he'd given him a million dollars.*

His father still cherished Pete the parrot, teaching him to say more words and phrases and even to sing part of the refrain of Austin's best-selling record, "Who's number one now? Who's number one now?"

Cameron knew the words all too well. He had written them the same night of the party after he had come home, angry and bitter, vowing he would one day be the star of a rock band as its front man.

You took the stage, you stole the show,
But fame only lasts for so long,
Then I became the leader of the band
And you were finally gone, gone.
Who's number one now, front man?
Who's number one now? I am,
Who's number one now, front man?
Not you, not now, only I am.

But he realized now he didn't know what he was thinking, because that never happened with the drummer.

Cactus Moon had played the often-requested song at concerts, and then Austin had asked his brother if he could record it.

How was I to know he'd actually get a deal with a major record label?

And then Ivy had gotten pregnant, and Cameron had seen that as an opportunity to rise above his brother in his parents' eyes. He had thought he would finally have something Austin didn't have, a grandchild for his parents to dote on and love.

But even his fame of being favored with a child was fleeting because of the miscarriage, and he knew in reality that his parents barely tolerated Ivy.

Who could blame them? Even I don't like her half the time.

As if conjuring her up like a voodoo doll, his phone buzzed.

The Grammys were over, and a rerun of NCIS had just come on.

It was a text from Ivy.

Cameron had encouraged his wife to go out for drinks with a friend that night after she had complained for hours that she refused to watch the Grammys.

"They're all just a pompous bunch of glory hounds, and your brother doesn't even deserve any of those awards, you do," Ivy had fumed for the past week. "It will make me sick to my stomach if I have to sit and watch those awards, especially if he wins one. We will never hear the end of it."

Since they only had one television, Cameron finally got tired of hearing her complain and handed her two twenties and told her to find a friend and go out for drinks.

Cameron looked down at the text on his phone. "Heard the news. Gag me. Be home soon. Love you."

He walked out to the kitchen to grab a beer from the fridge. After taking a few deep gulps, he finally texted her back.

"I know. Love you too."

The phone came alive in his hand and he saw that his mom was calling. He hesitated. *Should I pick it up? I really don't want to, but that means I'll just have to call her back.* He hit the green button on his cell phone to accept the call. *Let's just get this over with.* "Hi, Mom."

Eliza's words came out in a breathless rush. "Hi, honey! Did you watch the awards? Did you hear the news?"

Cameron tried to sound upbeat instead of sarcastic. "Yeah, Mom, I can't believe it, tell Austin that's great and—"

"Here, you tell him yourself."

And before he could prevent it, he was talking to his brother.

"Hey, Cam, did you hear? Did you watch?"

"Yeah, congratulations, little brother!" Cameron forced gaiety into his voice even though he was feeling the exact opposite.

"I wish you could have been here! You could have gone up on the stage with me!"

Yeah, right, like he would have taken me up on the stage, Cameron thought bitterly. *I should have been up there all by myself.* "Nah, this is your time to shine. When are you guys coming home?"

"We're going to an after-party to celebrate now with Dexter, who said LL Cool Jay, Bruno Mars, Lady Gaga, and a bunch of other stars are going to be there. Can you believe it?"

Cameron winced from the pain of the jealousy that stabbed his heart. "That's great. Hey, I gotta run, I have another call coming in." It was a lie, but he had to think of some excuse.

"Sorry about that, man I wish you could be here. We gotta run too, Dexter and Dad look like they're going to start without us. See you in a few days, love ya."

The connection broke. "Love you too," Cameron said into the dead cell phone, thinking, *I hate him with all of my being.* He swallowed the hard, concrete lump of resentment that lodged like a stone in the pit of his stomach.

A FEW DAYS LATER, Ivy told him that she had missed her period and was feeling a little nauseous and thought she might be pregnant again. A home pregnancy test confirmed it.

Ivy seemed overjoyed, but Cameron felt another resentment

creep in like a jagged stone and lodge itself into the growing rock pile inside.

Cameron was already working overtime to pay the bills and make payments on the few thousand dollars' worth of debt they had accumulated.

Ivy had been working at the local Macy's as a sales clerk some nights and on the weekends. The day she came home and told him she had quit because she just couldn't stand being on her feet for eight-hour shifts, Cameron thought he was going to lose it.

That day, Cameron decided he had to do something drastic and started gambling at the local casino.

It started with penny, nickel, and quarter slots at first.

He would win a pot or two one week and then plunk it right back in just to break even or lose a little.

Then he found roulette. It was addictive. When the little ball hit his number and he got paid thirty-five to one, it was a thrill like he had never felt before.

But just like the slots, he would win a little and lose a little.

And then he discovered black jack and finally poker. The stakes were a lot bigger but then so were the winnings.

When Ivy started to become suspicious of his whereabouts when two nights' "overtime" turned into a nightly routine, he tried to be extra attentive to her every desire, cutting back a night or two only to return to the thrill of the win.

One night he was up a thousand dollars in a poker game and couldn't leave the table, he was on such a hot streak. When he got home at midnight, Ivy was up waiting for him, eyes sparking with anger, arms crossed, standing there in the middle of the small living room as he tried to sneak in the door.

"Whoa, hey, babe, you scared me," he whispered, his heart skipping a beat.

Her black hair was tousled, falling down on her pink robe-covered shoulders, her face rosy with sleep. She had gained much more weight with her second pregnancy and was sort of pudgy all over, and he hadn't been attracted to her in moths. *But she actually looks a little sexy now*, Cameron thought for the first time in a long time. *Or maybe I'm just a little drunk from the cheap cocktails they were serving all night.*

Alarms went off in his head, but he turned them off and tried to hug her.

"Get. Your. Hands. Off. Of. Me." She uttered each word separately for emphasis in a deadly soft tone.

"Sorr-eee," Cameron said snidely. "I was going to tell you that you look sexy, but never mind." He tried to slide around her in an effort to get back to the bedroom, but her hand whipped out and clutched his upper arm like a vise, her nails knifing into his flesh.

"Where have you been?"

He made the mistake of looking into her icy blue eyes. If looks could kill, he'd be dead. "I was working overtime and, well, a few of us went out for drinks afterward. I was going to call to let you know, but I figured you'd already be sleeping and I didn't want to wake you." He tried to shake his arm free but couldn't. "Hey, you're hurting me, let go. I need to get to bed so I can get up for work. Long day tomorrow."

"Stop lying." Ivy's grip didn't relax for a second, and she continued to glare at him suspiciously. "I know where you've been going all of these nights. I saw the credit card bills. Do you think I'm an idiot?"

"Okay, fine." Cameron's anger rose, and he managed to pull his arm free. He stood facing her, ready to stand up to her now. "I go to the casino once in a while so I can try to win some money to get us out of the hole we're in. My measly income isn't covering everything and you're certainly no help now. I didn't know what else to do, I guess I felt desperate."

His anger dissolved into a deep desolation over what his life had become, his dream of one day being rich and famous as a rock band drummer crumbled now and blown away like dust. He sank onto the threadbare couch and put his head in his hands.

Ivy just stood staring at him, but her fury didn't dissipate. "Well, you've got to stop." He looked up at her, trying to find compassion, maybe a trace of the love they had once shown each other, but instead saw the unflinching coldness in her eyes. "I don't care what you need to do, maybe you need to go get some help or something, talk to that Dr. Fulton, I don't really care. Are you even taking your bipolar medication?"

Cameron's wrath returned, and he stood to face her again. He quickly tried to recall the last time he had taken his Lithium prescription. It had been several months if he remembered correctly. *But she doesn't need to know that. How dare she even ask me?* He hated when anyone questioned him about whether he was taking his medication or not, the way it made him feel like something was wrong with him, like he was inferior or messed up somehow. His parents had learned a long time ago not to ask anymore.

But not his wife. She just sat around here all day talking to her friends and complaining about what a rotten husband she had, eating snacks and letting herself go and daring to question him like he was the one with a problem, when she couldn't even work for a living.

He balled up his fist to keep from wrapping his hand around her neck. "Of course I'm taking it," he responded evenly, taking a deep breath. "And fine, I'll talk to Dr. Fulton if that will make you happy."

Ivy sighed, the fight leaving her now. Cameron stayed on guard but noticed her eyes started to look a little sleepy, her face a little puffy, and her shoulders sagged a little as she turned to go back to bed. *I really don't know how I got myself into all of this,* he thought hopelessly, feeling a wave of depression overtake the receding tide of manic agitation and aggression he had just felt.

That's the way it usually went, he knew. Extreme highs and lows, ups and downs, for bipolar people. Well, he could accept that. He didn't need any doctor telling him what to do or medicine numbing him out anymore. He could deal with his witch of a wife. Besides, once the baby was born, she'd be too busy to pay attention to him.

He smiled to himself. *I'll be fine if everyone just leaves me alone.*

»——►

IVY HAD ANOTHER MISCARRIAGE, this time earlier in the pregnancy, and she was even more devastated about it than the first time.

Cameron could do nothing to console her.

She only wanted her mother, who drove down from Flagstaff and announced she would be moving in to stay with them for a few weeks to take care of Ivy.

Cameron couldn't stand his mother-in-law, who, he came to discover, was even more spoiled than his wife, and he knew his life was about to become a living hell.

CHAPTER THIRTEEN

THE TRIP to the Grand Canyon started out innocently enough.

Alex and Eliza made all of the arrangements for their sons to go together on a camping trip for the weekend as a gift for Austin's graduation from Stanford that year.

Their plan was to leave early that Friday morning and drive up Interstate 17, camp that night in the Grand Canyon National Park, and then the next night in one of the state parks in the Oak Creek Canyon between Sedona, which they'd see on Saturday, and Flagstaff, where they'd hang out on Sunday before driving back home to Phoenix.

They had seen almost all of the state of Arizona as kids when they went camping with their parents, and had been to the Grand Canyon a few times, but they had never actually spent much time in Sedona or Flagstaff.

They knew that the Oak Creek Canyon was part of their heritage, that the Navajo Nation surrounded the entire area, and that it brought back memories for their mom and dad that were barely spoken about.

Cameron had been excited to revisit their native culture and to travel for the first time with his brother without adult supervision.

But when Austin picked him up in his black Chevy Corvette,

wearing designer jeans and a big, brass buckled belt and brand-new leather boots that Cameron guessed must have cost over a thousand dollars, he instantly realized this trip was a huge mistake.

He was wearing a worn tee-shirt and an old pair of jeans with a hole in the knees. And he wished he could have hidden the car he drove, but there it was, his used, banged up blue Ford Taurus, parked in front of their equally ugly apartment building. He felt his cheeks flame with shame and anger. How had life turned out so unfair?

But it was too late to turn back now. Everything was arranged and paid for.

As Austin prattled on about his next series of concerts and how he was cutting more records and hoped to get nominated for the Grammys again that coming fall, Cameron grew increasingly resentful with each mile.

And then his little brother started talking about his future with Megan, and Cameron had to roll down the window despite the ninety-eight-degree heat. He felt like he couldn't breathe and sucked in the hot, dry air.

"Hey, Cam, what are you doing, you're letting the air condition out of the car," Austin chided him.

"I don't feel so hot. Can you pull over at the next exit so I can get a soda or something?"

He bought a pack of cigarettes, even though he had given up smoking years ago when Ivy first found out she was pregnant.

He came outside, leaned against the stained concrete wall of the run-down gas station, and lit a cigarette, taking a long draw, inhaling and exhaling.

Austin was sitting impatiently waiting in the driver's seat of the car, bopping up and down to some rock song he had blaring loud on his stereo. His eyes grew wide as he looked over and saw his brother smoking.

He rolled down the window and shouted over at his brother, "What do you think you're doing?"

"Smoking obviously," Cameron said and felt a small smile play on his lips. "What's it to ya?"

Austin started the car, pulled over to the side of the building where Cameron stood, parked the car, got out, slammed the driver's door shut, and strode toward him.

"Why are you smoking? I thought you gave it up."

"I did, so what, we're all going to die one day, might as well enjoy the ride." He held out the pack at arm's length. "Want one?"

Austin scowled at him. "No, I don't want to start that nasty habit. I should tell Mom you're smoking, see what she'd say."

"You're such a baby. You always have been. If you don't like it, just leave me here and go on your own camping trip."

He saw the look of hurt cloud his brother's brown eyes, his eyelids drooping slightly. Austin turned and slowly walked back to the car, his shoulders slumped.

Cameron dropped the half-smoked cigarette onto the concrete and stamped it out with his work boot and strolled to the car, opened the passenger door, and got in.

He looked at Austin, who wouldn't turn his head but stared straight out through the windshield at the blank, dirty white concrete wall in front of them.

"Hey, man, sorry, I shouldn't have said that. It's just that all that talk makes me crazy sometimes. Can we just turn some music on for the rest of the ride?"

Austin sighed and then looked him in the eye. "All right. But you have to promise not to be a jerk the rest of the trip."

"Promise." The two bumped fists, Austin started the car, and they got back on the highway.

Austin cranked up the music, and they opened the sunroof and windows and soon they were both singing one of their favorite punk rock songs by the Ramones at the top of their lungs.

Maybe this will be okay after all, Cameron thought, the wind whipping through his hair. At least he didn't have any responsibilities this weekend. No work, no wife, no chores.

Once they reached the park entrance, they headed to the Grand

Canyon Village. They parked, got out and took a selfie to send to their mom and dad, then started the long trek along the south rim of the canyon. The sun shone through puffy white clouds in the bright blue sky, and the weather was perfect since it was much cooler up here than it had been in Phoenix.

They hiked for about two miles, enjoying the breathtaking scenery before stopping to rest and take some photos at a clearing where a small tour group stood listening to their guide.

Suddenly they were being swarmed by a handful of college-age girls.

"It's him, it's Austin Trellis!" one of the girls squealed, and the rest followed her lead, asking for autographs on notebooks, hats, and the backs of their shirts, and begging him to please pose with them for pictures. One girl in braces shoved her cell phone at Cameron, who had stood at a distance and was watching the spectacle from a few feet away. "Hey, can you take my picture with Austin?" she asked, and before he could refuse, Cameron was holding her phone in his hands and she was standing, smiling a big, cheesy smile, her arm around his brother.

Cameron took a few photos and handed the phone back to her but not before six other phones were shoved in his face, the owners all screaming, "Take mine next, take mine!"

Austin looked at Cameron, shrugged his shoulders, and smiled, obliging their demands. But more people started to notice the commotion and began to gather in the small alcove in the rock wall, which was meant to be a tourist stop for a handful of people, not a large crowd. Cameron felt claustrophobic, being bumped and pushed, and finally, he decided he had had enough. He shoved through the crowd, grabbed his brother by the arm, and led him away from the canyon wall and out onto the dirt path, yelling, "That's it, the party's over, I'm his bodyguard, let me through, that's all for today."

"We've gotta get out of here," Cameron told his brother, desperately looking around for a hideaway as a few stubborn, straggling girls tried to follow them.

He saw a tall, stocky park ranger approaching them and yanked Austin by the arm toward him.

"Is there a problem here, boys?" the ranger asked in a gruff voice.

"Yeah, we've got to get away from all of these people. Apparently my brother here is famous, and we're going to have to go on a more remote trail so we don't cause these commotions all day long."

"Famous, huh? Who is he?" The ranger scratched his scraggly beard, seeming disinterested.

"Well, famous to those girls gawking over there," Cameron said, pointing toward the growing crowd of onlookers who stood at bay due to the presence of the ranger.

"Austin Trellis." Austin held out his hand, and the ranger shook it, peering over his sunglasses.

"Never heard of 'ya, but okay, I'll take your word for it."

"I'm big with the young crowd, especially girls," Austin said, grinning. "My fans are actually pretty crazy sometimes."

He thinks this is all a big joke, Cameron fumed. *He's actually eating this up.* He told himself he'd have plenty of time to be mad later, realizing there was probably no time to waste as the crowd was growing, pointing at them, and still taking photos from where they stood a few yards away. Some were walking away, sneaking sideways glances at them. Probably trying to figure out how to get around this ranger dude and find them.

"You guys will want to head down that trail over yonder called the Bright Angel Trail. I'll rope it off and guard it, letting the crowd know it's closed for the day. That should give you a good head start, at least until they find a way to get to you. Luckily we're not expecting a big attendance today, but you never know. It's a long, steep trail that eventually heads down to the Colorado River at the bottom of the canyon, but I wouldn't suggest you go all the way down because you probably won't make it back before sunset, and you don't want to be caught here at night with just the clothes on your back."

Although they had never hiked it, Cameron and Austin knew about the trail. They looked at each and nodded.

⇒→

THE BROTHERS HIKED for a few miles down the trail, some-times side by side, often one in front of the other when the path got steep and narrow, mostly not speaking except to point out some-thing particularly scenic or beautiful like a hawk or flower or the way the light played on a rock formation, glowing in prismatic layers of reds, oranges, golds, and greens.

They each carried a backpack with water bottles, granola bars, and trail mix, enough to last them for several hours.

Save for a single hiker or a couple exploring together here and there, the trail was relatively quiet as the ranger had promised. Thankfully, the people on the trail were interested in exploring the canyon, not seeing some young punk rock star.

After two hours Austin, hiking ahead of Cameron, turned around. They were about halfway down the canyon and had come to a scenic bluff overlooking the Colorado River, which seemed to magically grow in size as they had gotten closer to it.

"Why don't we rest here?" Austin suggested.

Cameron, still holding onto the grudge that had started with the photo frenzy, rolled his eyes but acquiesced as he was feeling a little winded. *I shouldn't have picked up smoking again*, he chastised himself. *It's all Austin's fault though. If he would learn to shut his mouth …* "Fine," he grumbled.

They pulled out their water bottles and snacks and sat on a large, flat boulder in a clearing.

"That was pretty wild back there, huh?" Austin smiled, his dimples deepening.

"You loved it, didn't you?" Cameron wasn't smiling and was glad he was wearing sunglasses so his brother couldn't see the envy in his eyes.

"Nah…well, maybe a little. But hey, I came on this trip to be with you. Were you bothered by it?" Austin lowered his shades and peered over them, his brown eyes sparkling mischievously. "You were, weren't you?"

"Of course not."

Austin chugged on a water bottle. He had stopped teasing and was serious now. "I wish you could…well, that we could be playing together back in the band, that things would have turned out differently for you."

Cameron's ire rose. He could tell his brother was feeling sorry for him. *How dare he pity me when he's the one that caused it all?* "If you wouldn't have ditched the band, maybe we would be together. But I'm fine, don't go feeling sorry for me."

"Hey, why don't you come play in my band?"

Yeah, right, and be your back up while you get all the accolades. He thought of an excuse. "And what, leave my wife?"

"Well, yeah, maybe. Do you even love her?"

Cameron sighed and looked up at the jutting rocks above. Now he felt sorry for himself. The answer was no, he did not love his wife. But he wasn't about to admit that to his brother and allow him to feel even more superior than he did already, with girls fawning over him, tons of money in his bank account, on the brink of fame and fortune, while he was broke, working a job he hated, married to a woman he despised at times.

He lied. "Of course I do."

"Well, that's good at least. I love Megan too."

The words hit Cameron like a punch in the gut. "You love Megan?"

"With all my heart and soul. I'm going to ask her to marry me. I've wanted to tell you this whole trip but wasn't sure how you'd feel. Of course I want you to be my best man."

Cameron suddenly felt nauseated and fought to keep himself from upchucking the two granola bars, handfuls of trail mix, and bag of beef jerky he had just consumed. His insides burned. This was the most unfair cut of all. He took a deep breath. How could he? How could Austin love the one woman he loved?

And Cameron realized in that moment he had never stopped loving Megan McGee.

There is no way I'm going to let my brother marry her, he decided right then and there.

"Cameron, did you hear me?" Austin stood, walking over to his brother, his eyes curious as to why he sat seemingly in a stupor, not moving, not responding. "Will you be my best man? I'm going to propose as soon as we get home Sunday night. It's going to be a big wedding, that's what Megan says she's always dreamed of. I don't care one way or another, I'm just planning the honeymoon. It's going to be a surprise, don't say anything to anyone, but I'm taking her to St. Lucia and…"

Austin kept talking, a big, idiotic grin on his face, but Cameron couldn't see or hear him anymore. A dull thudding was in his ears, a pounding was in his head, his eyesight blurred, and hate filled his heart. Clouds gathered over the canyon and suddenly, lightning flashed in the distance.

"You don't look so good, bro, plus it looks like a storm's picking up," Austin chattered on. "I think we should start heading back."

Cameron walked over to a scrub brush and threw up into it. He wiped his mouth with his sleeve, drank down the rest of his water bottle, and still a little hunched over, turned to face his brother, who stood before him now, looking down on him with an expression of concern. Austin was a little taller, and his head blocked the sun. All Cameron could see momentarily was his face in shadow, his eyes still filled with pity.

"I feel better now." Cameron straightened and peered up into the sky. Already the clouds started to break up and patches of blue broke through and dotted the sky again. The weather always rapidly changed in the Grand Canyon. Cameron noticed the rocky ledges above once again, and his thoughts crystallized into a single vision. *I can end this.* One ledge overhung the rest, seeming to jut out over them like a diving board over a swimming pool. He looked down and saw the Colorado River churning.

THE SUN WAS SUPPOSED to set at seven-thirty p.m. Climbing

back up the trail, they had looked on their map and agreed they would stop at the visitor's center, where the majority of food stops and restrooms were located, to get more food and water to take with them to watch the sunset. Once they arrived at the center, Cameron would go into the deli to grab some sandwiches and drinks while Austin would secretly wait for him, remaining incognito, and then they would take their carry-out dinner to the remotest place possible to eat and watch the sunset before heading back to the campground where they had paid for a space to spend the night.

They planned that as they got close to the center, Austin would stuff his curls up under a bandana he had brought in his knapsack, wrapping it do-rag fashion, and then putting his baseball cap on top. With his sunglasses on and his jacket collar pulled up around his face, hopefully no one would recognize him and they wouldn't have to deal with the gawking girls and fans that had crowded them earlier.

It was already six o'clock, and they still had two miles to go before they'd reach the visitors center. Cameron was huffing for breath as the trail grew ever steeper, his brother hiking effortlessly ahead of him. "Hey, I need to stop and rest," he called, panting.

"All right, it looks as if there's a place ahead."

They reached an overhang. It was a small clearing overlooking the canyon and the river. A scraggly pine tree jutted out over the cliffs.

Austin stopped, standing precariously close to the edge to get a closer look at a bird.

"Hey, Cameron, come here!" he shouted.

Cameron stopped a few feet from his brother, winded from the climb, drawing deep breaths of air.

He looked up at the sky. The yellow sun was already taking on an orange cast as it began its descent to the horizon, the clouds becoming rosy with the promise of another amazing sunset.

He knew the ledge he had seen from below, the one that jutted out farthest over the pit of the canyon, was just ahead. They would make it at just the right time, when the sun would begin its descent, and the darkness of night would soon envelop the rocky crags and the blackening river and all of the secrets that would remain in the unseen depths below until it rose again to perhaps reveal them with the morning of a new day. And perhaps not, depending on if anyone ventured there.

"C'mon, we better move, we don't want to get stuck here in the dark." Cameron was desperate to get there, but his brother wasn't budging, his sight transfixed on the bird and what he apparently had in his beak.

Cameron's mind raced ahead.

He took a few steps ahead and peered out beyond the ledge Austin was standing on, into the canyon. He looked up and noticed the jagged edge of the ledge he had spotted. *If we don't move now we won't get up there in time. Austin won't want to stop again until we get to the visitors center.*

It was the plan. Cameron had always been a planner, had even been called "obsessive compulsive" by people who knew him, while Austin had always been the more relaxed, free-wheeling, eccentric, impulsive dreamer type. He knew Austin wouldn't want to miss the sunset, but his younger brother wasn't thinking about that right now, caught up in the moment. He was actually talking to the bird now.

Perhaps the plan had to change.

Cameron looked right and left, and seeing no one was in sight, strained to listen and heard...silence, save for the distant cry of a hawk, Austin's chattering, and the raven's offended squawks.

It would be over in a second. Drawing a deep breath of resolve, Cameron slowly inched toward his little brother until he was within arm's length and reached out his hand.

Austin turned just before Cameron's fingers touched his shoulder, his eyes filled with alarm.

CHAPTER FOURTEEN

AUSTIN THREW his arms around his brother and tackled him to the ground, just seconds before Cameron was able to complete the act of pushing him off the cliff overhang to his death.

For a moment, Cameron was knocked unconscious. When he regained his wits, he pushed Austin off him, enraged. "What are you doing?" he shrieked, rolling over and getting to his feet, brushing off the dirt from his jacket and jeans.

Austin lay on the ground, laughing so hard tears came to his eyes. Catching his breath, he sat up. "There was a huge spider on your shoulder, I was trying to save you." He laughed again and then sobered up. "Seriously, dude, it looked like a tarantula. You should have seen your face." And he was hunched over, laughing uncontrollably again.

He had one of those contagious laughs where, once unleashed, you couldn't help but laugh with him. But Cameron was so stunned —at his homicidal thoughts and at how his plan had instantly gone awry—that he couldn't even crack a smile.

He had no idea what I was about to do, that I was about to kill him, Cameron realized. *He didn't look afraid because he had no clue that I was going to push him over the ledge. He saw the spider. And he saw the look on my face as something other than what it was, one of surprise that he turned around, and of fear that he was onto me at that instant.*

None of it mattered now. His plan had backfired. He had failed. And he felt a mix of relief and disappointment so tangled up inside that it ached.

Austin stood up and brushed himself off. "Well, the critter's gone now. I guess we better go see that sunset."

THEY DROVE in relative silence back to the campground, both lost in their own thoughts and tired from the day.

The sunset had been really spectacular, like none either brother had ever seen before, with deep, dark streaks of reds, purples, and blacks slashing across gentler hues of yellow, pink, and orange. "God painted another beautiful sky," Austin had whispered reverently as they sat together on the big, flat rock at Yaki Point, a good spot to view nature's show.

About two dozen other people were scattered along the rim near them, but they were so focused on the sunset that they didn't even look in their direction. Cameron and Austin had waited until most left and the sky turned black and filled with stars before walking toward their car, flashlights from their backpacks in hand.

They used a lantern from the car to pitch their tent once they arrived at the camp space they had rented for the night. Since they hadn't made it to the visitors' center to get food in time to see the sunset, they had stopped at a restaurant in the Grand Canyon Village for dinner before heading to the campground in the Grand Canyon National Park. Once there they were so tired they didn't even bother to light a fire and sit and talk for a while as they had originally planned. Tomorrow night they'd do that, they agreed. Austin fell asleep as soon as he got comfortable in his sleeping bag and his head hit his pillow, but Cameron lay restless, thinking too much, and it took him at least an hour to fall into a fitful sleep, the Ambien that he took religiously every night as a sleep aid finally kicking in.

Cameron was up at five-thirty a.m., his usual wake-up time each morning to get ready for work. Even though he tried to roll over and fall back asleep on days off, it was as if an alarm went off in his head.

Might as well get up, start a fire, and make some coffee.

The sun started its ascent once more to begin a new day. Cameron sat in his camp chair, sipping his coffee, warmed by the fire he had made. He watched the sun start its climb over the treetops and into the sky and saw a sunrise almost as glorious as the sunset the night before.

Anyone observing him would have said he looked peaceful, but he was anything but, his mind churning, searching for ideas on what to do next to solve his problem: getting rid of his little brother once and for all, before he married Megan, before he became an even bigger superstar, before he stole even more of Mom and Dad's love away from what little was left for him, before he robbed Cameron of the shred of self-esteem he still had left. *Maybe then I will finally find some peace.*

Today marked three years since he had last taken his bipolar medicine, and although he was anxious to come up with a new plan now that his original one had been foiled last night, he still felt on top of the world. *Today will be the day it will all work out,* he decided triumphantly, knowing he was in the height of one his manic stages but not caring one little bit.

His thoughts were interrupted when Austin emerged from the tent flap, yawning and rubbing the sleep out of his eyes.

"Good morning, little brother," Cameron said cheerfully. "I've got some coffee ready for you." He had already had three cups, which had served to buoy his determination.

"Wow, Cam, thanks." Austin took the steamy cup from his brother's outstretched hand and sat in his camp chair, warming his hands around the mug and his feet by the fire, a blanket wrapped around his shoulders. Even in late spring and summer, it could get cold at night up here by the canyon.

"You ready to go explore Sedona?" *He's so clueless,* Cameron thought, smirking to himself.

"I need to wake up first." Austin looked at his wrist, obviously having forgotten he had taken off his watch. "What time is it anyway?"

Cameron laughed. "It's already eight-thirty, little bro, by now I'd have been at work for two hours already."

"Yeah, well, I've been a student, don't forget, sleeping in 'til ten some mornings, especially if I had a concert the night before."

"I didn't forget." Cameron's smile belied the sharp stab of envy he felt again over the difference in their circumstances and how their lives had turned out. But he knew he had to keep up his cheerful show for now. "Well, this trip is for you. Take your time waking up, and I'll make breakfast."

Living with Ivy, Cameron had become a pro in the kitchen since his wife had few cooking skills, not to mention no desire to be a housewife. Cooking was one of the few things in life he enjoyed.

Austin got dressed in the tent while Cameron scrambled eggs, potatoes, peppers, onions, ham, and sausage together in a big iron skillet over the flame.

There was a picnic table at their campsite, and they took their plates over to it and ate breakfast, listening to the birds and squirrels who darted around them.

"Dude, this is amazing," Austin said, wolfing down a mouthful. "How did you learn to cook like this? Mom didn't even cook this good. Don't tell her I said that."

"I won't." *I should, but I won't.* "And thanks. Ivy doesn't cook much, so I sort of picked it up. Guess I'm good at something."

"Maybe you should become a cook somewhere," Austin said, chomping into a piece of buttered toast.

Cameron knew he had been fishing for a compliment and was hoping Austin would have said something like, "Don't forget you're a great drummer, and a really good songwriter obviously, since the song you wrote helped me to win Best New Recording Artist at the Grammys."

But why would I expect that from my spoiled rotten little brother?

Once he's gone, though, people will notice me again, that I'm the one behind the music. He comforted himself with the thought.

THEY DROVE the two-hour trek south along the scenic drive to Sedona, the town that they thought as boys was just as neat as the Grand Canyon. Many tourists over time actually claimed it was prettier and just as breathtaking.

The sun was high in the sky when they drove along US 89 into the heart of Sedona. They had mapped it out and drove to see a few of the top spots—Cathedral Rock, Courthouse Butte and Bell Rock, the Chapel of the Holy Cross—before getting hungry again and deciding to stop for lunch in the downtown shopping district and roam around in the Tilaquepaque Arts and Crafts Village, which looked like a rustic European plaza with its cobblestone streets and mosaic fountains.

They ate at Café Jose's, chowing down on authentic Mexican fare, and then wandered into some of the New Age shops selling crystals and a wide assortment of mystic gifts and spells.

Cameron and Austin decided to split up, since Austin wanted to check out the touristy, tee-shirt shops on the main drag to get some gifts for friends, while Cameron said he wasn't sure what he was looking for but wanted to browse the more authentic, out of the way local stores around Tilaquepaque.

They agreed to meet in an hour at a designated ice cream parlor, and then venture on to hike the Red Rock State Park before hitting the scenic road up into the mountains where they would camp in Oak Creek Canyon.

Cameron really just wanted time alone to think so he could come up with a plan to deal once and for all with his little brother.

Right before they started heading their separate ways, they wandered past an exotic animals pet store, and Austin talked Cameron into venturing inside real quick before they went off shopping.

Cameron didn't have much of a choice since Austin tugged him by the arm.

Just a few steps into the store, Cameron saw why Austin was so excited. There in front of him was an African grey parrot, perched in his cage, selling for seven hundred and fifty dollars. "Look, Cam, it's just like the one I bought for Dad."

Suddenly, all of the memories of that night flooded back into Cameron's psyche, nearly suffocating him with shame. A hot flash of anger came over him, and for a moment, he was blinded by rage.

He inhaled a deep breath, cleared his vision, and exhaled.

"Remember how Pete talked that night and Dad was so excited and…" Austin's chattering faded in and out of Cameron's ringing ears. All he could hear was the sound of his murderous thoughts. *I hate him. He has got to go.*

"It's really warm in here, I've got to get some fresh air." Cameron walked briskly to the front door and out into the bright sunlight of Sedona's midday, where tourists strode happily by along the sidewalks of one of the most colorful cities in all of the world.

But all Cameron saw were shades of gray as he doubled over, nearly hyperventilating.

"Hey, what happened, are you okay?" Austin followed his brother outside. "I guess it was a little warm in there. They probably keep it that way for all of the tropical animals."

"Yeah, I guess I just got overheated. I'm fine." Cameron stood up and forced a smile. "C'mon, daylight's wasting; I'll meet you in an hour." And they parted to go their separate ways.

CAMERON WANDERED AIMLESSLY past the stucco walls of the Tilaquepaque village, which housed art galleries and glassware shops, local handmade jewelry boutiques, candy stores, and of course, the spiritual and hedonistic spas and new age shops.

He had walked up a hill and turned the wrong way, up a narrow, cobblestoned path that meandered away from the village, when he spotted a small neon store sign that said, "Trippin" in a dark store window that also featured other small signs advertising tattoos, piercings, palm and tarot card readings, Satanic rituals, weaponry, and snake bite oils and venoms.

Mesmerized, Cameron was drawn trancelike into the strange, narrow little store as if caught in one of the ancient Indian vortices in Sedona, which, if you got sucked into one, legends told, could offer spiritual healing, clarity and peace, or, if evil spirits lurked in one's heart, supposedly a more demonic calling.

The musky air in the store was dense, close, and smelled of smoke and incense. There was little light in the narrow, one-room shop, which seemed smaller than it was with the entire interior painted black.

Skull jewelry, drug paraphernalia and Native American art lined one wall of glass shelves, while the other wall of glass cabinets encased a variety of weapons including carved Indian knives and bows and arrows that sold for hundreds and thousands of dollars.

The store's sole proprietor, or maybe just its only clerk on duty, sat along the far wall with a headset on, bobbing his head to some type of music. He was young, maybe in his thirties, with long, stringy black hair, and wore a dirt-colored tank top and faded black jeans. He was clearly high on something, and Cameron hesitated before asking about the one advertised item that had piqued his interest in the store's front window, wondering if he should just beat it out of there.

A moment too late, he had no choice as the greasy young man looked up and saw him standing there. His brown, muscular arms were covered in tattoo sleeves. Cameron noticed belatedly that they were made up of various devil designs in red and black.

"Can I help you?" he asked, smiling, revealing tobacco-stained, uneven teeth that parted in his dark, unshaven face. He had been jamming on a stool behind the counter but stood now to greet his only customer.

"Uh, yes, um, I was curious about the snake bite venom you claim to sell that was on the sign out front?"

"Not claim to sell, do sell." The rough-looking man peered at Cameron through his red, slitted eyes. His smile vanished, and he looked almost menacing as he glared at Cameron now. "Why, are you interested in some?"

"Well, I just wanted to ask about it, you know, how much it costs." Cameron felt awkward and stuffed his hands in his pockets.

"Depends on what you're gonna use it for."

Cameron looked around him to make sure no one else was lurking in the store. He hoped he couldn't get in trouble just for asking the question. *Besides, this guy looks pretty wasted. He may not remember.* "What if I wanted to use it to inject into something to kill it?" *I didn't say someone,* he thought shrewdly.

"What, like you mean another animal or something?"

"Yeah, say like a rabid dog or something."

"Big or small?"

"Really big. I need to get rid of this thing. He's like Cujo in the Stephen King novel. You ever read it?"

"Yeah, dude, you're really sick, aren't you?" The guy was smiling now and suddenly animated, like he had woken up from his drug-induced stupor.

Great, we're actually bonding over killing something with snake venom, Cameron thought sardonically.

"Hold on." And with that, the store clerk disappeared behind a psychedelic curtain and re-emerged holding a locked glass box of tiny vials containing clear and yellow-colored serums. "We've got your cobra venoms, which might not work since their strengths vary." He pointed to the clear liquid vial. "And we have rattlesnake venoms." He waved his hand over the colored vials, the small amount of liquid in them a strange, Day-Glo, lime-yellow color, unlike anything Cameron had ever seen. "These babies are potent. The diamond rattlesnake venom could kill a person your size."

Cameron drew in a deep breath. "How much does something like that cost?"

"You serious, man?"

"Yes."

"Well, let me explain rattlesnake venom." The clerk cleared his throat, all business-like now, apparently aware his customer was quite serious. "It contains two types of toxins: hemotoxins, or the kind that attack blood cells and tissues and cause internal bleeding, which are sometimes fatal, and neurotoxins, which are more dangerous because they target the nervous system and can shut down organs and if untreated, can definitely kill you.

"Lately, they're saying the diamond-back rattlesnakes around here are becoming more dangerous because their venom has more neurotoxins than hemotoxins, but I don't think anyone knows why for sure. All I know is that this type here," the young man held up a vial of the chartreuse serum, which seemed to cast an eerie glow of light, "could be deadly."

"How long would it take to, um…work, you know, kill someone…I mean a big dog?"

"Could be a couple days, but could take just a few hours. I've heard if one of these rattlesnakes bites someone and they don't get to a hospital within a few hours, they're dead meat."

Nice choice of words, Cameron thought wryly. "I'll take it." He had his credit card with him that was linked to his personal account. He used it strictly to gamble and had recently won a few thousand dollars. Ivy, of course, was unaware of the personal credit line.

"By the way, name's Jake." The store clerk held out his leathery hand and shook Cameron's in a vice-like grip, flexing his tattoo sleeved muscles.

"My name's Robert," Cameron lied.

"Hey, Robert, you ever see what an animal looks like that's been bit by a rattlesnake?"

"Nah, why?"

"You don't want to see it then. People who are bit by rattlesnakes look like they been burned alive. Not a pretty sight. Really nasty."

"Well, this isn't for a person," Cameron reminded him, nervously handing him his credit card and checking his watch. "Hey, Jake, I'm kinda runnin' late to meet my brother, can we hurry this up a little?" He heard his phone buzz and looked at it. A text from Austin asking where he was. He responded, typing he was running late and would meet him at the ice cream shop in ten minutes.

Jake looked slightly hurt at first but then apparently realized the magnitude of the sale from his one and only customer the past half hour and got down to business. He peered at the credit card and then up at Cameron. "Cameron R. Trellis."

"Yes, I go by my middle name, Robert."

Jake carefully removed the vial, placed it into a small nondescript bag, and handed it to 'Robert.' "Do you have a way of injecting it into the dog?"

Cameron hadn't even thought about how he would do that and was grateful Jake's fogginess had worn off with the excitement of the conversation and that he had asked the question. "Actually, no, do you sell that too?"

"Sure do, here." Jake went back behind the colorful curtain and came out with a plastic-sealed syringe. "Usually this runs a few bucks, but hey, since you spent so much it's on the house."

"Thanks." Cameron slipped the syringe into the bag with the vial and put it in his backpack.

"Good luck with that mean dog out there. Hope it works."

"So do I." Cameron was almost out of the shop's front door when he turned back in. "I almost forgot, I need one more thing if you have it."

THEY HAD SET up camp that night at Slide Rock State Park after hiking the Red Rock State Park near Sedona much of the afternoon.

The brothers had witnessed another glorious sunset from the Airport Mesa overlook, the sun's rays bathing the red rock formations in fiery copper light.

Since Cameron had his plan ironed out in his head, he had decided to just relax the rest of the day and enjoy the scenery. Even Austin had remarked how calm his brother had seemed as they sat blissfully watching the sun put on its show.

Cameron hadn't even minded when Austin teasingly said, "Your medicine must be working."

They had built a nice campfire together, just like they had

learned to do in the boy scouts, and Cameron made a delicious supper of roasted beef, onions, potatoes, and carrots, which simmered together and made a hearty stew.

Then they had roasted marshmallows over the embers and made s'mores for dessert.

They had also toasted multiple times to Austin's graduation and success in the music business by downing "chasers," or shots of whiskey followed by chugging cans of beer.

"This has been the perfect trip," Austin said, licking the chocolate and marshmallow that stuck to his fingers, drunkenly laughing and swaying as he put his arm around his brother.

Cameron nodded and sighed with resignation and regret. *We are finally getting along*, he thought sadly. But then he willed himself to snap out of his present sentimentality. *Don't go all soft and weak, Cameron. Remember Dad and the parrot and the fawning fans and Megan. Just stick to the plan.* "Yep, it has." Cameron rose and gave a fake yawn, stretching his arms dramatically for effect. "I'm beat though." He looked at his watch which read ten o'clock. Great, the rangers would be off duty by now. It was time.

"Wait. Look!" Austin stood and pointed above, where a million stars flickered in the vast, ink black Arizona sky. The fire had died, enabling them to see the star show in all of its majesty. As Austin pointed, Cameron saw the flicker of light cross the sky, a shooting star that flashed then faded. "Make a wish." Both young men closed their eyes for a moment. "What'd you wish for?" Austin asked, slurring his words, grinning with intoxication.

Ah, if only you knew, Cameron thought slyly. "If I tell you it won't come true."

Austin shrugged and yawned. "Okay, well, itsh been a long day, so letsh hit the sack."

Cameron lay on his back staring at the top of the tent, listening to the sounds of nightfall around the tent grow louder, the crickets, frogs, an owl hooting, listening to his brother breathe, waiting until he could be sure Austin was fast asleep.

CHAPTER FIFTEEN

SOON, the sounds of the great outdoors seemed to fade, and all Cameron could hear was Austin's measured, level breathing and occasional snoring, which seemed like muted background noise compared to the sounds of the ticking of his wrist watch and the beating of his own heart.

He must be asleep now. Cameron was so impatient he felt like he was going to jump out of his sleeping bag if he waited any longer. Time to put the plan into action.

Cameron had spent the past hour waiting for Austin to fall sound sleep and also thinking of every last detail of his plan. He would need to go in stocking feet so as not to leave any footprints that could be traced back to his boots. It was cold, even for spring in the Flagstaff area, with temperatures reaching only into the forties. But at least he wouldn't get frostbite.

He put on the disposable gloves he had bought when he had run into a grocery store on the way to the campground, telling Austin they needed to stock up on more beer, which fortunately, Austin had plenty of around the campfire that night on his big brother's urging. Cameron encouraged his brother to celebrate and had pretended to do multiple chasers with him, pouring him shots of whiskey and handing him cans of beer. He cleverly thought that if Austin had a lot to drink, his blood alcohol level would show up on a coroner's report and indicate that his reflexes and motor skills were compromised, making him more susceptible to being bitten by a snake... and then being unable to run for help.

If he was drunk, authorities could also deduce that he had stumbled or fallen and tumbled down to the stream at the bottom of the hill where his body would be found, the final resting place Cameron had selected. Feeling twinges of compassion for his little brother, Cameron hoped the alcohol would also numb some of the pain he might feel.

But most importantly, I've got to remove any signs that can be traced by the police or a medical examiner back to me. His manic scheming side quickly overruled his depressive soft side, his disorder kicking into high gear in his fragile psyche. Cameron had always been captivated by TV shows like *Law and Order, Criminal Minds, NCIS,* and others that dealt with solving crimes. *And now I get to play suspect and detective.* He felt a superior sense of satisfaction.

Cameron dumped his shots when Austin wasn't looking and only consumed two beers, emptying the cans later when he offered to clean up, Austin clearly too wasted to help or to care. Cameron needed to stay completely sober and clear-headed for his mission.

A few yards from their campsite, which he had selected because it was the most isolated of them all, he had found a short but steep embankment in the densely wooded forest which led down to a small, slow moving stream about six feet in width and about a foot deep. Cameron had thought the plan through down to the very last detail. To keep his brother from feeling, or crying out from, the violent pain of the snake bite, he would place Austin's unconscious body face down into the stream so that he would ultimately die from a mix of the snake bite and drowning. This way death would be certain, foolproof, and hopefully not painful.

It was time. Cameron slowly climbed out of his sleeping bag, careful to be as quiet as possible, and dressed in sweatpants and a sweatshirt, pulled a ski cap he had packed for cold weather down over his forehead, and put on his oilskin leather jacket, lifting up the collar flaps around his face, just in case anyone were to stray into this remote section of the woods.

Then he reached for his backpack, unzipped it, and pulled out its secret contents: the snake venom, the syringe, and the third thing he had remembered to ask Jake for before he left the store—an anesthetic of some sort. He had been in luck that day. Jake said they carried chloroform in the back of the store, which they used to knock out the snakes before drawing their venom. For the right price, Jake had said, he could sell him some. To knock the dog, of course, unconscious so he wouldn't feel the awful pain.

Austin was a sound sleeper once he dozed off, but Cameron also knew he needed to keep him that way. Cameron knelt over his brother, doused a rag with the chloroform, and held the wet rag over his brother's sleeping face for a few minutes until his breath slowed and he was unconscious. Cameron next reached into the bin holding all of the camping gear and supplies and pulled out his all-purpose hunting knife. Its medium-sized, pointy, serrated blade gleamed dully in the faint moonlight.

He would need it as well.

Moving with panther-like stealth, he quickly unzipped Austin's sleeping bag. His brother was wearing the same tee-shirt and jeans he had worn around the campfire, obviously too drunk to change into anything else for bed. Cameron pushed up the bottom hem of the jeans to expose Austin's foot and ankle, used his flashlight and his fingers to find a vein, held his breath and injected the deadly snake venom, praying it would work rapidly and well.

After wrapping the syringe and empty vial in another rag to later dispose of, Cameron took the knife in his hands. He pushed the point of the blade into Austin's foot right at the injection point, making a tiny hole to mimic the mark a snake's fang would make, then carved another tiny hole in his skin about an inch apart.

Cameron cringed as blood trickled from the wounds. *Don't worry, he's unconscious. He won't feel a thing*, he said to soothe himself. He quickly pulled down the cuff of denim over Austin's ankle and zipped the sleeping bag up around his brother's sleeping body.

He opened the tent flap and looked around to make sure there was no one lurking around in the woods. All was eerily dark and quiet, except for a sliver of moon that lent just enough light for Cameron to see the way and the melodic song of nature's creatures in the night.

Dragging his brother's body out of the tent and into the woods was made easier by the slippery nylon of the sleeping bag. Leaves rustled and branches cracked underfoot, seeming to cause a loud cacophony as Cameron hauled the sleeping bag and its contents to the crest of the hill and then down to the bank of the stream.

Cameron stopped to catch his breath, not realizing he had been holding it nearly the whole time for fear someone would hear him and foil his plan. He had no idea how he would possibly explain what he was doing. Hopefully he wouldn't have to now, since the plan was almost complete.

He unzipped the sleeping bag and rolled his brother's immobile body out onto the forest floor. And then something he didn't count on started to happen. Austin started to make noises, apparently waking from his stupor. Although his eyes were still closed, he started to emit a low groan. *He's probably starting to feel the pain of the snake venom coursing through his veins,* Cameron thought, trying not to panic, momentarily wondering if he should stop, rethink this whole thing, call 911.

It is too late, bro. His ego overruled his heart. *This is already happening. C'mon, pull it together, it's no accident that you've come this far, it will all be over in a few minutes and then life will go on, better than ever, with the universe in balance once more.*

Austin moaned again, jogging him back to the present, causing another terrifying realization. If he were stirring now, the cold water of the stream would definitely wake him all the way and he would cry for help. What to do?

He needed to get more chloroform. His heart racing, Cameron bounded up the hill, wincing when his right foot hit a patch of sharp brambles. He ignored the shooting pain, ran to the campsite, tore open the tent flap, and grabbed his flashlight, turning it on only long enough to find the soaked rag. He doused it again with the anesthetic liquid, crumpled it in his hand, careful to hold it away from his own face, and ran back down to his moaning brother.

Please don't wake up, he prayed and held the rag over his brother's nose and mouth until his groaning and whining stopped. Austin stilled, his breathing barely perceptible. "There, there, that's it, it's okay little brother." Suddenly realizing he was faintly whispering the words aloud, Cameron jerked his head right and left to make sure no one was nearby to hear him.

His eyes adjusted to the faint moonlight, Cameron looked once more at his brother's prone body, now finally and blissfully quiet. He pulled up Austin's pant leg to see his ankle, and noticed the "snake bite" wound had begun to spread into an ugly patch of pink and gray blisters fanning out from the two "fang" holes. It did look like a burn wound, and Cameron had to look away. He hoped he wouldn't have to see the end result of his handiwork but knew that was probably a futile wish.

Once he made sure Austin was unconscious again, Cameron racked his brain trying to think of a way he could render his brother unconscious longer just in case he woke up again from the chloroform. He couldn't keep running down here with the rag.

Then it hit him. *Brilliant.* He found a rock in the steam bed nearby and, taking a deep breath to fortify himself, struck his brother in his temple, hard enough that he would remain unconscious and not wake up once the chloroform wore off again, long enough that he might "drown peacefully" in the stream.

I should have thought of that in the first place, he scolded, then congratulated himself. This way, anyone who found Austin would see that he hit his head on a rock, which made him lose consciousness and wasn't able to feel the snake bite nor the drowning. Investigators would never suspect he had been drugged or in a stupor from chloroform. They wouldn't know if the rock, the water, or the snake bite ultimately killed him, but they'd know between the three he never stood a chance. It was the perfect trifecta.

As he laid the dark, jagged rock to the side of his brother's head, watching his sibling's blood disperse into the water, Cameron prayed that Austin didn't feel the pain of the rock or the suffocation or the snake venom. *I'm not a monster after all*, he reminded himself. And with that self-justification and a silent foxhole prayer, Cameron gently rolled the body of his little brother over, carefully placed his torso face down into the cold water of the stream, grabbed the sleeping bag and chloroform rag, and retreated back to the campsite.

Once safely back on site, seeing no one else from any neighboring campsites had stirred, Cameron, still wearing the plastic gloves, lit a small fire in a metal container usually used by smokers and burned the rag and the syringe, and then buried the needle and the vial several feet below the ground's surface. He kept the knife but cleaned it well with some rubbing alcohol and antiseptic wipes from the first aid kit they had packed.

Back within the safety of the tent, everything back in place, Cameron tried to fall asleep, feeling a little relieved that everything was finished.

He looked over at Austin's sleeping bag and then it dawned on him. His brother's blood from the fake snake bite wound might be inside. Cameron quickly found his flashlight and searched inside the sleeping bag. There, at the bottom, was a dark smear that looked like it was probably blood.

Cameron took the knife once again and cut away a swatch of the flannel material where the blood stain was, hoping it would look like a natural tear. He lit it on fire and burned it to ashes as well.

Hopefully he wouldn't have to explain any of this but better to be safe than sorry.

Finally, Cameron laid his head down on his pillow to try to rest. But even though he had taken twice his normal dose of Ambien, the sleeping pills had little effect, and his overactive mind churned.

He finally took a third pill and mercifully fell into a fitful sleep.

CAMERON AWOKE to the morning sun blazing down on their little tent, feeling suffocated, sitting up in a cold sweat.

It was going to be another hot one in Arizona, even for the northern parts, the weatherman predicted.

Cameron could barely breathe, he was so hot, and quickly peeled off his sweatshirt and sweatpants, replacing them with a fresh tee-shirt and shorts. He checked his wristwatch. He could barely believe his eyes. It was already nine a.m. He couldn't believe he had slept that late.

Groggy from the Ambien and suffering a headache from the stifling heat that had accumulated in the little airless tent, Cameron momentarily forgot what he had done the night before and looked next to him for his brother.

Then he suddenly remembered the events of the night before, and a chill pricked his skin, giving him goosebumps despite the warmth of the sun. There was the sleeping bag a few feet away, but no brother inside.

Cameron shook his head, trying to clear his thoughts, but his temples throbbed. He reached for some acetaminophen and swallowed three down with the remnants of a nearby water bottle.

I shouldn't have taken that third sleeping pill. Get your act together, man. And then he heaved in a deep breath and listened. He heard nothing, save for the chirp of some blue jays, the distant screech of a hawk, and some far-off rustling in the woods, although from the opposite direction than the hill and stream. He slowly exhaled, willing himself to calm down. *No one knows.* He kept repeating it in his head as a mantra, allowing himself to feel a little relief.

No one knows. Until you let them know.

Cameron started a fire, humming to himself, pretending Austin had simply gone for a walk, probably to relieve himself, and that he would be right back.

He put the kettle of water on for coffee, meanwhile picking up the empty beer cans that lay littered around and tossing them into a trash bag hanging from a nearby tree. He spooned some instant coffee in his mug and poured in some steaming water, inhaling the aroma, which helped wake him more fully.

After taking a few sips, he looked down at his cell phone and called his brother. A normal thing to do if he didn't show and he was trying to find him. The cell phone hummed within the tent. *Austin must have left it behind*, he would say.

It was nine-thirty by then. He started shouting, hoping most campers were the typical early risers and had already left for wherever they were going. "Austin! Austin!"

After yelling a half dozen times with no response, he sat down in his camp chair, drank down the rest of his coffee, and dialed 911.

He didn't have to try too hard to force a modicum of fear into his voice, his heart racing. "Um, I'm at the Slide Rock campgrounds and I have a missing person report. I can't find my brother anywhere," he said, his voice quavering a little.

"Please state your name and your exact location including the campsite number," the woman's voice on the other end crackled.

After Cameron gave her all of the information she requested, he asked what would happen next and when help would arrive.

The stern but polite woman told him she would send a National Park Service ranger, but that it wasn't considered a police emergency until a person was missing for more than twenty-four hours.

Cameron thanked her, hung up, poured himself another cup of coffee, and waited for the ranger to arrive. About ten minutes later, a weathered white man who looked to be in his sixties drove up in an official park service Jeep, talked into a handheld radio, and then got out of the vehicle and strode up to Cameron, who was now pacing in front of the fire. Beside him walked a German Shepherd, leashed and harnessed.

Cameron worriedly greeted the ranger shaking his hand. "I haven't been able to find my brother since I woke up this morning and that was an hour ago. I hope you and maybe your dog can help?"

The ranger introduced himself. "I hope we can. My name's Ranger Rick Frazier, and this here is Toby." The tall, lanky but well-built park ranger spoke in a slightly southern, gravelly drawl. The dog sat obediently by his master's side. "Tell me the last time you saw him, son."

Cameron recounted their evening the night before, how they had a few drinks around the campfire after dinner and then went to bed in the tent, and how he had woken up that morning around nine and noticed Austin was missing and had called his name, searching in the surrounding brush and woods before calling the emergency hotline.

Ranger Rick took notes in a small notepad while Toby sat quietly. Cameron noticed his eyebrows raise as he looked around the campfire when finding out the boys had been drinking, but other than that, he didn't appear suspicious about anything amiss. After he seemed to be satisfied he had all of the answers he was seeking, the ranger flipped his notebook shut. "Do you mind if Toby here sniffs an article of his clothing and then we do a little search for your brother?"

"No, of course, we need to find him." Cameron forced a little impatience into his tone. He ducked into the tent and emerged with Austin's sweatshirt.

Ranger Rick held the sweatshirt to the dog's nose and after the shepherd caught a good whiff, laid it down on a camp chair and gruffly commanded the dog, "Let's go, Toby."

The dog pulled at the leash, and the three of them headed into the woods.

It didn't take long for Toby to find the trail that headed into the forest at the top of the embankment and then lead his master down through some brush to the bottom of the hill and the stream bed.

Cameron trailed the ranger and his dog by a few feet, picking his way more gingerly through the forest's undergrowth. He was wearing his camping boots, but his foot ached from the cuts made by the brambles the night before.

The dog barked loudly, and Ranger Rick shouted back to him, "Mister Trellis, I think we found something." Cameron hurried to catch up to them but was stopped in his tracks by the ranger's next command. "Stay right there, Mister Trellis, don't come any closer yet."

Cameron stood still, but his heart felt like it was going to pound right out of his chest cavity. He concentrated on taking one breath at a time and could feel wet stains growing under his arm pits and a trickle of sweat run down his back. He wiped his dripping forehead with his shirt sleeve. A minute seemed to pass like an hour. He could hear the ranger and his dog about five or six yards up ahead but could barely see them through the thick trees and brush surrounding them. He knew Toby was sniffing something on the ground. He knew what...who it was.

And a million little questions shot like needles through his head. What if Austin's death appeared suspicious? What if the ranger, or his dog, discovered the truth, that the death was a murder made to look like an accidental snake bite? What if they somehow traced it back to him?

Suddenly Cameron's whole throat was parched, and he fought to breathe and swallow in the dry heat of midday. His head throbbed, the pain medicine and caffeine long worn off. He needed water, his mouth was too dry to form any words. Fear paralyzed, immobilized him, and he involuntarily began to shake.

What if Austin wasn't dead? What if he was writhing in agony? Would he recall what he did to him? Maybe he had been awake or at least aware during some of it and would say something?

Reason gave way to terror, his vision started to blur, and he felt like he was going to pass out when finally, the ranger called out to him again. "Mister Trellis, please come here, but walk very slowly." As Cameron, trembling now and covered in a cold sweat, walked toward the man and his dog, the ranger kept talking to him in his slow, southern drawl. "We have found someone here by the stream. It's hard to tell, it looks like he was bit by a rattlesnake. I want to warn you, Mister Trellis that he's not alive. It may be your brother and you may not want to see him like this but I will need you to identify him."

Cameron was now upon the scene and even though he knew what to expect, one look at the body, facing up now that the ranger had overturned it, made him turn his head into the woods and have the dry heaves. He wiped his mouth with the back of his hand and slowly approached the spot where the ranger squatted next to the body and the dog sat, ears perked, at attention.

He barely recognized Austin even though he knew it was him.

All of his younger brother's exposed area—his face, neck, arms, hands and feet—were swollen, bruised, and blistered, the skin shades of black, gray, purple, red, and pink as if he had been beaten and then burned in a fire.

At least his torso and legs were still covered by muddy, wet clothing so they were not visible. Cameron bent over his brother's face, still framed by curly, wet black locks, and saw with horror that Austin's eyes were staring back at him, although they remained unseeing, vacant, dead now, the life and light in them snuffed out for eternity.

What have I done? When he had envisioned the scene played out in which the police and he would come across his brother's dead body, Cameron had figured he would have to pretend to feel and show his loss and would have to put on the best performance of his life, wailing and crying fake tears.

But the scene played out for real now. Cameron didn't have to play act at all as he crumpled to the forest floor and wept.

CHAPTER SIXTEEN

CAMERON SAT BACK at the campsite around the fire pit in his camp chair, covered in a light blanket despite the afternoon heat.

He had changed into dry clothes and sat in his gym shorts and a fresh tee-shirt, but he just couldn't seem to get warm although the temperature reached eighty degrees that spring day in the mountains.

The ranger was in his jeep, Toby safely in his cage in the back. Ranger Rick talked on the car radio to the state police, who were apparently en route along with a coroner to transport the body to the morgue.

Cameron was thankful that Rick Frazier had called his parents for him to tell them the news that their youngest son had died, apparently the victim of a rattlesnake bite. They had asked to talk to Cameron, but the conversation lasted less than two minutes, as his mother could barely speak she was so distraught, and his father just wanted to make sure he was okay and told him they would drive to Flagstaff to meet him as fast as they could and then would meet him to drive together to the morgue and make arrangements.

Cameron had packed all of his and his brother's belongings into the Chevy Corvette and was smoking a cigarette when the ranger wandered over to him after finishing his call.

"Son, again I'm real sorry you have to go through this." The tough man's weather-beaten face and marine haircut belied a warm heart. "In my thirty-seven years as a park ranger, this is one of the worst snake bite cases I've ever seen."

He questioned Cameron a little bit after they arrived back at the campsite, leaving Austin's body at the stream but out of the water so it wouldn't decompose further and covering it with a tarp to ward off bugs and other animals. Cameron had suggested they bring it up to the campsite, but the ranger said that even though it was a clear case of snake bite, the police and coroner would have to investigate the scene before removing the body to the morgue.

The ranger stood with his hands on his hips, shaking his head. "We gotta start doing something more out here to protect people from these diamondbacks. They seem to be getting more deadly as time goes on. Can't explain it, but that's what seems to be happening. Why, just last year two people died in Arizona after being bit by a rattlesnake. One plumb fool owned one and it turned on him."

"I just wish I could have found him earlier and saved him. I feel like this is my fault."

"No, son, this ain't your fault no matter how you look at it. Nothing you coulda done. Your folks will just be glad you're okay."

My folks. Cameron did not want to face his mother and father, not at the morgue, not ever, but he knew he would have to sooner or later. He had thought that through too, how he would lie to them, like he did to the ranger and like he would have to do again with the police and coroner once they arrived and questioned him.

I'll just stick to my story, he kept reminding himself, playing it over and over again in his head like a broken record. *I woke up around nine a.m. and looked over and saw that Austin wasn't in his sleeping bag. I just figured he was out, you know, taking a leak in the woods. The night before we had come back after spending the day in Sedona and made a fire, then I cooked dinner, we ate, and we had a little celebration of Austin graduating and us being together on the trip and all. We had a couple of shots of whiskey and chased them down with a few beers. We had a few s'mores. Then we put out the fire and went to bed. I took my Ambien like I do every night, and I was out cold. I never heard him get up. I'm not sure what time it was. Like I said, the next thing I knew I woke up and he wasn't there. I made some coffee and waited for him to come back so I could make us some breakfast. I usually do the cooking since I'm good at it. Anyway, he never came back. After about twenty minutes or so I thought maybe he had gone for a little walk. After close to an hour, I realized something was wrong and I started to call for him and I walked into the woods looking for him and then I called 911, and they sent the ranger, and...I shouldn't have let this happen, I'm his big brother, I'm supposed to look out for him. I know there's nothing I could have done, I guess, but still...I just can't believe he's gone...*

CAMERON'S PARENTS arrived nearly three hours later at their meeting point, the Coconino County Morgue located within the national forest.

Cameron was waiting on a bench in the lobby of the nondescript foyer when he saw his parents walk, and then run, toward him. They threw their arms around him together, and his mother broke down, sobbing on his shoulder.

His dad had tears streaming down his face. "We are so happy to see you, Son." He gave Cameron a broken smile through his tears. "Thank God you are okay." Eliza didn't say anything and just kept her arms wrapped around Cameron for minutes. Growing uncomfortable and starting to feel suffocated, Cameron finally extricated himself from his mother's grip and took her hand to lead her and his father up to the receptionist desk.

Cameron signed in with a young female receptionist who looked and sounded pleasant but business-like. No doubt she was used to seeing emotional displays in her lobby every day. The young lady, dressed in a gray suit and white blouse, stood and extended a slim, manicured hand to greet them and then escorted the three Trellis

family members into an elevator and down two floors to the basement level. The receptionist's heels clicked ahead down a sterile
looking hallway and into an even more sterile looking white room
where a technician, dressed in hospital scrubs, greeted them politely,
taking over for the young lady.

The technician, a middle-aged man who introduced himself as
Doug, led them to a wall of numbered metal rectangular doors,
almost like big mailboxes, stopping at number six-forty-two.

"Mr. and Mrs. Trellis, Cameron, this is not going to be easy.
Austin's body was very badly damaged from the poison of the snake
bite venom, and if you've never seen anyone who has suffered a
deadly rattlesnake bite, you may not want to see your son," Doug
said with his stoic demeanor, although he showed a tad bit more
emotion than the receptionist. "He may look as if he was badly
burned in a fire because the venom travels through the bloodstream
and eats away at a person's tissues and even skin from the inside out,
causing blisters, bruising, and discoloration. Plus, he was lying face
down in a bed of water for quite some time, which caused his face to
also become swollen and further discolored. If you don't want to see
him, that is perfectly understandable."

"I've already seen him," Cameron said softly, and his parents
looked at him in surprise. "With the ranger," he added quickly. "I
don't want to see him again, if that's okay?"

Alex and Eliza looked down, not saying anything, but the coroner's assistant nodded. "You can either wait outside in the hallway or
stay here in the room but just turn away."

Cameron said, "I'll stay here" and walked to a far corner of the
room and just bent his head, looking down at his feet.

"Mr. and Mrs. Trellis?"

"I want to see him." Eliza spoke for the first time in the past
hour. "He's my son."

"Yes, me too," Alex said, putting his arm around his wife's
shoulder to support her.

"Okay." The coroner's assistant unlocked the bin and slowly
pulled it out, revealing a body with a white plastic bag covering it.

He slowly unzipped the bag from the top, down about a third of the way, revealing only the head, neck and shoulders.

Eliza started to shake and sob, leaning on her husband for support, crying into his chest. "My baby..." she wailed with despair over and over.

"That's him...that's our Austin," Alex whispered, closing his eyes.

Cameron felt a little sadistic but couldn't help himself from looking up briefly to take a peek. *At least his eyes are closed,* he thought. But other than that, he looked the same as he had at the stream bed when Ranger Rick called him over to identify him.

ELIZA AND ALEX drove home the next morning after having a quiet dinner with Cameron at the restaurant in the Little America Inn in Flagstaff, where all three of them stayed that night following their traumatic day visiting the morgue and making initial arrangements back home with the local funeral parlor.

Austin's body was transported via train to the funeral home back in Phoenix to be prepared for burial. Eliza and Alex had decided to have a closed casket ceremony at St. Augustine Church followed by a catered lunch in the parish hall.

Cameron drove Austin's Corvette home by himself, savoring the time alone on the open road for the most part. Occasionally during the three-hour drive he let his feelings wander into the darkness of guilt and remorse but tried to pull his thoughts out of the abyss by turning on the radio or stopping for a cold drink at a truck stop or gas station.

He didn't regret what he had done. He just missed what could have been.

We should have been stars together. Cactus Moon should have become famous. I should have stuck with Megan instead of leaving her and falling for Ivy. I should have finished college. And if Mom and Dad had given me an equal amount of attention, affection and support, none of this would have happened.

Cameron blamed his parents, mainly his father, for what he had done, but seeing them run to him at the airport and having them fawn over him at the restaurant the night before had helped relieve some of his anger and hurt.

Maybe things would be different now that he was the only child. They would be grateful that at least he survived, they had said so last night, and he would make them proud now, build his career, maybe even find his own record label, give them grandkids one day.

Cameron had called Ivy once he was comfortably resting in his hotel room and told her everything. Well, almost everything, leaving out the part that he would take to his grave as a secret, the fact that he had killed his brother.

No one will ever find out, he had promised himself once he had found he was definitely in the clear with the ranger, the police and the coroner. Their investigation had shown that the death of Austin Trellis was an accidental act of nature, a poisonous rattlesnake bite that had gone untreated because the victim had fallen down the side of a forest hill after having been bitten, hit his head on a rock, become unconscious, and fell face first into a stream where he had either drowned, or died of the deadly venom, or a combination of both.

Ivy had sounded somewhat sad and sympathetic, although Cameron guessed his wife was forcing her feelings over the phone a bit. She had never liked Austin that much, especially the night that he broke the news that he was dating his big brother's old girlfriend.

Seeing Cameron bothered by that revelation had caused a week-long fight between them. Just like he did, Ivy had a terrible jealous streak, which may have been part of the reason he was initially attracted to her.

His wife's lack of sincerity oddly comforted him that night as he took his Ambien and went to bed, able to finally get a good night's sleep in the solitary comfort of his own hotel room.

"THE GRACE of our Lord Jesus Christ and the love of God and the fellowship of the Holy Spirit be with you all," Father Timothy

Franklin exclaimed from the back of Saint Augustine Roman Catholic Church to the congregation who stood facing him.

Light from the arched doorway streamed in and around his tall, silhouetted frame draped in his liturgical vestments, his arms raised, causing him to look like an angel or prophet.

"And with your spirit," the Catholics in the pews said in return.

Fr. Tim sprinkled the dark bronze casket before him with holy water. "Austin Trellis died with Christ and rose with Him to new life. May he now share with Him eternal glory."

The kindly yet authoritative priest nodded, and a pall was placed over the coffin by two of Austin's friends from college who had flown in to attend the funeral.

The procession toward the altar then began down the church's main aisle. Two young altar servers walked slowly in front, one carrying a cross and another a candle, and were followed by a lector carrying the Bible, Fr. Tim, and then the casket on wheels, flanked on either side by Austin's friends from home, school, and his musical career including Max and Charlie.

Cameron sat with Ivy and his mother and father in the first pew to the left. Directly behind them sat Megan McGee and her parents, Ivy's parents and Aunt Doli, and over to the right, Dexter Poseidon and several members of the Stardust label, a few of them stars in their own right. Eliza's friend Marsha and a few of her coworkers sat behind them, and the church was also filled with coworkers and friends of Alex. Cameron saw a few friends he and Austin had grown up with in high school whom he recognized, along with Max's and Charlie's families.

He had downed several cups of coffee but was only able to swallow a few bites of the omelet Ivy had kindly made him that morning.

This day was going to be long and hard, he knew. *But once it's over, it's over,* he told himself. *Once and for all, and life will go back to a semblance of normality and we will be a family again, Mom and Dad, Ivy and me, and our children to come.*

We'll have three or four children and celebrate holidays and life will be good again. Cameron focused on images of the future he pictured in his head. Christmases, Thanksgivings and Easters with kids running around, laughing, playing—

His dreams were interrupted by a strange small sound next to him, growing louder until it filtered through the fog of his fantasies. It was his mother. Eliza Trellis sat between her son and husband on the hard wood pew, trembling and emitting a soft sobbing sound as the casket inched closer. As it came into view and stopped next to them, the pallbearers taking their seats, Cameron and his parents could look at nothing else but the cloth covered-casket, and Eliza could no longer hold back her emotions. Her shoulders shook as she cried aloud.

Oh God what have I done to her? Cameron closed his eyes, holding back the sting of his own tears, praying for the Lord to take away his mother's pain.

Fr. Tim blessed the casket, making the sign of the cross over it, praying, "Lord God, source and destiny of our lives, in Your loving providence You gave us Austin Trellis to grow in wisdom, age and grace. Now You have called him to Yourself. As we grieve over the loss of one so young, we seek to understand Your purpose. Draw him to Yourself and give him full stature in Christ. May he stand with all the angels and saints who know Your love and praise Your saving will. We ask this through Christ our Lord. Amen." And then he stepped up onto the altar with the servers and lectors to begin the funeral Mass.

Cameron was, for the first time, grateful for the rituals and rote prayers and actions of the Mass, so that his mind wouldn't wander off into the abyss of remorse. Just get through one prayer, one reading, one kneeling, one song at a time.

Fr. Tim delivered the homily, which also doubled as a eulogy. He had known the Trellis family for the many years they had attended St. Augustine's.

And finally, the mass concluded when one of the recording artists, Jay Greene, who was Austin's age and had been a good friend of his, sang a soulful rendition of "Amazing Grace" from the pulpit that left everyone in tears.

"Amazing grace how sweet the sound that saved a wretch like me. I once was lost but now am found, was blind but now I see." The young, black singer's powerful voice quivered and then lingered a moment in the still, incense laden air of the church. Then the entire congregation applauded, which Cameron noticed brought a small smile to his mother's lips.

The power of song, Cameron thought, and for a minute his mind wandered down that dark hallway of envy that had caused him to be standing here dressed in his hot, black suit and itchy, starched collar and tie in the first place. *One day I'll play the drums again. And they…those smug singers and producers sitting across the aisle will be applauding me, Cameron Trellis. And my mother will be smiling for me.*

THE BURIAL AT St. Francis Catholic Cemetery had been relatively quick as the hot June sun beat down on those gathered, the tent over the plot offering the only relief from the intense heat.

Fr. Tim was mercifully brief and then invited everyone back to the church's parish hall for a lunch catered by the women's Sodality of Saint Augustine.

About fifty or so of the guests feasted on the buffet of lasagna, casseroles, salads, and desserts. There was also an open bar, and Alex and Cameron helped themselves along with other guests to multiple rounds of cocktails, beer, and wine.

Alex stuck to hard liquor, preferring scotch and soda, while Eliza had a few glasses of wine and Cameron mainly drank beer, although he downed a few shots of whiskey when no one was watching.

Marsha and Dexter were the last of the guests to leave the wake party. Marsha helped Eliza pack up some of the leftovers to take home while Alex talked to Fr. Tim, thanking him for all of his help that day, and squaring away the bill for the lunch.

Cameron attempted to take advantage of that and sidled up to

Dexter, who was standing alone at the bar nursing a beer. He tried hard not to slur his words. "Hey, Dex, you know I still play the drums and would love to write some more songs and maybe do a few recordings...records...with ya," he said. "You know I wrote most of Austin's hit songs, and, well, I'd like to—"

Suddenly Marsha walked up to them in her short black dress, black stockings and pointy black heels, her red lips parting in a ravishing smile, and Dexter was lost in her charm. The two of them had been chumming it up and charming each other the past few hours. Cameron seethed with rage as the record producer completely ignored him, abruptly turning away from him and gallantly bowing and offering the lady his arm to walk her to her car.

And with that, they were gone, leaving Cameron alone with his parents.

Ivy had gone home an hour earlier, complaining of one of her migraines, which seemed to start the minute Cameron introduced her to Megan, who didn't stay long at the lunch either, much to Cameron's dismay.

Cameron grabbed a beer from behind the bar before it was wheeled away and sat, gulping it down, trying to wash down his anger, although the alcohol only had the opposite effect, fueling his already inflamed temper.

His mother and father walked up to him and sat at the table.

"Don't you think you've had enough to drink, Son?" Alex's tone was calm yet firm, but to Cameron it came across as condescending.

"Well, you had plenty to drink today, too, so you're not one to talk, Dad."

"Cameron!" Eliza scolded her son. "You need to apologize to your father for back talking him right now."

"Well, it's true. How can he sit there and tell me I had too much to drink when both of you had your share?"

Now Alex became irate. "That's no way to talk to your mother, or either one of us. This whole thing has put a strain on all of us. The least you can do is be compassionate where your mother is concerned. Austin...this...has been especially hard on her."

"Oh, and you don't think everything's been hard on me my whole life?" Cameron rose as he spoke, his voice getting louder. He loosened his tie and slammed his beer bottle onto the table, sending the frothy remains spilling over the rim. "I had to look after Austin my whole life, be the big brother, while no one looked out for me."

Alex rose and stood face to face with his son, matching Cameron's anger with his own.

"Well, where were you the night Austin was bitten by a rattlesnake?"

Eliza, sitting holding her head in her hands, gasped sharply. "Alex!"

"No, I'm serious, Eliza. Where was Cameron? Why didn't he hear Austin cry for help? Was he drunk then too?"

Cameron balled his hands into fists, and it took all of his self-control not to slam one into his father's face. "I'm responsible for my brother?" he shouted. "For Austin dying? That's what you're saying, isn't it? Isn't it?"

His father backed up a foot and glared into his son's eyes, as if searching for the truth, and then his brown eyes widened in horror at finding it in the malicious, challenging gleam in Cameron's eyes. Alex's next question came out in a choked whisper. "Are you, Son?"

"Yes! Yes, I am." Cameron stood triumphantly, flashing a wicked grin.

Eliza stood and looked up at her son, her eyes glazing with fresh tears. "Cameron, you're not serious?" she asked.

"What have you done?" Alex stepped back and away from his son, staring at him as if he no longer knew him.

"And you know what?" Cameron rolled up his dress shirt sleeves and put his hands on his hips, proudly defending himself and his actions. "I'm glad I did what I did. You and Mom needed to be taught a lesson, that I matter too." Cameron now gesticulated wildly. "My whole life you've favored Austin over me, and his plan to marry Megan would have just made things worse. I couldn't take it anymore. This is all your fault, Dad." He pointed to his father, and although her head was buried in her hands now and she couldn't see him, he then pointed to his mother. "And yours, Mom. Not mine."

He turned and stormed out of the banquet room, leaving his parents to wallow in their shock and despair.

III

ELIZA

CHAPTER SEVENTEEN

SHE JUST WANTED TO DIE, to fall asleep and never wake up again.

But apparently, God wasn't listening to her prayers anymore. Answers to prayers had ended a long, long time ago, in fact, back when she was a little girl, as she recalled.

If there ever was a God at all, she thought dismally, her eyes closed. Her memory of where she was and how she got there started painfully to penetrate her psyche like broken shards of glass, and she wanted to block it all, to shut down altogether but couldn't, her sensory perception betraying her.

She felt her bare legs beneath the hospital gown under the stiff, white sheets in the patient bed in the psych ward of Banner Hospital. Fr. Tim and her husband had brought her here in a wheelchair when she had a severe migraine attack the night of the funeral brought on by the sudden and overwhelming stress and grief of hearing the news…

It was the very place she had taken her oldest son not too long ago. *My son. Cameron. Who killed my other son Austin. The son we just buried.*

And the tiny shards of pain became daggers stabbing her heart and soul.

She opened her eyes, fighting through the agony that ripped through her head. She reached for the button she vaguely remembered the nurse showing her, the red button that you hit when you felt the pain become unbearable. Her hand shook uncontrollably so that she had to concentrate with everything in her.

A different nurse briskly walked into her room and checked the plastic bags that dripped pain medication and fluids through the IV lines hooked into her arm.

"What seems to be the problem, Mrs. Trellis?" the middle-aged, stocky nurse barked in a voice that was much too loud for the small room. "Are you feeling more pain?"

Eliza slowly nodded, since it would hurt too much to speak, pointing to her head with the index finger of her left hand, the one not rigged up to all of the bags and machines.

The nurse bustled around her bed, busily checking her charts and re-checking the medication pumps. "Well, it doesn't seem time yet to give you another dose of Dilaudid, but I will come back in twenty minutes; you just try to relax and breathe." The nurse exited, dimming the light, turning her already colorless world to a darker shade of gray.

Tears of pain trickled involuntarily from her eyes, and she was amazed that she had any left in her. *God, just let me die*, she prayed, but her hope and faith in anything, including a quick death to relieve her of her suffering, were also long gone.

AFTER THREE DAYS of psychiatric observation, counseling, and pain medication, Eliza was released from the hospital with prescriptions for Percocet to take as needed along with Zoloft for her depression and anxiety. She was also encouraged to see a psychotherapist on a regular basis and attend a support group for parents who had lost children.

But they haven't lost a child at the hands of another child, she thought when the doctor on call handed her the slip of paper with contact information on support groups in her area.

She knew Alex was just waiting to talk to her about Cameron's revelation until she was strong and well enough to come home.

And now here she was, propped against pillows, her legs outstretched, comfortable in her own home sitting on her couch in her living room, still feeling completely devastated and miserable.

And here he was, sitting in the recliner facing her, ready to discuss the truth.

She didn't know if her heart could take it, but she did want to get the confrontation over with.

"Honey, I know you just got home and all, but I think we need to talk about what happened at the funeral lunch. About what Cameron said." Alex hunched forward, his fingers nervously clenched together, obviously trying to pick the right words to say to her, obviously anxious to discuss the matter.

"Did you talk to him more while I was in the hospital?" Eliza was afraid to hear the answer but needed to know and was filled with a shred of hope. *Maybe he wasn't telling the truth, maybe he was making it up to get their attention, maybe he hadn't killed Austin.*

"Briefly, yes, over the phone, not face to face. I asked him if he was telling the truth, whether he really did somehow…cause the death of his brother." Alex shifted uncomfortably in his chair, clearing his throat. "He said he did. He told me he—" a sob caught in Alex' throat as he continued to relay the painful details. "He staged the snake bite to look real. He injected rattlesnake venom into Austin's foot and dragged him to the stream to die. He made sure that Austin wouldn't feel any pain by putting him to sleep with chloroform a few times and said that he was truly sorry."

"Oh, God," Eliza crumpled forward, choking on her grief.

Alex got up, came over to her, and sat next to her, wrapping her in his arms, rocking her back and forth. She wanted to battle him at first, to hit and scratch and kick and bite and let the grief-turned-rage out on someone else, to turn on him and what he was saying. But she didn't have any more fight in her, instead she sank into his embrace, like a drowning victim finally gives in to a lifeguard, and let him hold her, contain her.

Maybe if I shrink instead into a tiny ball of nothing, I can shut out my feelings, shut out reality. But she knew that was only a temporary respite, and suddenly she felt like she was suffocating and pushed him away. She got up off the couch and started pacing wildly, hyperventilating, angry now at Alex, at Cameron, at Ivy, at the world, at herself.

"How could we let this happen?" she shouted at her husband, her head starting to throb. "This is our fault. Looking back, I can see how you, we, always favored Austin. How we gave him special attention even when he was little. And you were so hard on Cameron. Even at your birthday party, you were rough on him and all happy with Austin. And then the Grammys…this is all our fault."

Now Alex stood up, also irate, barely keeping his tone level. "We can't blame ourselves, Eliza. We did the best we could as parents. And you can't pin this all on me either. Cameron is a grown man, and I know he feels somehow like he's been cheated in life, but we got him help after he tried to overdose. It's not our fault he stopped taking his medicine."

Eliza could hear herself shrieking now, as if another woman, a witch, had possessed her. "You know whose fault this is besides ours? Ivy is to blame too. If she hadn't gotten her hooks into Cameron, trapping him by getting pregnant…"

"That's true, but still, Cameron is a young adult now."

"He's still my baby boy. He should have been a star too. Life just hasn't been fair for him. We weren't fair. God hasn't been fair."

Alex let her rant for a few minutes until she had exhausted herself and sat on the floor, heaving ragged breaths of regret and remorse. And then he broached the subject that was still the white elephant in the room. "Do you think we should report this to the police?"

Eliza sat up straight and then abruptly jumped to her feet, and grabbed her husband's tee-shirt in her fists, pulling herself up on her toes so she could look him in the eyes, which she saw widen in surprise.

"Don't you dare ever say that again," she whispered frantically.

"Of course we can't do that. He would go to jail for the rest of his life."

"But what about doing the right thing? Our son committed murder."

"I don't care about doing the right thing, I care about protecting our son." She unclenched her fingers, smoothed her husband's shirt over his chest, and stood facing him, arms crossed with determination. "You and I are the only ones who know about this, right?"

"Well, I'm not sure if he told Ivy."

"I would hope not."

"What do you propose we do? Just keep the information to ourselves? I don't know if I can ever look at him again."

"He's our son."

"He killed our other son!"

"What are you saying, we kill him too? Because that's what will happen. He'll rot away in a prison cell or be beaten up and killed or commit suicide or maybe even be executed by the death penalty. I couldn't live with myself if any of that happened."

Eliza recalled the news headlines about Arizona's execution in 2014 of Joseph Rudolph Wood, III, who died of lethal injection in the state prison complex in Florence. It was called a "botched" execution when the procedure, which should have taken ten minutes according to experts, turned into a two-hour ordeal in which Wood gasped and snorted for over an hour like a "fish gulping for air" one media witness reported. It took fifteen shots of the drug cocktail to finally kill him, even though one dose was supposed to be sufficient. An *Associated Press* reporter wrote that Wood gasped more than six hundred times.

Wood was on death row for killing his twenty-nine-year-old estranged girlfriend, Debbie Dietz, and her fifty-five-year-old father, Eugene Dietz, in 1989 by shooting them in their family-run auto body shop. He was also convicted of aggravated assault against a police officer for turning his gun on the cops, who shot him nine times.

Certainly my son isn't a hardened criminal like that. He made a mistake because we favored his brother, caused him to be jealous, never loved him enough. A big mistake but certainly a mistake he regrets. And that he doesn't deserve to die for.

"Well, I can't live with myself knowing the truth," Alex said defiantly.

"Please, Alex, please tell me you'll keep quiet about this, please, for me." Eliza pleaded with her husband now, like she had done so many times before when she had begged him to stop gambling, to forgive her for buying dresses and shoes out of their budget, to take it easy on Cameron when he was bad. But this…he had to listen to her or, she didn't know what she'd do. She sat down on the living room sofa and started to weep.

After a few moments of silence, he finally spoke up. "Okay, but on one condition."

Eliza smiled at him through her tears. *I'll agree to anything.* She nodded.

"He needs to leave here and never come back."

And suddenly all of the memories of when her father kicked her out of the Navajo Nation, turning her away forever from her home, her mother, her sisters, her family and friends, her people, her heritage, came flooding back. She had buried the pain for so long, but now the scars were ripped open and bled again, fresh wounds as raw as if they had just been inflicted.

But she knew her husband. She saw the resolve in his eyes. He would not budge on this. "Okay," she agreed, and fresh tears started to fall down her face.

Alex picked up his cell phone sitting on the coffee table and dialed their son's number.

She heard Cameron answer with a tentative "hello?" Eliza felt helpless as she listened to the conversation. Her husband had put his phone on speaker mode so she could hear.

"Hi, Cameron. I'm calling to tell you we talked about your situation and we've decided not to say anything about any of this to the police or anyone else."

He sounded so formal. Like this was a business transaction. But better he talk than she. *I would lose it.* She sat on the sofa just listening, her fist in her mouth to keep her from crying out to her only son.

"I am so sorry for all of the pain I've caused you and Mom." Cameron's voice sounded small, as if he were a kid again who had eaten candy before dinner or gotten in trouble in school. *He's still my baby boy.* "Thank you both."

"But, Cameron, this is on one condition. Your mother and I think it will be best if you leave Arizona—the Southwest in fact—for good. By the way, does Ivy know about…about everything?"

"No, I haven't told her any of it. I want to protect her from knowing. You and Mom are the only ones. I wish I had never told you, but I can't undo that. Mom said she wants me to leave?" Eliza heard despair in her son's voice now and felt a fresh stab of guilt for betraying him. *No, I don't, but it will be better than the alternative.*

"Yes, Son, we decided everything together. Your mom is here with me but is too upset to speak right now. We don't care where you go, but as far away as possible would be good. We need to… distance ourselves from all of this. I was thinking the East Coast, New York City, in fact, would be a good place for you to start fresh, get lost in the crowd so to speak."

"You mean you want to distance yourselves from me?" Eliza heard Cameron's voice rise an octave in self-defense. "Dad, I don't know how I can just move east and find another construction job, especially in New York where everything is built up and out. And construction is all I know. There's not even any land left to build on. And the cost of living there is through the roof. We'll never make it on our own. Not to mention Ivy will have to leave her family behind and won't understand why."

"Well, Ivy will just have to stick by you as her husband now, won't she?" Eliza detected a hint of frustration in her husband's voice. "And I know a few people from my company who work in New York City. I'm sure they can help you find a job there."

Eliza looked at him, stunned. Had he planned this all along?

"When you get to New York, go into Manhattan and report to

the offices of a construction firm named Krause and Sons. Tell them who you are, that you are my son, and that you are looking for a job. They work for my company, ABC Oil. We're one of their biggest clients. They will find work for you."

He planned this whole thing, she realized. He just needed her to back him up.

There was silence on the other end for a minute. Cameron was obviously thinking. "Okay, but can I see you both before we move, to say goodbye?"

"I think it would be best if you just go," Alex told his son gruffly. "And be grateful that you're getting away with all of this."

"Can you tell Mom goodbye for me?" Eliza heard Cameron sniff back his tears and felt a deep ache resurrect within her from a place she assumed had grown numb. She reached her hand out toward her husband, and he gave her the phone.

She could barely get out the words but knew this was her only chance. "Hi, Cam," she said in a choked whisper. She took the phone off of the speaker mode, looking at her husband, who nodded his assent. *He can at least give me that.*

"I'm so sorry, Mom," Cameron whimpered. "For everything. You know, I will pay the price the rest of my life by being sorry for what I did, living with the guilt and shame."

"Me too, Cam." Eliza started to cry into the phone, but felt her husband staring at her with a look of impatience. "I'm sorry too."

"Mom don't blame yourself, this is all my fault. And don't worry, I'll be okay, I know this is probably for the best."

Eliza sniffed and looked up at her husband. "When do you think you would leave?"

"I guess I'll talk to Ivy tonight. I'm sure she can find a job in New York. She's always talked about wanting to go there. I don't think she'll have too much of a problem with it. I'll just tell her I found a new, great-paying job there, I guess. It sounds like Dad has all this figured out."

Yes, it did. Eliza glared at Alex. But then she thought of the image of Joseph Wood being injected fifteen times as he sputtered and thrashed and reminded herself this was the only way.

"I guess we won't get to say goodbye in person. I don't know if Dad will be okay with it, but maybe you can come out and visit once we get settled in. But please don't call me. I think it will be easier on all of us. I'll text you once in a while. I just don't want Dad getting angry with you. Please tell him I said goodbye. And thanks again…I love you."

"I love you, Cam," she whispered. "I love you." And the phone went dead.

IT WAS four months after Eliza last talked to him when Cameron finally called her. He had texted her sporadically every now and then —when they arrived and found a place to live in an apartment complex, when he got the job with Kraus and Company as a dry wall hanger, when Ivy got a job in a Manhattan dress shop, to wish her a happy birthday—and now her heart jumped when her phone rang and she saw it was him.

"Mom, I'm calling to tell you the good news. Ivy is pregnant. And I…we want you to come out to visit when your grandson is born."

"It's a boy?" For the first time in months, Eliza could feel again, and her heart sang with joy. And then fear instantly crept in to take its place. *What if she has another miscarriage and the baby doesn't make it? What if he's born and something happens and he dies? I don't think I could take it.* Eliza bit her lip, trying to will the thoughts from her mind, reminding herself that this wasn't about her.

"Yep, Ivy got an ultrasound when she went to the doctor and he confirmed it's a boy."

Eliza swallowed hard and forced a note of happiness into her voice. "Honey, that's exciting, when is she due?"

"The doctor told her she's due next March. She's already four months pregnant. We wanted to wait to tell anyone until we felt pretty sure this time that she won't miscarry. What do you say, would you like to come out and see your new grandson when he's born?"

"Well, sure I'd love to come out." Alex would just have to get over it.

As if reading her mind, Cameron asked with hesitation, "And Dad? Do you think he'd want to…you know, come out? Or will he be okay with you coming out?"

"Oh, honey, I don't think…he probably won't be able to get off work." Eliza disguised the truth. Ever since Cameron had left, they hadn't spoken a word about their son or daughter-in-law except the initial news Eliza relayed when they found an apartment and subsequently landed their jobs. This code of silence was what Alex requested from her, and she never talked about their son's occasional texts. She knew her husband wouldn't want to visit their son if he couldn't stand to even talk about him anymore. Eliza just hoped he wouldn't have a major problem with her visiting New York.

And if he does…well I'll figure something out.

CHAPTER EIGHTEEN

ELIZA FINALLY TALKED to Alex on Christmas Day to tell him the news that their son and his wife were expecting. It had been a cold Christmas season that year in more ways than one. The weather was unseasonably cold in Phoenix, but mainly, the air between Eliza and her husband had cooled ever since the unspeakable death of their younger son.

They found they had little to talk about except for their jobs. Eliza still worked at the local library although she had received a promotion to branch manager, which brought more hours and more pay. She liked her job and was grateful it provided a sanctuary of sorts, a place for her to escape and distract her from the hole in her soul, the chasm of grief that had opened inside her with the loss of both sons. If she focused all of her efforts on managing her staff, sorting and filing books and CDs, answering emails and calls, hosting events and occasionally burying her head in a book on her lunch break or at night so she could review it, she could trick her mind into forgetting, if just for a few moments, that she was the mother of a son who was murdered and of a son who was banished because he was to blame.

Alex still worked at ABC Oil Company, and while he still didn't particularly like his job, he had acquired enough seniority and a large enough pension and stock plan that he looked forward to retiring at age sixty-five and providing for himself and his wife in their old age. Unlike the Native American culture, where families took care of the elderly, Eliza and Alex would obviously not be cared for by their children and had no other family to turn to for help should they become sick or frail.

They only had each other. And for Eliza, even though she was healthy at age forty-five and didn't dare think about the future since she knew it would only add to her grief, home was a very sad and lonely place since her husband still worked so many hours and they seemed to have so little in common anymore.

And of course, there was their secret, which they couldn't share with anyone else but each other. And since Alex, just like his father before him, refused to acknowledge the existence of his son, that secret was buried forever.

Eliza had attended a few sessions of one of the support groups her doctor had recommended. But instead of feeling a common bond or being able to relate to the other men and women in the group, she felt increasingly different and isolated, since she had a secret she couldn't dare share. Instead of lightening the load by sharing her story and grief with the others, Eliza always felt that, even when she spoke, she was holding back. And that burden would rise slowly but surely, like a heavy iron anchor that was dragged to the water's surface, only to be plunged again to the dark, secret depths of the ocean. It was exhausting and after five meetings, she couldn't do it anymore.

That cold Christmas morning in their home, the first without their sons, was so bleak that Eliza didn't even want to get out of bed, much less celebrate.

She and Alex had bought a small artificial tree, only because it seemed like they had to have some kind of Christmas decoration should anyone stop in. She still hung out with her friend Marsha from time to time, but even they had become more distant, since the bubbly, vivacious redhead became increasingly exasperated with her mournful friend. It wasn't that Marsha wasn't sympathetic or compassionate, but that she had limits on the negativity she would allow into her own life.

When Eliza and Alex woke and saw the gray, drizzly, chilly Christmas morning outside their bedroom window, they both crawled back under the covers. Alex went to the kitchen around ten to make coffee, then Eliza joined him to exchange the handful of gifts they had bought each other.

The six wrapped packages under the tree were a sad sight in themselves. Eliza pulled her terrycloth robe tighter and wrapped a blanket around herself to ward off the chill. They hadn't bothered to turn the heat on the night before, not expecting the temperature to dip into the low forties. It was only expected to climb to fifty degrees that day.

Alex handed her a steamy cup of coffee, kissed her on the cheek, and wished her a Merry Christmas.

Eliza tried her very best not to cry and quickly wiped a stray tear when her husband turned from her to get a present from under the tree. He sat next to her on the couch and handed her the gift, a small box that held a pretty silver and coral bracelet inside.

So she could stay covered up and warm until the heat finally started to work in their house, Alex brought all of the gifts over to the sofa, and they exchanged and unwrapped them slowly, one by one, making a big fuss about each, knowing this was all there was and then they'd be left with the yawning, dreary day stretched before them with nothing to do but cook and clean and watch TV and wait for it to be over.

They were so bored after watching a rerun of "It's a Wonderful Life" that Eliza suggested they make love and then take a nap. It had been so long, months actually, that the act seemed somewhat mechanical and dispassionate. But at least it was something to pass the time.

Afterward, lying in bed, Eliza brought up the subject of the baby.

"Honey, thank you for making Christmas okay," she said, stroking her husband's bare chest with her fingers.

"My pleasure, thank you for all of your gifts," he said playfully, smiling contentedly, his black hair tousled against his pillow.

He is still handsome. And he really has been very attentive and loving today, knowing I would be hurting without our children to cele-brate what used to be my favorite day of the year. I guess this is the perfect time to break it to him. Here goes…

"I have another gift to share with you." She held her breath, summoning all her courage. "We're going to have a grandson."

A range of emotions played across her husband's lean, angular face. He opened his eyes, his smile vanishing, and looked at her. Surprise registered in his dark brown eyes, and then a fierceness. Eliza guessed it was a mixture of resentment and determination to stay the course and not let any other feelings in. His brows knitted into a frown.

After a long minute of silence, he propped himself up on one elbow, looked directly into her eyes, and said, "We are not going to have a grandson because we have no son."

Eliza sat up, drawing the bed clothes up over her.

"How can you say that? You know we still have a son and daugh-ter-in-law and now they are going to have a baby boy. And while you can block them out all you want, I can't. I still don't excuse what Cameron did, but I have forgiven him. I know you can't, or won't, and I have made peace with that. Just like you will have to make peace with the fact that I am going to visit them in New York City to see my grandson."

"Eliza, I forbid you to do that." Now Alex climbed out of bed, pulled on a pair of sweatpants and a sweatshirt, and stood stub-bornly at the foot of their bed, hands on his hips. "I am adamant on this. If you go to New York, I swear I'll—"

"You'll what?" Eliza challenged him. "You'll divorce me? I'm all you have." She sighed, and her tone softened. "You're still my whole world. But God is bringing this new life into it now, and I think I can open my heart again to find a little more love to share with him too. He could bring the healing we both need."

"I don't need any healing, I am fine with the way things are. Just you and me."

"I'm not fine, Alex." She should try a different tactic. "I know you're my husband and I will respect your wishes." She paused for that statement to make an impact. "But if you deny me knowing my grandson, I think I'll be so broken-hearted that I don't see how I'll go on. I promise I won't speak of Cameron or his wife or baby if that's what you want. You won't see any pictures or hear any reports. I will keep everything to myself. I won't even stay overnight so you won't even know I'm gone. Just think about it."

Alex frowned but didn't say anything as Eliza heard the clock on their bedside ticking for what seemed like an eternity. Several minutes passed by in silence until he finally replied. "All right, but I don't want to see or hear anything about it."

It. He was referring to their new grandson as an "it," a small detail that wasn't lost on her. *Maybe he'll come around in time. But who cares, I have his blessing to go and the rest doesn't matter.*

Eliza exuberantly hopped out from under the covers, knelt at the foot of the bed, and threw her arms around her husband's neck in gratitude, forgetting for the moment that she was still unclothed. They wound up under the covers again, this time feeling their passion and love rekindle like it had many years ago.

WHEN CAMERON CALLED her to tell her that her grandson, Mason Elijah Trellis, was born, eight pounds, two ounces, in the middle of the night at Harlem Hospital, Eliza felt as though a tiny candle of hope, love, and life had been re-lit inside her, at least temporarily. Perhaps this new baby boy would be her reason to look ahead to the future and not stay trapped in the despair of the past and present.

Cameron had called his mother closer to the delivery date to find out if she was coming. She asked him to let her know as soon as the baby was born and told him she'd fly out three days later to visit them, then fly back to Phoenix later that night.

Eliza took a taxi straight from JFK Airport to the big apartment complex where her son's new family lived just outside of Harlem and arrived at two in the afternoon to visit her newborn grandson.

She finally arrived at her son's apartment feeling anxious but determined. She tried to ignore the squalor of the neighborhood, the trash overflowing from the garbage bins on the side of the yellowed stucco apartment building, the handful of hoodlums hanging out on the corner. The dingy hallways inside smelled faintly of urine and smoke, and she was relieved Alex had not come with her.

And she tried to disregard the fact that she had to climb four flights of cement stairs since the rickety, old elevator was broken.

She just wanted to see her baby grandson. She knocked on the apartment door, ecstatic and nervous, and she heard the door unlatch and then saw her son, sleepy and disheveled, as he opened the door. Her heart warmed as his expression turned from wary seriousness to a grin of delight to see his mother.

For a second Eliza noticed the apartment's drab, cluttered, windowless interior but then all that mattered was the little bundle in the arms of Ivy, who was sitting on a threadbare upholstered brown sofa in the middle of what appeared to be a sparely furnished yet cluttered living room.

"Congratulations," Eliza said, barely able to contain her joy and excitement. She awkwardly bent over and embraced an exhausted but happy looking Ivy.

"He's sleeping, but you can pick him up and hold him," Ivy said, patting the cushion on the sofa next to her for Eliza to sit.

Eliza's heart danced—for the first time in nearly a year—when she first held her grandson, looking down on his little cherub face. *He looks just like his daddy*, she thought, gazing at his tuft of straight, jet black hair, tiny nose, creamy caramel skin with touches of pink on his cheeks, and dark brown eyes.

She had thought she had known what love was, but it was nothing compared to this. She rocked her precious baby grandson back and forth in her arms.

They ordered in pizza, which Eliza insisted on paying for, and she stayed for a few hours until Ivy yawned and stretched around five p.m. and said she needed to take a nap. Ivy had nursed baby Mason and then explained that she always tried to sleep when the baby did, hinting it was time for Eliza to go. "You'll want to leave to catch your flight," she said.

It was much too short a visit, but Eliza reminded herself to be grateful that she had had any opportunity at all to see her grandson and her son.

She hugged Cameron tightly in the apartment doorway as she reluctantly left, wishing she had also had more time to talk one on one with him.

"Let me know when you need me to babysit," Eliza called over his shoulder to Ivy, who started to look impatient as she watched them, still sitting on the couch, holding a now fussy Mason in her arms.

"We will, Mom," Cameron said softly, a hint of sadness in his eyes as he looked into her own. "Thanks for coming, Mom, it really meant a lot."

"I love you, Cameron," she said and tiptoed to kiss him on the cheek.

"I love you too, Mom." And with that he slowly shut the door, and Eliza wiped her tears so she could make her way down out into the dusk where her taxi waited.

ANOTHER YEAR WENT by during which Eliza secretly kept in touch with Cameron and his little family by Skype whenever Alex was away.

Cameron had informed his mother that he had worked really hard and had twice been promoted within the construction company, first to a superintendent position and then to a project manager.

He explained that some people had quit the company, or been fired, when they had vehemently disagreed, based on their political views, with the firm's successful bid on a new mixed-use housing and retail development that involved partnering with government entities to build a new "sanctuary city" type of community.

"I didn't care one way or another about the political angle. All I know for sure is that we really needed the money, and I took advantage of the sudden openings to move up the ranks and get ahead," Cameron had told her proudly.

While her son didn't have strong political leanings, Eliza figured her conservative Republican husband would be upset by the news.

She decided not to tell him, hoping he wouldn't find out, but her secret was short-lived.

Alex found out when he read about the government's sanctuary city project in the paper and then saw it on the national news. He angrily slapped the newspaper down onto the coffee table and turned up the volume on the TV. As was his usual daily routine, he was dressed for work and having his coffee and breakfast while watching the news.

"...where several 'sanctuary towns' are now cropping up in new areas of the country..." Eliza walked into the living room to ask her husband if he wanted more coffee when she heard the Fox News announcer, and suddenly realized why her husband was upset, although she played dumb.

"You won't believe this," he said, pointing to a paragraph midway through the article on the front page of the *Arizona Republic*. "Listen to this." Alex proceeded to read the piece to her.

"While in the past, cities in the United States have been deemed 'sanctuary cities,' or cities which permit residence by illegal immigrants to help them avoid deportation, now the nation is seeing newly constructed little 'sanctuary towns' crop up across the landscape,"Alex read aloud.

"In the past several decades, ever since the existing city of Berkeley, California became the first city government in the U.S. to pass a sanctuary resolution in 1971, many existing big cities declared 'sanctuary' status, setting aside millions of dollars to support programs for illegal immigrants," Alex continued reading. "Many other big cities like New York, Chicago, Philadelphia, Las Vegas, and New Orleans followed suit, adopting sanctuary ordinances banning city employees and police officers from asking people about their immigration status."

Alex put the paper down. "This is why Stewart should have never been elected," he said. "The former administration had all but quashed these stupid programs, saving us billions of taxpayer dollars. And why should we pay for LA and New York to allow illegal immigrants in? They almost cut me out of a job. These sanctuary cities are a blatant disregard of our laws here in America." Alex looked up at Eliza to see if she was still paying attention and then scowled, picking the paper back up to continue reading.

"This is where it gets interesting," he said sarcastically. "President Stewart has promised to open the floodgates again to not only allow federal and state funding be provided for existing city governments to become sanctuary cities once more, but to support building brand new little sanctuary towns or communities in outlying plots of land that would include the construction of low-cost or subsidized housing and schools for poor legal and illegal immigrants alike."

And then Eliza saw her husband's eyes grow wide and his face redden with rage as he read on.

"A handful of these new 'sanctuary towns' or pre-fab suburban developments are now under construction, offering attractive and affordable alternatives to cramped city apartment dwellings, including 'Gray Rock,' Michigan, 'Slade,' Illinois and 'Mason,' New York, the latter interestingly named after Krause & Sons' construction project manager Cameron Trellis's young son Mason Trellis…"

Alex grabbed the remote and flipped the TV off, then turned to his wife, his face flushed with anger. "I can't believe Cameron would do this to me!" he exclaimed.

"Why does it hurt to build these new towns?" Eliza asked innocently, unaware of the pros and cons of sanctuary cities, having a tendency to stay out of politics, although she was well aware of her husband's conservative views. "Isn't it a good thing to build more housing since New York City is busting at the seams? I mean, look where our grandson is living. Now maybe Cameron and Ivy will be able to afford to have their own little house or townhouse with a yard where Mason can play." She was just trying to understand it all, but her question seemed to infuriate her husband even more.

"You don't know what you're saying," Alex said, visibly attempting to hold his fury in check. "First of all, taxpayers like you and me are the ones paying for all of this. Second, sometimes the illegal aliens these towns and cities harbor aren't only illegal but can be dangerous, like criminals or even terrorists. Third, my company is headed up by conservative Republicans who would never support this. Need I remind you, the same company which helped Cameron get a job in the first place. ABC Oil is already suffering the consequences of this new Stewart administration with an infiltration of illegal immigrants coming across Mexico's border, applying for jobs at competitors' companies which are paying them far less. And now, this is just another nail in our coffin. This is like a slap in their face, and in mine. When they see this…well, I might very well lose my job. I have to tell my boss that I had nothing to do with this." Suddenly he was grabbing his suit jacket and briefcase and scrambling out the front door.

ALEX WAS BROODILY quiet at dinner that night. He told Eliza he had managed to speak to his boss and let him know that he'd talk reason into his son, and that he was completely against the sanctuary town of Mason. "But at least I was able to be honest when I told them my son and I have been estranged for over a year and that Cameron's decisions and actions were completely out of my control."

Alex then bluntly stated that once again, he would like Eliza to have absolutely no contact with Cameron, which meant no contact with her grandson.

Eliza's heart splintered once again, the old wounds of separation and loss splitting it open, but she refused to let the monster of grief consume her. Arguing with her husband, and losing, would do that, she believed, and she decided to play along with him, submitting to his demands for the time being, realizing she would probably have to break that commitment if and when the opportunity presented itself.

Later that night, while she was watching a sitcom rerun to distract her mind from the depressing reality of her life, Alex walked in and interrupted her show, saying, "I talked to him."

She immediately muted the TV and gave him her full attention. "You talked to Cameron?"

"Yep. And of course, he refused to budge on rethinking the construction of a sanctuary city, or town, or whatever you want to call it. Not only is he heading up construction of this fictional town of Mason, New York, he and Ivy are going to move there once it's finished."

Eliza felt a surge of relief. They would at least be living in a better home to raise Mason.

"And that's not all, would you believe Ivy is pregnant again? That's all she knows how to do apparently, have more babies."

Eliza initially felt the sting of the scorn behind his words, but the joy and hope that sprang forth inside her overrode that. Another baby, another grandchild! She would have to find a way to see them without Alex finding out.

"How is Mason?" she dared to ask.

"He's fine, Cameron said. We didn't talk long, but I did ask." Alex's frown softened a bit, and she remembered why she fell in love with him in the first place. "I can't believe he's one-year-old already."

He remembered Mason's birthday. Eliza's heart warmed with the realization that her husband hadn't completely shut out their son and grandson. Of course, she had remembered and sent him a birthday card and gift card for Cameron and Ivy to buy him something. She had asked them to buy him a toy and tell him it was from his Grandma and Grandpa Trellis.

She wondered what they bought him and if she would ever get to know him, if her grandson would ever know her and how much she loved him.

CHAPTER NINETEEN

NAMED after both of his grandfathers, Kyle Alexander Trellis came into the world on a snowy November morning in Mason, New York.

Eliza had tried to arrange to fly into New York, had cajoled Alex until he was okay with her visiting the first week of December, but the East Coast had been blasted by a blizzard named Snowstorm Haley and had been blanketed by a foot of ice and snow that had forced the airports into closing for several days.

It turned out that Eliza's library branch was expanding at the same time and was having several grand re-opening celebration events the next week so that she couldn't take off from work.

Eliza and Cameron talked, and arranged that he and Ivy would bring Mason and the baby out to Phoenix for a brief visit with both of their families that Christmas.

Of course neither Ivy nor her family knew about the Trellis family secret, and Ivy's parents had flown out to New York on several occasions to visit the little family.

Every time Cameron had spoken of these visits with his in-laws, pangs of jealousy hit Eliza that Joan Brown had a normal grandparent-grandchild relationship with Mason and she did not.

Once she had been so bitter about it all, she had brought it up to Alex at the dinner table.

"And whose fault is it?" Alex barked. "Not mine and certainly not yours. It's Cameron's fault that we don't have a relationship with him or his family. Don't you think I wanted to be a grandfather one day?"

Eliza started crying then, her anger melting into grief once more, hurting not only for herself but for her husband. Life was so unfair.

Alex stormed out of the room that night, and Eliza never broached the subject again. She stuffed down her jealousy and bitterness along with her grief, anger and sadness until they were all tangled, melted and hardened together like a ball of steel wool compacted into a bullet that lay lodged in her heart. One false move and that bullet could kill her, but she dared not act on her feelings anymore.

Rather, she started to numb them with painkillers left over from her stay at the hospital, which she refilled every now and again when she had one of her migraines.

ALEX REFUSED TO ALLOW CAMERON, nor his wife and children, to enter their home. Eliza was forced to make arrangements to see her grandsons at the Browns' family Christmas gathering on Christmas Eve.

It was extremely awkward for Eliza since she hadn't seen Ivy's parents since the wedding nor met any of the rest of Ivy's family before, and especially since she was going to the Browns' dinner solo, but it was her only chance to meet her new baby grandson.

Her husband, meanwhile, couldn't make the visit, coming up with the excuse that he was called away to work on an emergency oil shortage. Even though it was true an unseasonably cold December in Phoenix had caused a fuel shortage, ABC Oil Company was only one of several suppliers of oil, and they could have operated without him most likely. But Alex eagerly agreed to help send out the oil truck fleets and manage deliveries on Christmas Eve so that it all operated smoothly.

Eliza decided to put on her best show that night, summoning all of her strength to be as courteous and social as she possibly could be, even though she wasn't feeling it. She wore her best slacks and a red sweater and some costume jewelry—she still didn't really own anything expensive—and her hair was short now. She didn't have to fuss with it too much. *I look like a grandma.* Eliza smiled to herself in the bathroom mirror while she applied some red lipstick. *A young grandma though.* And while she was nervous to go alone to meet the Brown family, she was excited for the first time in a long time to get out of the house where she had stayed cooped up for so long.

Savoring being out and about, Eliza drove slowly the half hour from their home in Glendale to the newer, more artsy town of Scottsdale where the Browns had moved when they retired together a year ago.

Kyle Brown answered the door of their stucco house, nestled in the suburban neighborhood of Scottsdale, known as "the West's most western town." He warmly welcomed Eliza into their upscale, nicely decorated home, surprising her with a hug as if they were old friends or at least close-knit family.

She was a bit flustered when she approached her son and his wife since she hadn't seen them for so long, but once she saw her new baby grandson in Cameron's arms, she forgot about where she was or who else she was with and just wanted to hold him.

Cameron proudly laid baby Kyle into Eliza's arms. He looked just like his bigger brother who hovered nearby.

"Mason, do you remember Grandma Trellis?" Cameron asked. Mason stood next to the living room sofa where Eliza sat holding the baby while Joan and Kyle were in the kitchen preparing their big Christmas Eve dinner. The two-year-old looked up at her with big eyes, not smiling but not frowning either, just blankly staring up at her.

He didn't, Eliza knew, but she still tried to reach out to her grandson to give him a hug with her free arm. The toddler drew away shyly, although she caught a playful gleam in his eye.

"Mason, give your Grandma Trellis a hug." Ivy walked into the room just then and scolded him as he ran to her and hid in the fold of her long skirt. He played peek-a-boo by coming out, looking at Eliza, then ducking back in.

"That's okay, he hasn't seen me in a while," Eliza offered, feeling a little embarrassed but instinctively knowing not to push a two-year-old.

Ivy sat in a nearby chair, learning forward, warily watching her husband and mother-in-law smile and coo over the baby while her ornery older son ran around with an action figure in one hand and a toy dinosaur in the other.

Eliza refocused her gaze on Kyle's cherub face. He lay so peaceful, his eyes closed, sleeping in her arms.

Out of nowhere, Mason jumped next to her and made a "rah" sound like a monster trying to scare someone. Eliza was startled and tried to pretend she wasn't ruffled by her older grandson's actions, but the baby started to cry and all of a sudden, there was a flurry of activity as Ivy stood from her chair nearby, took Kyle from her to soothe him, and Eliza was left empty-handed and feeling confused and inept.

"Mason, you just scared your brother and your grandmother!" Cameron yanked Mason by the arm into a nearby corner of the room and firmly sat him down. "You need to sit in time out."

Eliza watched helplessly as Mason glared at her. *He thinks this is my fault*, she worried, feeling uncomfortable, wanting to fix everything. "Cameron, that's okay, he didn't scare me," Eliza said.

"Mom, he needs to learn his lesson, please don't interfere with that." Cameron also glared at her, and Eliza felt double-teamed…no, triple-teamed as she noticed Ivy was also looking at her with a reproachful stare.

She swallowed, wanting to shrink into the sofa and disappear.

Her discomfort heightened again when they were all gathered around the big dining room table to eat the lavish turkey dinner Joan Brown had prepared with a little help from her husband and their part-time housekeeper and cook.

Ivy's equally beautiful older sister and her husband and their two sons and Joan's sister and brother-in-law and their three children who all lived locally rounded out the number of people at the dining room table to fifteen. Eliza's anxiety grew as the room suddenly seemed loud, teeming and overwhelming.

She tried to make small talk with those gathered around the table near her and evasively dodge as many questions as possible, like "how come Cameron's dad hasn't seen either of his grandsons yet, isn't he just dying to see them?" And "you haven't been out to see Mason, New York? Why, it's a lovely town your son has constructed, like one of those quaint downtown main streets with shops and a fire station and cute little houses." And "what type of gathering does your family have for the holidays?"

They just didn't know, didn't understand. Eliza chose her answers as wisely and ambiguously as she could.

"I know it's terrible, my husband works so much but he's going to try to see them soon," she said, when she was really thinking: *He has no desire to see our son nor his family, since Cameron killed our other son Austin and along with it, any hopes of having a normal life ever again*; and, "Unfortunately I had plans to fly out to see the new town many times, and of course had a plane ticket to go see my son and his family a month ago, but then that blizzard hit and the airport was closed," when she really knew: *The town of Mason is a sham which almost cost my husband his job, and my husband and I really don't believe in sanctuary cities that give asylum to people who break the law*; and "Our families aren't that close, and we don't always see them at Christmas," when the sad truth was: *We don't have any family besides each other, and we really don't celebrate Christmas anymore, since Christ seems to be missing in action when it comes to our lives and the tragedies we've suffered.*

The evening was so exhausting that when Eliza got home, she crept into bed beside her snoring husband and took two pain pills instead of one, along with a sleeping pill, hoping she would be blissfully knocked out and sleep for twelve hours, or at least halfway through Christmas Day.

If the day starts later it will go by quicker was her last thought before closing her eyes. She didn't much care anymore about Jesus' birthday or God sending His only son into the world or the "reason for the season."

THAT SUMMER MARKED three years since Austin died. Eliza preferred to think of her son's passing that way. That he died. Not was killed or murdered.

And when she thought of Cameron, she tried to think of him lovingly, as any mother would her son, that he had moved East to seek better opportunities for himself and his family. She even told other people that story, showing photos of her grandchildren to acquaintances on her infrequent trips to the grocery store or hair salon, commiserating with other grandparents that she didn't get to see them often enough, but that was okay because they were making a better life for themselves.

That she was proud of her son, he had moved up within his company and was a construction foreman, a good son and father. Not that he was a killer, a murderer…a fugitive that she was protecting, which made her an accomplice in a crime.

No, she had somehow trained her mind to tread softly or entirely around the harsh realities of the past. And when her memory tripped on the truth, despite her forbidding it not to, daring to wander down that stark, black path, she grabbed her bottle of painkillers to stop it.

Days blended mundanely and monotonously into nights. Eliza went to work, came home, sometimes had dinner with Alex, once in a while dined alone, and then watched a television show or two, read a few pages out of a novel, or simply went to bed.

When her occasional migraines turned into frequent, although milder, headaches, she started taking her Percocet along with her antidepressant medication every day.

And when she ran out of her prescriptions, she went to a different doctor or emergency room to tell them she was having another migraine so they would fill them. She knew she had become addicted to the drugs but didn't know how to stop.

Eliza was desperately unhappy and knew it was because she felt desolately lonely. She hadn't seen Marsha for nearly a year, and eventually her friend just stopped calling her.

Every day became an endless stream of coffee, pills, work, and TV. And every night, when the nightmares came, she had a stiff drink or two to help her fall back asleep.

She had isolated herself from the world, save for her husband. And even her relationship with him became so ambivalent that it eventually ceased to even be a real marriage anymore.

Eliza had gone on a crazy roller coaster ride of pulling Alex close when she needed someone to vent to, cry with, yell at, hold for some type of relief or comfort…and then of pushing him away when her pain subsided because after all, she reasoned, he was part of the problem, had helped cause the pain she was feeling.

And Alex eventually became worn out from his wife's push-and-pull routine and distanced himself from her. He seemed to be able to compartmentalize his life much more efficiently, to work during work hours, to play golf or poker or whatever it was he did during the weekend hours, and to sleep at night as long as Eliza didn't interrupt his schedule.

One night he confronted Eliza and told her he needed to get off the ride.

"I need to sleep in a separate bed, a separate room," he told her squarely as she stood in her pajamas, brushing her teeth. She looked up into the bathroom mirror and saw reflected the cold, hard look of determination in his eyes as he stood looking as handsome and distinguished as ever in his dark gray suit, pressed white shirt, and Armani tie. He had just come home from a late-night business meeting—or that's where he told her he had been. He smelled faintly of cologne still, her favorite that she had given him for his birthday.

Unable to continue to look in those eyes, the same ones that had undressed her so lovingly, passionately before and now stared at her with indifference and disdain, she averted her gaze into the sink, but not before she caught her own reflection. In it she saw her own lifeless brown eyes with the faint gray circles underneath, her wan skin that was starting to sag a little, her colorless lips framed by vestiges of toothpaste foam, her dull, graying brown hair that she hadn't brushed that day.

No wonder he doesn't want to sleep with me, she mocked herself with disgust. *No wonder he's probably sleeping with someone else at the office.*

Eliza spit out the toothpaste, rinsed her mouth, and said into the sink, not daring to look at him lest she show any emotion or that she cared at all, "Fine."

"Okay then," he said simply in return and turned and left to begin moving his things into the boys' old bedroom, which they had had redecorated into a guest bedroom to try to remove the memories, just in case one of them ever had to venture in there.

For a time like this.

She waited until he left for work and broke down sobbing.

ELIZA WAS BROWSING in a local bookshop to buy her husband a copy of the *Sports Illustrated* swimsuit issue which he said he wanted for Christmas that year when she bumped into a tabletop book display, and one of the books fell onto her foot.

It was a heavy hardback, and her big toe smarted a little. Mildly annoyed, Eliza bent down to pick up the book, glanced at the cover, and saw it was an English language edition of "Diyin God Bizaad," the Navajo Holy Bible.

Suddenly, memories of her parents reading it to her as a child flashed back to her, and her heart was laden with sadness and nostalgia.

Without thinking, she carried the Bible with the magazine to the counter, almost laughing out loud at the contrast of the two, paid for her items, and went home, wrapping the gift for her husband and opening the book to read.

That night, for the first time in a long time, perhaps in years, Eliza dared to pray.

*God, please keep my family safe, please let them know I love them,
please heal me from my addictions, please help me love my husband
more, please let me know and do Your will, whatever that may be…*

A FEW WEEKS LATER, Eliza contracted a stomach virus and
stayed home from work for three days, voraciously reading the Bible
she had bought.

She skipped over parts that were difficult to comprehend,
sticking to the stories that were more entertaining, legends she had
almost forgotten about that her mother and father had read to her,
stories about David and Jonah, Solomon and Ruth, and of course
Jesus of Nazareth.

Feeling a little better, she went back to work on a Friday, but felt
sick all over again over the weekend, and by Monday, had to drag
herself from bed to go to work.

After two weeks straight of feeling weak, tired, and nauseated,
the intuition that maybe, just maybe, she could be pregnant started
to dawn on Eliza.

But that can't be, she told herself, trying to reason her way out of
a panic that started to seize her, filling her thoughts.

While she had never taken birth control pills, Eliza had been
very careful throughout her childbearing years, always using the
"rhythm method" since her cycle had always been regular.

Plus we haven't been intimate lately…well, there was that one time.
She hadn't been interested in making love for so long that she had
almost forgotten the one night she gave in to performing her "wifely
duty" when Alex asked. And besides, they slept in separate rooms.

The third day her period was late, Eliza really started to be afraid.
She went through the motions at work that day, her mind racing,
trying to figure out what she would do.

*I can't start another family. I'm too old. This would be terrible
timing. Maybe I'm just late because I'm stressed.*

Like a ping pong ball, her thoughts batted back and forth
between deciding pregnancy wasn't an option—it had to be impos-

sible since she had just celebrated her forty-seventh birthday—and the very real, stark truth that it was possible, could be probable, and that she wouldn't be able to cope if it was, in fact, a reality.

She was so panic-ridden that every morning for a week, after Alex went to work, she got on her knees at her bedside and prayed to God to please spare her from an unwanted pregnancy and allow her to have her period.

My boys are twenty-eight and twenty-five, Lord, she pleaded silently. *Well, correction, would be. Austin is with you now. I'm a grandmother for crying out loud. This can't possibly be Your will.*

And yet a teeny, tiny piece of her heart beat with the thrill that it might be. *What if I am going to have a baby? He, or she, would be a fresh start.* But then the most terrifying of all thoughts chilled through her. *I can't handle raising a child all over again when I've failed so miserably in the past. If I were to lose another child, I would kill myself.*

She couldn't be pregnant, but if she were, Eliza wondered if she would have the courage and strength to actually have the child. Or if she should just take the easy way out and terminate the pregnancy. Abortion was against everything she believed. Would she tell Alex, or would she just have a procedure? She had heard about those "morning after" pills. Maybe that would be the way to go.

And what about all of the pain pills she'd taken? Maybe she'd already done enough damage. She couldn't be pregnant, God wouldn't allow a baby to be born defective just because she'd become a pill addict.

Addict. Eliza suddenly admitted to herself that this was what she had become.

Baby or not, she would have to stop taking pain pills. She made a vow to God, still sitting on the top of the toilet seat, that if He could arrange it that she not be pregnant, she would agree never again to take any type of drugs, no matter what, and to start seeing Dr. Paulus again for counseling.

Eliza took the pregnancy test on the first Saturday in October. It was her tenth day late.

She hadn't breathed a word about her conflicted thoughts and emotions or even the possibility that she might be pregnant to Alex. *There won't be any need to alarm him if I'm not,* she reasoned, still praying.

She waited the two minutes, impatiently tapping her foot on the tile bathroom floor, her heart thudding. She wanted badly to take a pain pill just to calm herself down but instead forced herself to go out to the kitchen and pour herself a glass of milk, which she drank with a muffin, even though she had been trying to lose a few pounds again after the holidays. *I have no willpower,* she had thought when she bought the muffins, but now all she could do was scarf it down. *Losing weight is the least of my worries now.*

She went back into the bathroom and said one more fervent prayer before taking a peek at the pregnancy stick. She sat down on top of the toilet seat, weary of being sick and worn out by her constant battling thoughts and emotions, and said a quick silent prayer.

God please don't let me be pregnant.

She opened her eyes and turned the stick over.

There it was, a light blue plus sign.

She was going to have a baby.

CHAPTER TWENTY

AS SHE SUSPECTED, Alex didn't take the news well at all at first.

Since it was Saturday, he had slept in while she took the test. She had sat on top of the bathroom toilet seat for what seemed like an hour, dumbstruck by the little blue plus sign.

She had a new life growing inside her. And once she knew it, she also knew she couldn't snuff it out with an abortion or morning after pill or any other method. While Eliza was paralyzed by fear of what raising a new child would mean for her and her husband, she also knew that the guilt and grief she would suffer if she committed such an act would kill her much more swiftly than her fears about having the baby ever could.

As soon as she heard Alex stirring, she went into the boys' bedroom where he lay sleeping, curled on his side on the double bed. Just like a little boy. And her heart warmed toward him. She glanced around and noticed the *Sports Illustrated* magazine in the wastebasket where Alex had apparently tossed it. Good, right where it belonged.

Still dressed in her nightclothes and glad she had randomly selected her silk nightie instead of her oversized old tee-shirt last night, she slid into the bed next to him and rubbed his back. She saw the left corner of his mouth turn up contentedly.

"Nice way to wake up," he said, rolling over. They both sat up, propping pillows against the headboard behind them. His sleepy eyes showed suspicion at first, and then mischief. "To what do I owe the pleasure?"

"Alex," she began and hesitated, unsure how to even tell him. "I have something to tell you that's a bit shocking."

She watched his smile and the glint in his eyes disappear. "It's not Cameron or his family?"

"No." At least he asked about them. *Here goes, now or never.* "It's me. I'm pregnant."

Her husband's eyes grew big and round, his eyebrows knitted into a frown and his jaw tightened. "Are you sure?" he asked after a few moments of silence.

"Of course, I wouldn't have told you if I wasn't. I know this is a shock to you. It's a shock to me too."

"And…I hate to ask you this…but…are you sure it's mine?"

Eliza couldn't believe he was asking her that question. She felt as if her husband had jabbed her with an ice pick. "How can you even ask me that?" She sat up straight in the bed, pulling away from him. "I shouldn't even justify it with an answer, but yes, of course it's yours. I am really hurt that you would ask me. I have never been unfaithful to you, and now I'm wondering, since you asked, if you can say the same thing?" She got out of the bed and stood there, arms crossed, challenging him.

"I'm sorry." Alex also got up, walked around the bed, and put his arms around her. "I'm sorry, you're right, I shouldn't have asked you that. It's just that…well, we haven't had sex that much…I guess it was that one time…wow, how did this happen?"

She looked up at him with tears in her eyes, still feeling the bite of his words, and hurt in her heart. "You didn't answer my question."

"I have never been unfaithful to you either. I love you, Eliza."

"Can you love this baby? Should we even have it?"

Alex gently put his hand on her belly. "If you can love him or her, I can too. Wow, this is just…shocking. I don't know what else to say."

And his simple gesture made Eliza's doubts about whether or not to bring a new life into the world vanish once and for all. Seeing the truth in her husband's eyes, that he did love her despite everything they had been through, was enough for her to choose for her baby to live. "I know." Eliza hugged her husband tight. "I'm not sure what to say or how to feel about it either. We've already been through so much, but I guess God has brought us through everything and He'll help us through this too." She pulled back and looked at her husband, allowing herself to feel joy. "Who knows, maybe I'm carrying the next president of the United States or a pope even."

Alex laughed, and the rich, warm sound, one she hadn't heard in a long time, made her smile through her tears. "I guess anything is possible."

Eliza felt a wave of nausea wash over her, and she ran to the bathroom. Fortunately, she didn't throw up the muffin or milk, and she walked slowly back to their shared bedroom, where Alex stood waiting, a look of concern on his face.

"Why don't you just get back in bed?" he said. "I'll cancel my golf game today and take care of you for a change."

"Will you come back here…will you come back to sleeping here with me?" Eliza asked hesitantly, hearing her voice come out just above a whisper. She was trembling, and Alex sat down next to her on the bed and put his arms around her, warming her, calming her.

"Of course I will. You're my girl."

Eliza allowed her fears to melt into him, weeping tears of relief.

ALEX STILL DIDN'T KNOW about her pill addiction, and Eliza wasn't about to tell him unless she had to.

She hoped that her obstetrician would be able to help her and her husband wouldn't have to find out. She went alone for her first prenatal checkup with Doctor Marvin Malone, her new doctor now since his partner, Eliza's former obstetrician, had retired. He was younger and slicker than his older, soft-spoken mentor had been, and Eliza wasn't entirely fond of him, but since he was Dr. Manning's associate, she figured he couldn't be all that bad.

Dr. Malone recommended Eliza be put on Suboxone to help wean her off of her addiction to the Percocet and curb her desire for the pain pills, and to keep both mom and baby from going into withdrawals. Going off any drug cold turkey, he explained, could prove fatal for the fetus.

He had also told her that her pregnancy was considered "extremely high risk," but that if she followed all of his orders, she and the baby would be "fine."

Dr. Malone scheduled a series of blood panels to test for any fetal abnormalities, plus monthly check ups and multiple ultrasounds. He added that if it were discovered she had high blood pressure or any other problems, she would most likely be put on bed rest during the third trimester.

Eliza was alarmed that Dr. Malone told her to stay on the Suboxone, a narcotic used to treat opioid abuse, throughout her pregnancy. He explained that going off of it would cause more distress on the baby than if she stayed on it.

She went home that night and searched the internet for possible side effects on a newborn from the drug. Lots of moms weighed in their opinions and discussed the outcomes they experienced by staying on Suboxone, and none reported having a miscarriage or any abnormalities. *Who's going to report having an abnormal child though?*

Eliza decided that, in addition to making a neonatal appointment with an obstetrician-gynecologist, she needed to start seeing Dr. Paulus for counseling to really get back on track not only physically but also mentally, emotionally, and spiritually. She needed to find a way to let go of the constant fears that plagued her.

Dr. Paulus was able to fit Eliza in the following week. She sat in her chair across from Eliza, seated in the middle of the couch.

The lithe blonde doctor, as usual professionally dressed in her customary suit, smiled at Eliza. "Welcome back," she said, and Eliza knew she meant it.

Soon Eliza was pouring her heart out and had used most of the box of tissues next to her. "I'm really sorry our hour is up," Dr. Paulus said, taking Eliza's hand in her own. "Can I make an appointment for you to come back next week?"

"Yes, I would like that," Eliza said.

"Meanwhile, I'd like to suggest something I believe would be a big help to you," the counselor said in her soothing voice.

"I don't want to make you late for your next appointment." Eliza was nervous now, still feeling raw.

"That's okay, I can take a few more minutes with you. I came across this recovery retreat." The doctor riffled through a stack of papers on her desk, retrieved a flier, and handed it to Eliza. "It's a spiritual weekend retreat being led by a really great priest who is a friend of mine and has been in addiction recovery himself," Barbara Paulus said. "I was asked to attend and give a workshop, but I can't make it now because I have a conflict. Since I already paid for my room and meals, I could send you for free in my place. I think you'd get a lot out of it."

Eliza stared at the paper, specifically at the name of the retreat director who was leading this spiritual event.

It was none other than her own pastor, Father Tim Franklin.

ELIZA PULLED into the parking lot of the retreat at the Cathedral Rock Lodge and Retreat Center in Sedona and sighed. She was starting to have doubts already about coming on this recovery retreat, despite the gorgeous scenery around her.

Not knowing anyone else attending, she had driven herself up the long, lonely stretch of Interstate 17 that fall Friday afternoon. She played music intermittently from her car radio and her I-phone music library. Anything to keep her mind off of the last time she had made this same trek. *The day we found out our son was dead and had to identify his body. The worst day of my life.*

As she got closer to her destination, her fears grew like weeds inside her. *What if I feel sick again?* Her nausea with the pregnancy had subsided and finally dissipated, but still she couldn't be sure it was gone. *What if something happens with Alex?* They had been getting along well lately, sleeping together again, but still she could never be certain that he wouldn't wander while she was away, into the casinos or the arms of another woman. *What if I don't fit in?* She was pregnant, had a drug addiction, and was hiding a secret that would be so horrifying if exposed that she could be thrown in jail and face total abandonment and isolation. *What if someone finds out what Cameron did to Austin?* This was the greatest worry of all.

Eliza got out of her car, closed her eyes, and sighed. Breathe in faith, breathe out fear. She reminded herself of the meditation mantra Dr. Paulus had taught her. The sun was warm on her face, and a soft breeze enveloped her. Up here in Sedona, the air was about twenty degrees cooler than it was in Phoenix. She put on the jacket she had thrown in the front seat and headed in to the retreat center.

Feeling a bit calmer she surveyed her surroundings. The recovery retreat coordinators had rented the entire lodge facilities as well as the nearby Moondance retreat house and several campsites at Camp Avalon, which were both affiliated with Cathedral Rock, to accommodate the twenty-five attendees. Dr. Paulus had booked a single room in Moondance which was where Eliza would be staying.

Wow. Eliza had wheeled her suitcase up to the entrance of Moondance, a unique structure with a majestic blend of Asian and southwest architecture framed by lush green landscaping. It stood at the foot of Cathedral Rock, the breathtaking red rock formation shaped like its name.

Eliza had contended with hardly any traffic and had arrived ten minutes before the check-in time, but that was no problem according to the friendly young girl behind the welcome desk. The girl warmly greeted her and quickly processed her registration, handed her a welcome package, and pointed her to her room.

She walked into the room with its Native American motif and felt instantly at home. An Indian quilt covered the wood-framed double bed, reminding her of the one that her mom had made for her as a young girl. Wooden beams arched along the ceiling above her, and several carved animals were scattered across the dresser, much like those her father had made that she had played with as a child and then sold with her mother and sisters at the market.

Eliza sat on the bed, forgetting her fears for a moment as she opened the welcome package, which outlined the itinerary for the weekend: Friday night welcome dinner and opening remarks by Fr. Tim; Saturday morning and afternoon workshops on prayer, meditation, and working the Twelve Steps with an evening bonfire meeting under the stars; and Sunday breakfast and closing mass service. There were also times set aside for free time which could be spent hiking, swimming in the camp's indoor pool, or taking a relaxing stroll through the gardens onsite. And there was a sign-up sheet for yoga classes, guided tours through Red Rock State Park, or half-hour one-on-one talks or confessions with Fr. Tim.

Eliza decided not to become overwhelmed and to just take the retreat one day, or better yet, one hour at a time.

BY THE TIME Sunday morning came, Eliza felt a little more content and peaceful. She had learned a lot about meditation and focusing on her recovery from pill addiction through the workshops and Twelve-Step meeting, gotten some much needed rest and relaxation, and even made a few new friends.

She surprised herself as she passed by the room where Fr. Tim was hearing the last few confessions before the closing mass. She looked at the sign-up sheet and found herself signing her name into the last available time slot. She had heard in one of the workshops that "we are only as sick as our secrets." That saying had stuck with her, gnawing at her insides, still leaving a gaping hole in the newfound cloak of serenity she was trying to wear.

Fr. Tim stood when she entered the room, warmly shook her hand, and asked her to sit in the chair facing him. Here at the retreat, Fr. Tim seemed to look more like a man than a priest, donning jeans and button-down shirts for most of the weekend. Today, since it was Sunday, he wore his clerical black shirt with the square of white collar along with a pair of slacks and tweed blazer.

A soft-spoken, gentle man in his early sixties, Fr. Tim was tall and thin with salt and pepper hair and glasses, and usually seemed very serious and authoritative to most parishioners when he preached at mass on Sundays.

Eliza had spoken with him years ago when she had gone to confession at Saint Augustine's after her bout of rage over Alex's gambling addiction, and of course often stopped to wish him a good day and shake his hand after masses when she used to attend.

But here in this setting, as she sat face to face with him, Eliza felt like she was seeing the priest for the first time. She noticed the twinkle of recognition in his eyes before he bowed his head, indicating she could begin.

She closed her eyes and blessed herself with the sign of the cross. "Bless me, Father, for I have sinned. It has been, well, a few years since my last confession. I'm not sure where to start." Even with Fr. Tim she was a bit tongue-tied, having had so many tragic events occur in her life in the past few years.

After a few awkward moments of silence, Fr. Tim encouraged her. "Just begin where you wish to begin, Eliza," he said sincerely, looking at her with his kind, hazel eyes and then bowing his head again to listen.

"A lot has happened since my last confession. My son Austin… he died in an accident…no, that would be a lie, but I've kept the lie so long that it seemed to be true after a while. And I know I can tell you anything, Father, but, well, you see, Austin was killed. By my other son, his older brother Cameron. It was made to look like an accident and my husband and I have kept it a secret for fear Cameron would go to prison for life or worse yet, get the death penalty and…I felt guilty because we did play favorites, I think, and gave Austin a lot more attention when they were growing up. I think the whole thing was partially my fault, and now he has a family of his own and has moved far away, and I just hope he will be able to do a confession with a priest like you someday. And well, now I am pregnant again and at first I begged God not to be pregnant, and I even considered having an...well, you know, terminating the pregnancy but I didn't, and now we're scared to death of having the baby, but we decided it was the right thing to do and now, well, now I'm addicted to painkillers which I took to get over the migraines and depression I had after my son died and I didn't want to go on and there seemed no other way. And Alex doesn't even know any of this because I've been afraid to tell him and..." Eliza broke down weeping. Father Franklin handed her a box of tissues from a nearby table.

"Eliza, it sounds like you've been through an awful lot in the past few years, more than most people go through in a lifetime, so don't be too hard on yourself." Fr. Tim took her hand in his, and she wiped her nose and looked up into his benevolent eyes.

I probably look like one hot mess. The thought at least made her smile a little. "Still, I feel bad about even considering...well, you know, an abortion." She felt like she was sinning just saying the word out loud.

"But you didn't act on it, and that, Eliza, is God at work in you."

"Yes, but now I might be harming him, or her, by taking these pain pills, although I've started to wean myself off of them, and I'm only two months pregnant, still..."

"Remember you're not a bad person trying to be good, you're just a sick person trying to get well. Perhaps after church today you should go home and talk to your husband about all of this. I'm sure he'll understand and support you."

It would probably be one of the hardest things she would have to do. And she had done a lot of hard things. But at least it sounded like a plan. Eliza nodded.

"I would be honest with your husband about everything going forward. And as for Cameron, well, I'm sure God has a plan for him and hopefully he will confess one day, even if it's just to a priest. But your son is an adult, capable of making his own choices, and what he did was in no way your fault. And I'm very sure Austin is in heaven right now smiling down on us all."

Eliza suddenly missed both of her sons and felt the unfairness of it all burn like lava in her gut. "I just don't understand—" She had difficulty finishing her sentence, not willing to admit she was angry with God to one of His earthly representatives.

"You don't understand how God could be so unfair," Fr. Tim finished her sentence. "And you're probably angry at Him still, right?"

How did he know? Eliza felt her cheeks flush with guilt and shame. "Yes, I am. But I feel terrible saying that out loud. I know it should be the other way around, that God should be angry with me, but I just can't help feeling this way."

"Eliza, it's okay to be mad at God," Fr. Tim said softly and took her hand in his own. "God can take it. He wants you to bring all of you—your anger, guilt, all of your emotions—to Him so he can help you, heal you and forgive you because He loves you so very much."

Fresh tears fell, but these were tears of relief that perhaps she could find some serenity in her life after all and that she could be forgiven.

"Eliza, for your penance, I want you to go get some professional help with your addiction, and to pray for God's grace and love for this child, and I will keep you and your husband, son, and baby in my prayers as well. Do you remember the Act of Contrition?"

"Not too well I'm afraid."

"Let's say it together then, shall we?"

And the two prayed aloud together, "Oh, my God, I am heartily sorry for having offended You. I detest all my sins because I dread the loss of Heaven and the pains of hell. But most of all because they offend You, my God, who are all good and deserving of all my love. I firmly resolve with the help of Your grace, to sin no more and to avoid the near occasions of sin. Amen."

"I absolve you of all of your sins in the name of God the Father, the Son, and the Holy Spirit." Fr. Tim made the sign of the cross with his right hand over her bowed head, and she made it along with him. "Go be at peace with the Lord, Eliza."

"Thank you, Father." And Eliza felt a joyful gratitude and sense of release as the heavy burden of guilt, remorse, and doubt she had been carrying for so long was lifted from her soul.

She knelt in one of the pews of the small chapel that had been set up for mass, and her spirit soared with the voices around her as they sang the opening hymn of praise.

CHAPTER TWENTY-ONE

AFTER LEAVING THE RETREAT, Eliza drove straight home that Sunday afternoon to talk to Alex. She walked in the front door, interrupting him as he watched a basketball game on TV.

She told him about her headaches and anxiety, about the pain pills and anti-depressants, and how she really tried to get off them once she had found out she was pregnant, but that it had been really hard. And she told him how reading the Bible and seeing the obstetrician, her therapist, and Fr. Tim had all helped her along the way.

"I'm so sorry Alex. I know how disappointed you must be, and I won't blame you for being angry. I so wanted things to be different this time, with this child."

Alex sighed and then stood up and turned off the television.

"This is all so much to take in." He crossed his arms and shook his head back and forth. "I just don't know how much more I can take."

Eliza tried hard not to cry, but it was impossible. "I'm sorry," she said through her tears.

"Will the baby be okay?" he asked softly.

"The doctor seems to think so." Eliza sniffed.

"Well, all we can do is hope for the best then." He looked at her with sadness in his eyes. But Eliza thought she also saw a trace of love.

Alex held out his arms and she let him hold her.

ELIZA WAS NEARLY five months pregnant when she went in for her third ultrasound.

Fortunately, the ultrasound and another series of blood tests showed no abnormalities, but Dr. Malone still recommended Eliza have an amniocentesis because of her age. At forty-eight, she was much more prone to being at risk of having a baby with birth defects or genetic disorders, drugs or no drugs.

It was a choice for her to make, and Eliza refused, not wanting to run even a slight risk of having a miscarriage and not wanting to know the outcome of such a test. She believed that if she and Alex found out anything was wrong with their baby, they would be under even more immense stress and most likely would have the baby anyway.

After her refusal, it seemed that Dr. Malone was a bit restrained, even guarded, when they spoke. Still, there was nothing that could take away from the joy Eliza felt when the ultrasound once again showed the beating heart.

Alex went with her for all of her tests and prenatal checkups after the first one. He told his wife that he wanted to be more involved with this child, since he hadn't been so much with his other sons.

Eliza wasn't sure if it was because he felt guilty for the past and partially responsible for the fate of their two older sons like she did, but she knew to question him might embarrass him to the point where he might do an about-face and shut her out. She decided to let go of her need to know his reasoning. Whatever it was, she was just glad he was with her to hear the latest news.

"Mr. and Mrs. Trellis, do you want to know the sex of your baby?" The young, chipper technician smiled at them, ready to burst with excitement.

Eliza looked at Alex, and they both nodded in unison.

"It looks like you're going to have a boy!"

Another son! While Eliza knew she could never fill the place Austin still held in her heart, she was overjoyed with the news. A fresh start at doing things right, at being a better mom. She squeezed her husband's hand and looked up into his dark brown eyes, glistening with tears of happiness like her own.

"We're going to have a son," she whispered, her voice choked with emotion.

"A son," Alex murmured, repeating the words aloud. "Wow. What should we name him?"

"How about Stephen Paul?" Eliza suggested. She had thought about names every day for the past few months, and it just seemed to fit. The name Stephen meant "crown." He would be their new little prince. And Paul was the English form of Paco, her father's name. *I still love him*, she reflected, sorely missing both of her parents.

"Stephen Paul, I like it." Alex smiled at her. "I love it. I love you."

The technician had quietly stepped out of the room to allow the couple to enjoy their newfound discovery.

ELIZA STILL HADN'T TOLD Cameron and Ivy the news that she was pregnant, hoping to somehow tell them in person.

Finally, the opportunity presented itself a few weeks after the ultrasound when Cameron called her, asking her if she could please find the time to come out and babysit, it was urgent.

"Is everything all right with Ivy?" she asked, concerned.

"Yes, it's just that we need to get away, and her parents are away in Europe for the month," Cameron replied, tenseness in his tone.

"Okay..." Eliza hesitated, unsure what could create such urgency.

Her pause caused Cameron to blurt out the truth. "Mom, listen. Ivy and I have been having problems in our marriage," he said. "The boys are fine, although I'm sure they feel the tension between us."

"What's been going on, Cam?" Eliza couldn't help but be curious. She was still his mother. Better to ask than to jump to conclusions.

"It's me, mom, it's my fault, I blew it." Cameron sighed into the phone. "I had an affair. It was a one-night thing, but Ivy found out, and I swore to her it would never happen again but…she's really been struggling with it. I just thought that if I take her away somewhere romantic, we could rekindle things between us somehow, I could make it up to her."

Oh Cameron, why? Eliza wondered with exasperation. *Why do you do the things you do? Why do you sabotage yourself and hurt everyone else in the process?*

"I hope you can, Son, and yes, I think I can arrange to come out this coming weekend, although I could only stay for two or three days." She needed to save all of her time off from work for when baby Stephen was born, but she couldn't tell him that, at least not over the phone. "Who was this other woman, why—"

"It was Megan McGee, Mom." And suddenly Eliza knew why, he didn't have to say anything more. As much as Eliza had always liked Megan, and disliked Ivy over the years, she still wouldn't have wished this for her son, who now had a family to defend and protect, or her daughter-in-law, who was a wife and mom just like she was.

"Oh, Cameron, how could you?"

"She was visiting New York," Cameron explained, his words tumbling out in a rush. "I found out through a mutual friend that she would be in the city for Fashion Week. She works as a scientist for one of the lead fabric manufacturers and was attending as a VIP or something, and I just wanted to have lunch with her, but we both had too much to drink and we went back to her hotel and one thing led to another. We both know now it was a huge mistake. I didn't tell Ivy…well, you know, that the affair was with Megan."

"You didn't tell her about…your brother, did you?" Eliza could barely bring herself to ask the question.

"No, Mom, you and Dad are still the only people in the world who know, and who will ever know," Cameron whispered. "Look, I've gotta go. Ivy will be home any second. I'm watching the boys right now, and Kyle is starting to fuss because he's hungry. Can I count on you to fly out this Friday?"

"Sure, Cameron, I'll be there."

"Thanks, Mom. I don't know what I'd do without you."

Eliza sadly hung up the phone and absent-mindedly rubbed the growing little bump on her tummy.

"I DON'T THINK it's a good idea for you to go all the way to New York in your condition." Alex was mowing their little grass plot that was their back yard, weeding the small flower garden, and pruning the bushes and trees. His face was red and sweaty.

Eliza walked out the back door with a glass of cold water which she handed to him, and they both sat down in the newly purchased patio chairs. Alex had worked hard the past few months in what little spare time he had to fix up the back yard so they could finally enjoy it, just the two of them. He had chucked the old, rotting swing set, given the fence a fresh coat of paint, put pavers in to make a patio, and planted a bed of flowers around the one tree in the back. "Time to start enjoying our life, just the two of us," he had said one night after they finished paying the monthly bills and realized they had a little surplus to spend.

That was before they knew about the baby. But Alex was determined to keep up the yard. To both of them, it was almost symbolic of their new phase of life, their new little family, a fresh start.

"Let Cameron figure this out," Alex added, gulping the water, wiping his sweaty brow with his tee-shirt sleeve. "He got himself into this jam, let him get himself out of it."

"But I want to tell him in person about the baby, he has a right to know." Eliza sat across from her husband at the patio table, determined to go to New York no matter how mad Alex might get over it. "And more importantly, I want to see Mason and Kyle. Besides, I am feeling great, so this is good timing."

"I don't know why you even ask me since you always do what you want anyway," Alex said, agitated.

I didn't ask, Eliza thought, but kept quiet, knowing she had won.

SHE RANG the doorbell of the neat, cookie cutter house on the cul-de-sac of the suburban neighborhood that looked like any one of millions of similar communities across the country.

But the quiet façade hid terrible secrets.

While families moved in and out of Mason, New York, the TV news stations had started reporting that a growing terrorist element was sprouting within its borders, protected by the sanctuary status bestowed by the president of the United States herself.

Eliza had kept up with the news on the newly built sanctuary towns of Gray Rock, Slade, and Mason since her son had headed up the construction of the third. She had read with impartiality the liberally slanted news stories, championed by her son, on how these new towns would not only spare the deportation of innocent undocumented immigrants who sought refuge in the United States, but also would house low and middle class working people who merely wished to be able to afford their own homes and to raise their families in nice neighborhoods.

And she had read the conservative news stories, applauded by her husband, which reported how these new sanctuary towns, like the older cities that ruled themselves as "sanctuary cities" before them, were not only breaking the law by harboring illegal immigrants but also shielding criminals, even terrorists in their midst, which threatened the very essence of these same towns. Doing so made them unsafe for those same working-class people and their families.

Perplexed and unsure of her own opinion, she had turned to her Bible to seek answers. Eliza found that it was true that the concept of sanctuary cities, or "cities of refuge" originated in Chapter 35, verses ten through fifteen of the Bible's Book of Numbers, in which God instructed the Israelites: "When you cross the Jordan into Canaan, select some towns to be your cities of refuge, to which a person who has killed someone accidentally may flee. They will be places of refuge from the avenger, so that a person accused of murder may not die before he stands trial before the assembly...so that anyone who has killed another accidentally can flee there."

She knew from her Bible readings that God's intent was to have His people protect those who may be innocent of intentional murder, ensuring they stood a fair trial before having their lives taken since He had also instructed His people through Moses in Exodus to take a life for a life, an eye for an eye, and a tooth for a tooth.

Ironic, she thought, that Cameron, who killed his brother intentionally, constructed a place of sanctuary in which he was actually being harbored. And even more ironic, she had come to realize, in a society today which had laws to protect people from vigilante justice and punishment without fair trial, that these same sanctuary towns and cities were protecting law-breakers who intentionally wanted to kill others.

My grandchildren may be in danger, Eliza thought, *and Cameron is working to build walls to house the very people who may harm them. I need to talk to him, make him see they should move away from Mason. But how?*

All of these thoughts were swirling around in her head when Cameron answered the door.

CHAPTER TWENTY-TWO

HE GAVE her a big hug and welcomed her inside.

She was wearing a lightweight, cotton jacket over her blouse since it was much cooler in New York than in Phoenix that June. Plus it would hide her secret news for the moment, until she was ready to tell them.

Mason ran up the hallway from the kitchen to see who was at the door and peered around his father's legs up at Eliza with big, brown eyes.

"Hi, Mason, how's my big boy doing?" Eliza cooed, bending down and holding out her arms to give her three-year-old grandson a hug, but he buried his face in his dad's pant leg.

"Come on, Mason, don't be shy." Ivy walked up behind Cameron and gave Eliza a light hug, but Mason merely peeked out between his father's legs and then hid from view again.

"Sorry, Mom." Cameron reached down and grabbed his son's arm, trying to drag him out to greet his grandmother. "Mason, you're being mean to your nana. She came a long way to see you, the least you can do is give her a hug." But the toddler yanked his arm free of his father's grasp, shrieked and ran away down the hallway.

Ivy berated her husband as she left to follow her son. "Cameron, you're going to make him cry."

"Well, you're babying him too much, he'll never go to anyone if he can't go to my mom."

Eliza tried not to feel hurt. "No problem, he hasn't seen me for over a year. I'm sure he'll warm up in a bit."

The three adults went into the kitchen at the far end of the hall.

"Where's my little bugger Kyle?" Eliza asked.

"He's up taking a nap in his crib, but I thought I just heard him stirring, I'll go get him," Ivy said. "Cameron, get your mom something to drink and I'll be down in a minute."

Cameron dutifully fixed his mom a glass of iced tea, and they went into the adjoining living room where Mason was playing with army soldier toys.

Eliza was exhausted and sat down on the sofa, content to just watch her grandson play. She instinctively knew better than to force him to give her a hug, remembering her own children being shy around virtual strangers. "By the way, your new home is really nice." Eliza noticed that, although it was cluttered with toddler's toys and baby bottles and the like, the cottage home was a far cry from the dingy, messy apartment her son and his family had lived in before. Still, since she and Alex didn't approve of the town itself, she held her praise in check.

"Thanks, Mom. How was your flight?" Cameron handed her the cold drink and sat down next to her.

Eliza quickly changed the subject. "Fine. Listen, Cameron, before Ivy gets down here, I have some news I wanted to share with you." Cameron looked at her with concern. "It's good news, don't worry. At least I hope it will be good news for you, although it may come as a shock." Eliza took a deep breath and exhaled. "I'm pregnant."

"Mom, how can...oh my gosh, are you going to have it?"

Eliza felt like he had slapped her across the face, and it took her a moment to recover from her son's brazen question. "Yes, Cameron, your father and I were surprised at first too, but now we're actually looking forward to having another child." She tried but couldn't read the emotions that rippled across her son's face. "How do you feel about it?"

"I just can't believe...I mean, I'm going to be thirty, my sons will have an uncle who's actually younger than they are. I don't know, Mom, is it, aren't you...?" He left his questions dangling but Eliza knew what he meant to ask.

"I'm not too old, it's perfectly safe for me to have a baby, and your father and I are happy about it and want you to be happy too."

"I just don't know if I can be, but I'll try."

Ivy walked into the room holding five-month-old Kyle in her arms. "I heard the news. You forgot you left the baby monitor on." She looked from Cameron to Eliza. "That's great, we can be moms together."

Eliza felt a quick pang of jealousy looking at her daughter-in-law sitting in the living room chair, playfully bouncing baby Kyle on her knee, so young and hip and attractive. She had gotten her hair cut short and looked lean and trim after working out for the past few months at the local gym which offered free fitness programs for new moms, paid for in large part with government tax dollars. Eliza suddenly felt old, fat, frumpy, and unsure of herself, sitting there in her jacket and stretch nylon pants. Ivy had applied some makeup and changed into a girlish, blue print dress that hugged her figure, and black high heels that accentuated her long, toned legs for her date with her husband.

Remember the reason you're here, Eliza reprimanded herself. *You're still a grandmother too, and you're here to help.*

Ivy tickled Kyle's belly, and he giggled. "Do you want to hold him?" Ivy offered.

"Of course," Eliza said, trying to start over. "How's my little guy?" She touched her baby grandson's cherubic cheek with her finger, and he gurgled and smiled, a dimple folding in his chubby face. And Eliza forgot the whole conversation as love warmed her heart.

Mason suddenly sprang up from where he sat playing on the

floor and warily approached Eliza, apparently curious what she was doing holding his baby brother.

"Hi, Mason," she said, but the little boy frowned and crossed his arms, then turned his back to her.

"He's just acting out," Cameron said, standing and grabbing his son under his arms, lifting him up and then plopping him down in the corner of the room. "Mason, you're going to sit in time out until you're ready to say hello to your grandmother and be nice to us."

Mason started to cry loudly. "Just ignore him, Mom, he does this all the time. He'll stop in a minute. But if he acts up tonight while we're out, you'll know this is how we handle it."

Oh my, I hope I can handle him, Eliza thought.

Ivy stood and took her husband's arm. "I guess we better get going, we have seven p.m. dinner reservations. Thank you so much, Eliza, for babysitting tonight. Tomorrow night I'll make us all a nice dinner before you have to head back home the next day."

Ivy and Cameron kissed Kyle then walked over to Mason, who was now sitting quietly facing the corner, looking around every so often to see if anyone was paying attention to him.

"Mason, you can come out of time out," Ivy told him.

Her grandson turned and looked straight at her with a pout. Eliza couldn't help herself and fished in her purse and pulled out a small chocolate bar she remembered she had stowed away in case she felt a sugar low during her trip. She noticed Cameron roll his eyes but held it out to her grandson, who bounded over to her and eagerly took it.

"Thank your nana," Cameron instructed him.

Mason smiled at her. "Thank you, Nana," he said in his sweet little boy voice then hugged her.

All was well with the world in that single instant. Eliza ignored her son and daughter-in-law's frowns of disapproval at the bribe.

"We left a list of instructions here for you," Ivy said, pointing to a piece of paper on the kitchen counter.

As if I've never done this before. Eliza smiled to herself.

"Kyle takes a bottle with four ounces of formula before he goes to bed, and Mason can watch a half hour of TV after his dinner. I left you a menu to order in if that's okay with you." Ivy placed some cash on the counter. "That should cover it. Mason likes chicken fingers, and please order anything you would like."

She bent down to kiss Mason, who was now clinging to her leg. "Bye, baby, Momma's gonna miss you."

"Thanks, Mom, this means a lot, we won't be gone long." Cameron hugged her. "We're just going to dinner in the city. Call me on my cell if you need me."

Eliza wanted to hold onto her son a second longer, but suddenly they were gone.

Mason immediately marched into the living room and turned on the television with the remote.

Eliza sat back down on the sofa to play with Kyle. *I guess it won't hurt if he watches his show now,* she thought, giving the baby a plastic rattle to chew on.

But then she noticed with horror that the show on the TV screen was one of those shoot 'em up Westerns, and there was an Indian pulling out a huge knife and holding it to the pale white throat of a young woman who had obviously been taken hostage.

"Mason, I think this is the wrong channel," she said and clicked through various stations, trying to find a Disney cartoon or something more age appropriate.

"Mommy and Daddy let me," he said defiantly, glaring at her from his stance in front of the television.

She certainly hoped not. Eliza took the remote and changed channels, finding a cartoon.

"It's my show!" Mason wailed. He turned around and tried to grab the remote from her hand, but Eliza quickly lifted it out of his reach. This made him scream even louder, startling Kyle, who in turn started to cry sitting on her lap.

Before Eliza even had a chance to stand up and tell Mason to stop screaming or she was going to sit him in time out, her grandson lunged at her and started punching her and the baby with his fists.

Eliza deflected the blows as best she could from the baby, using her body as a protective shield, but Mason landed two punches in her side. He was small but wiry and strong for a three-year-old, and Eliza winced from the pain but managed to stand up with Kyle still in her arms.

"Mason Alexander, you stop right now!" she shouted at the top of her lungs, causing Mason to stand still and stare at her with his mouth agape. Then he started sobbing, curling up on the floor with his arms cradling his knees, his head bowed, tears falling.

What should she do now? She had finally calmed Kyle, and she let Mason cry while she rocked her younger grandson in her arms, soothing him. Mason's sobs finally subsided, and he walked into the living room and started playing with his toys, as if she wasn't even there.

They ate dinner quietly, Kyle in his high chair and Mason in a booster seat at the kitchen table. Eliza just ordered a big container of chicken tenders. After her grandson's outburst she wasn't even hungry but managed to force down a few bites.

He was out of control. She wished she had listened to Alex, her side still hurting a little. He could have really hurt his baby brother. Or the baby inside her.

She wondered if she should tell Cameron and Ivy but decided not to once she successfully managed to read both boys a bedtime story, tuck them both in, Mason in his big boy bed and Kyle in his crib, and sing them both to sleep.

They had enough stress between them, she didn't want to add to it. Besides, hopefully this was a one-time incident. Tomorrow was a new day, and they were all supposed to go to the nearby park and playground that had just opened in town to have a picnic. And she would be home the day after that. She could survive that long.

Cameron and Ivy got home around ten to find Eliza sound asleep under a blanket on the couch.

ELIZA HAD FELT a bit of nausea, cramping, and heartburn

throughout her pregnancy, but nothing compared to the pain she started to feel that day at work.

She was almost seven months pregnant, in her twenty-seventh week, when severe cramps seized her as she stood at the library counter checking some information on the computer for a customer.

Eliza gripped the mouse so hard in her right hand she almost cracked it, clutching the rim of the counter with her left to steady herself when her knees buckled from the pain.

The customer, an elderly woman, looked at her with concern.

"Honey, are you okay?"

"Um, excuse me, I'll be right back." Eliza asked her assistant standing nearby to help the little old lady and then walked as fast as she could into the ladies' room.

Once in the stall, she doubled over from the pain in her abdomen and saw that she was spotting. *Oh God, not now, it's not time, it's too early.*

But then another cramp—a contraction?—made her cry out loud.

She took her cell phone out of her pocket and dialed Alex, asking him to hurry to pick her up, she might be going into early labor. Then she went to the employee lounge in the back of the library where her office was located and tried to get comfortable, sitting in a cushioned club chair, waiting for her husband to come.

Ten minutes later, Alex arrived, helped her into the front passenger seat, and then sped to the closest hospital, Saint Joseph, where she had had Cameron and Austin. It wasn't where she had planned to have Stephen. She had wanted to have a new experience at Banner Hospital. But right now, time was of the essence.

She tried to focus on breathing as Alex whipped through two yellow lights and a red light, swerving around slow-moving cars to get her there.

"What happened?" he asked, his eyes on the road.

"I don't know, I just started feeling cramping this morning and it kept getting worse as the day went on. And then I noticed some spotting." Eliza winced as another cramp clutched her insides. "Oh,

Alex, I hope the baby is okay. I never told you this, but when I visited Cameron and Ivy, Mason got really angry while I was babysitting because I wouldn't let him watch this violent television show, and he hit me really hard in the tummy with his fists. I was protecting baby Kyle, but—"

"Oh Eliza, you should have told me." Alex raised his voice but then lowered it again when Eliza started to cry. "Shhhh, it's okay. That was a few weeks ago so I'm sure that didn't hurt the baby or else you would have noticed something before now. I'm sure the doctor will be able to help. Don't cry, Eliza, I didn't mean to yell, I'm scared too."

Eliza sniffed back her tears, trying hard to hold it together.

They arrived ten minutes later at the hospital's emergency room entrance, and Alex got a wheelchair for his wife and checked her in. Within minutes, Eliza was whisked into a room for examination.

Alex had already called Dr. Malone, who met them in the obstetrics unit. His tough demeanor had seemed to soften when he saw they were in such distress. He told the couple that they shouldn't worry, the hospital had an excellent neonatal unit were Eliza to go into full labor, but that perhaps they could slow the contractions down meanwhile with medications.

After checking Eliza's cervix, Dr. Malone told her and Alex that she was partially dilated, but he would try to slow down labor with magnesium sulfate. Eliza needed to be admitted and immediately put on bed rest to try to prolong the onset of labor and give the baby more time to mature.

"Is it possible an injury could have caused me to go into early labor?" Eliza hesitantly asked the young doctor, lying propped up in the hospital bed, tears of fear stinging her eyes.

"It is possible. Why, did you sustain an injury during your pregnancy?"

"Well, my younger grandson hit me pretty hard in the stomach a few times about a month ago," Eliza said. "But I felt fine the next day and really didn't feel anything abnormal until this morning." Eliza saw Alex scowl in her peripheral vision. "He's only two-and-a-half and didn't mean to hurt me, he was just throwing a temper tantrum."

"It's possible he could have caused a little damage to the placenta or uterine lining at that stage in your pregnancy." Dr. Malone quickly added, "But the baby is pretty well protected, so I would think that it probably didn't cause you to go into premature labor. However, there's no way to be positive. We'll do an ultrasound right away to make sure the baby's all right."

Eliza breathed a sigh of relief when she looked at the screen and the ultrasound showed her baby's beating heart. She and Alex saw for certain that indeed they were having a baby boy and they smiled at each other through tears of relief that their baby looked healthy so far.

A SEEMINGLY ENDLESS stream of nurse and doctor checkups was stressful but at least broke up the time Eliza otherwise spent worrying nonstop about the baby each day of her hospital bed rest.

Dr. Malone examined Eliza a few times a week. Eliza and Alex also met with a NICU doctor who counseled them about all of the dangers of an early delivery: developmental delays, learning difficulties, the risk of brain and other neurological complications, breathing and digestive problems, deformed limbs or organs, or worst of all, a still birth.

The doctor told Eliza she would have to be given a series of steroid shots of Betamethasone in the backside to build up her baby's lungs in case of an early delivery. The shots were extremely painful, but Eliza told herself they would be nothing compared to the emotional agony she would face if the baby didn't make it.

As if hearing the list of horrors wasn't enough, Eliza added to her own anxiety by worrying about the Suboxone and the real possibility that if this baby died, she would not be able to go on.

She turned once again to reading her Bible along with novels and magazines, as long as they weren't related in any way to high-risk pregnancies and premature babies.

Eliza sometimes felt like she could scream from the constant unwanted thoughts and questions that assaulted her brain, raining like bullets on an already war-plagued battlefield. Was today the day the baby would be born? Would he be okay? Would he have a birth defect? Would she be able to love him if he did? Would he make it? And what if he didn't? Would she be so overcome with the heavy burden of guilt and grief that she would have to end her own life too?

Eliza was starting to sink into a deep depression. Dr. Malone assigned her a mental health counselor as well. Sometimes she just sat in her therapy session and cried for an hour, and then fell asleep back in her hospital bed from emotional exhaustion.

ELIZA HELD ON, praying every day that God see her and her husband and their unborn baby boy through. Somehow, she made it through the five weeks of torturous bed rest it took to get to thirty-two weeks.

"You made it," Dr. Malone told her, grinning widely for the first time since she had met him. She had made it to the significant landmark where a baby could be born without all of the dire consequences predicted with premature births. "You're a champion, Eliza."

And that same Tuesday night in June, her water broke, and Stephen Paul Trellis was born eight weeks early.

Eliza and Alex got to hold him briefly, both weeping tears of joy and relief. He had all ten fingers and toes and weighed a solid five pounds. But baby Stephen was whisked all too quickly away and placed in the Neonatal Intensive Care Unit.

Dr. Malone reassured his patient that even though he had been born prematurely, her baby was totally healthy, that he would receive great care, that they would be able to visit daily, and that Eliza would be able to nurse him in just a few weeks.

Once she was home a few days later, Eliza got on her knees every morning to pray for her little guy to grow, to be healthy and whole, and to know he was loved.

"God, I know I messed up with my other two sons," she prayed. "Please help Alex and me to raise our little Stephen into a child who knows and does Your will, who will do good in the world, who will walk in Your ways. And please tell Austin I love him and think about him every single day and that I miss him, and also please love and care for Cameron, Ivy, Mason, and Kyle."

Although Alex refused to forgive Cameron for Austin's death, or now to forgive Mason for possibly threatening the life of their newborn son, Eliza prayed to also find enough forgiveness in her heart for both of them, as well as for Ivy, whom she believed had trapped her older son and started the whole chain of events in the first place.

God help me forgive all of them and focus on being a good mother this time.

The one person she hadn't forgiven yet was herself, but Eliza refused to go back to pain pills. Instead she started seeing a counselor to cope with all of the pain and suffering she had been through. She wanted to be relieved of all of her resentments, including the ones she still had against her husband and herself.

Meanwhile, little Stevie, as they fondly called their tiny son, came home the second week in July.

Weeks passed, and he continued to grow and thrive. All seemed well in the world, and Eliza was finally looking forward to their new little family enjoying the upcoming fall and actually celebrating Thanksgiving and Christmas holidays for the first time in years.

Then the phone call came from Alex's sister Doli, who said that Eliza's mother was very sick, and they needed to come to the Navajo reservation as soon as possible.

Wenona Becenti was on her deathbed and asking to see her daughter one last time.

CHAPTER TWENTY-THREE

LITTLE STEVIE WAS in his car seat fastened to the back seat of their Dodge pickup truck. Although he was four months old, he was still tiny, but was finally starting to catch up to what should be his normal weight and size.

Alex drove the entire three-hour trip, leaving Eliza to think too much. She started to succumb to all of the fears that plagued her. *What if Papa and Mama change their minds and don't want to see me after all? What if Mama dies before we get there? How can I take it if only Mama wants to see me, not Papa? What if they ask about Cameron and Austin? Will I be able to cover up the truth with my parents?*

Eliza was grateful that Alex's sister Doli had kept her parents and sisters informed about her family over the years. They knew Austin had died from a snake bite, and Cameron lived with his wife and two sons in New York. She hoped it would make the reunion easier, with fewer questions for her to have to answer.

But Eliza didn't know what to expect of her family or the Trellis family when they arrived that beautiful mid-October morning. The drive into the Coconino National Park forestland was stunning, as the aspen trees glowed golden in the late afternoon sun when they arrived at the entrance of the native Navajo village.

Stephen was sound asleep in the back of the car. Alex turned off the ignition and looked searchingly into Eliza's eyes. "You sure you're ready for this?" he asked.

"As ready as I'll ever be," Eliza answered, memories of her childhood, of her teenage years, her dates and ensuing troubles with Jack, her father's anger, disappointment and her subsequent banishment playing back in her head like an old movie reel.

She took a deep breath and exhaled. "I feel scared to death to go in there, but I know it's the right thing to do. At least I have you with me." She smiled, and Alex looked at her lovingly.

"And your little guy back there who is probably going to get cranky when we wake him up."

Eliza looked back at her son, his cherubic pink face peeking out of his knitted navy sweater and adorable matching crocheted hat they had received from Marsha. She had bought at least a dozen outfits when she had come to visit the baby. Marsha was a good friend. She was always all in. Eliza realized she was lucky to have her, lucky to even have a friend.

"Ready?" Alex asked, giving her hand one last squeeze.

"Ready."

HER MOTHER LAY PROPPED up on a hospital bed in the living room. When Eliza saw her, she knew she was too weak to climb the stairs to her bedroom anymore. A fire burned in the wood stove in the corner, no doubt making the room comfortable for her but almost unbearably hot for others.

But Eliza couldn't feel a thing besides her heart pounding in her chest as she approached her mom, who drew in ragged, rasping breaths, her gray, wispy hair fanned out on the pillow beneath her head.

The lung cancer had taken its toll, and Eliza nearly gasped when she saw her mother's face looking so worn, wrinkled, and wan, the color of wheat almost.

Her father stood in the shadowy corner of the great room, waiting for them, his hulking presence silently filling the space. The

Indian chief had lost weight in his old age. He was dressed in a light-weight, short-sleeved plaid shirt and blue jeans, which looked like they might fall off him if not for the leather belt with the silver buckle emblazoned with a bear, the symbol of courage, strength, and leadership. But thin as he was, his tall and foreboding stature still commanded respect.

Eliza tried to recall her dad's actual age. He must be in his late sixties or early seventies now, she realized.

Alex laid down the car seat, which doubled as a carrier seat so the baby could stay asleep for as long as possible. He stood in the shadows of the perimeter of the room, warily keeping an eye on his father-in-law but not saying anything.

Eliza quietly approached her mother and took her papery, knotted hand in her own.

"Hello, Mama, it's me, Eliza…Anna," she said softly, almost whispering. She ignored her father, focusing all of her energy on radiating positivity toward her dying mother, not wanting any negative spirits to encroach upon them. Although she had been indoctrinated with the Catholic faith in her adulthood, had even made all of her sacraments in the church, Eliza had still held on to her native Indian beliefs in spirits and all of the rich folklore and legends of her childhood as well.

Her mother's eyelids fluttered, and then finally she opened her eyes. They were watery, cloudy, and red-rimmed, but they were still the fierce yet compassionate, inky dark eyes of her mama that she remembered from her childhood, that she'd recognize anywhere, that had so often appeared to her in her dreams.

"Anna…" A small smile turned up the corners of her mother's mouth.

"Yes, Mama, it's Anna. I heard you asked to see me, so here I am."

"That's…very good." Her mother gasped, taking in short breaths of air between her words.

"And Alex…Achak…is here with me, Mama, and also our baby who I want you to meet."

Her mom's eyes glittered, and she held out her bony arms toward the swaddled bundle. Eliza took off the baby's hat and folded down the blankets so the baby wouldn't be overheated and gently laid her son in his grandmother's cradled arms.

"Oh, Anna, he's beautiful," Wenona whispered, stroking the infant's black curls, which looked just like Austin's had when he was born. "I'm so glad you came." She started to cough spasmodically. Eliza took baby Stevie back into her own arms and looked over toward her father, who still remained standing silently, arms crossed, just watching.

"Hi, Papa," she said. "Do you want to meet your new grandson Stephen?"

The grandfather clock in the right corner of the huge, oak-paneled room ticked loudly in the seemingly endless interlude of silence.

Then her father came alive, it seemed, walked slowly toward her, and embraced both his daughter and grandson with his long, sweeping arms.

Eliza wept into her father's broad shoulder, hugging him tight with one arm, still holding the baby in her other.

Paco Becenti stepped back a few inches to appraise his grandson. Then Eliza carefully laid baby Stevie in her father's outstretched arms.

"Hello, little shash." Love warmed her heart hearing her father call Stephen a little bear. *That means he's accepting him as part of the family, which means he's also accepting me back into the fold.*

And the baby, eyes wide open now looking up at the weathered, grinning face of his grandfather, smiled and then gurgled out his first laugh, which to the Navajo people, was one of the greatest honors that could ever be bestowed upon one of their own.

ACCORDING TO NAVAJO CUSTOM, a celebration would be in order now, and phone calls were made to all members of the Becenti and Trellis families to come from near and far for this most important of ceremonies—the baby's "first laugh" ceremony—and word spread through the local Navajo village.

Instead of staying for two days as originally planned and spending just one night in their favorite cozy motel before returning home, Alex, Eliza and Stephen were put up in a spare bedroom in the Becenti house for a week to allow everyone to convene from all parts of the country for the ceremony.

Unbeknownst to her husband, Eliza had called Cameron to tell him about it, but he had saved her the agony of letting Alex know she invited their eldest son when he told her he couldn't get off work that long, plus Mason was sick with chicken pox.

Probably for the best, she had thought in retrospect, relieved that they weren't coming after all. Poor Cameron would likely be grilled on the details of Austin's death, which would have been very difficult to bear. Her family didn't mean to be overbearing, they just were, Eliza realized. She liked to think of them as over-caring.

The day of the ceremony arrived, a crisp fall day with a bright blue sky.

Since Paco had been the first person to make the baby laugh, tradition called for him to be the official host of the party.

Eliza and Alex had both been to a Navajo "laughing party" before, but this was different. *This is our baby*, Eliza thought excitedly. Although she questioned some of her family's old-fashioned ways growing up, she had always thought the celebration of a baby's first laugh was a beautiful ritual since it symbolized the child's joining humanity as a social being.

About a hundred guests gathered—friends, family members, and neighbors—at the hogan in the Becenti's back yard.

Thankfully Doli ran an event-planning business, and she had taken over the coordination and preparation, calling in her troops to decorate the grounds with balloons and dreamcatchers of all colors. They made the canopied tents look like rainbows hanging above the dozen or so picnic tables scattered in the clearing around the hogan.

The festivities began when Paco Becenti, dressed in full Indian headdress and Native American garb from head to toe, held baby

Stevie's hand, and together they held out a piece of rock salt and a small gift bag, which had coins and candy in it, to each of the guests who stood in a receiving line to greet the baby and his grandfather and family.

Wenona had been brought out to the ceremony, wrapped in blankets and seated in a wheelchair, Eliza's two sisters attending to her.

Alex's mother stood at the end of the receiving line next to Paco and Wenona since she was also the child's grandparent, and Eliza and Alex were at the end of the line.

Tradition held that each guest was to congratulate the family members and accept the gift and eat the piece of rock salt, thereby receiving the generosity of the child, who was symbolically learning to be gracious and giving. The guests also brought plates of freshly cooked food for the party, and after passing through the line, they laid them on the buffet tables in the hogan.

At one point, when there was a break in the line, Eliza observed her father holding the baby, talking to an elderly woman who was an old friend of the family. The proud grandfather held out his grandson, and his face was beaming with joy.

Perhaps he was never proud of me, Eliza thought, *but today he is very proud of my offspring, and that counts for something.* She smiled at Alex beside her, who was also looking down the line at her parents and at his mother. He smiled back at her, and Eliza hoped she could finally erase all of the past hurts, fears, regrets, and resentments she had harbored with this one precious memory she was capturing and holding close to her heart.

After all of the guests went through the receiving line, they gathered to give thanks for the meal. The minister, a medicine man named Black Horse, said the blessing over the food: "Father God, please bless this food we are about to eat which has come from Your hands through your faithful servants to our table today in honor of the child, Stephen Paul Trellis, who has blessed us with the gift of laughter which You also have bestowed on Your people. And thank You for all of your many gifts this day, Amen."

Long buffet tables in the hogan were now covered with native dishes brought by the women from the village such as grilled meats, corn on the cob, rice and beans, okra and squash, succotash, mixed berries and cream, goat milk pancakes, corn bread, and more. Everyone fixed a plate and sat down to eat at the round tables that were spread throughout the hogan and clearing around it, some soaking in the warm sunshine.

Eliza sat with her husband, their parents and siblings, and of course, the star of the day, little Stevie, who was busy napping after all of his socializing. It was almost as if they had never left. Eliza reminded herself to stay in the present moment and not hold a grudge about all of the time she had lost with her family.

Conversation was kept light around the table since this was supposed to be a joyous feast, but afterward, her sister Dena, whom she had always been closest to, walked with her into the house to help bring in some of the leftover food, intimating that she wanted to talk.

Dena lingered in the kitchen as Eliza set a stack of dishes in the sink. "We were really sorry to hear about Austin," her sister said, hugging Eliza tight. Her older sisters were both beautiful, with clear, tanned complexions, slim yet shapely bodies, dark brown, expressive eyes, and long, jet black hair. Eliza had always felt like the black sheep as the youngest, with her wavy, dark brown hair and lighter brown eyes, both of which she was told she had inherited from her father's side of the family.

Eliza fought not to break down crying. "Thank you, Dena. It was really hard, but I finally got through it, and now I have Stephen."

"I know, he truly is a beautiful baby." Dena took Eliza's hands in her own. "Like his mama."

"Thank you, I think he's a blend of both of us."

"I'm also sorry we never got to meet Austin or Cameron. So was our mama."

"Did Papa ever say anything about them...about me?"

Dena looked down at the oak floor sadly. "No, he was so stubborn. You have no idea how hard it was growing up with him towering over us all the time." She pantomimed a big bear growling, which made Eliza giggle, and soon they were both laughing together like in the old days.

"Here, I have a picture." Eliza retrieved her wallet out of her purse and pulled out a photo she had taken when Austin and Cameron were nine and twelve, looking innocent, happy, full of anticipation to seek all of the promises the world had in store. Cameron looked like a young, boyish version of her sisters with his straight black hair and dark, coffee brown eyes, while Austin looked more like his mom, with curls and lighter brown eyes the color of milk chocolate. She sighed. "They were…good boys."

Dena smiled looking at the photo fondly. When her sister's eyes filled with tears, she quickly handed it back and changed the subject. "How long will you stay with us?"

"I guess as long as Papa and Mama will have us." Eliza hugged her sister again. "It's so good to be home."

"It's good to have you back home." Now Dena had tears streaming down her cheeks. "Happy tears." She smiled, wiping them away. "We better get back out there or they'll think we were kidnapped."

They emerged into the bright sunshine in time to see everyone gathering in a big circle around a ceremonial campfire site next to the hogan.

It was time for the ceremonial blessing of the baby, which reminded Eliza of a Christian baptism.

Eliza found Alex, who was holding little Stevie in his arms, and they proceeded to the center of the circle to join the medicine man.

Black Horse placed his hand over the infant's forehead. "Stephen Paul Trellis, given 'Shilah' as your tribal name, which means 'brother,' you are surrounded today by friends and family who love and cherish you as your heavenly Creator does. Thank you for giving us the gift of your laughter, which was placed inside you by God to give to others. May your days be filled with laughter, peace, and love, and may you be a joy to those who come to know you. Amen."

Off to the right, Eliza saw there was a small band of three teenagers, two boys and a girl, who started to sing.

A slight pang of regret nudged her heart, remembering the boys of Cactus Moon and the many garage practices, mischief, and truly good music they had enjoyed together. They could have been really good one day if...*but then today is a time for new beginnings,* she reminded herself. *Remember the good and forget the rest. God somehow has a plan.* She needed to hold her baby. She gently lifted him from his daddy's arms and held him close, breathing in his mild, sweet baby scent.

The girl in the band sang with a voice as beautiful as church bells ringing, her multi-layered voice starting out in a low alto and rising into a high soprano, joined by the band's drummer playing the bongos and the other young man playing a deep bass guitar melody. Her voice soared above the music, like a bird flying free, to the song.

Little child, when you were first born,
The world prayed while you were asleep.
Little child, when you would cry out,
The world would hear you and weep.
Little child, when it heard your laugh,
The world sang with all of its mirth.
Little child as you face some trials,
Remember we loved you from birth.
Little child, as you go through life,
Always be grateful, always true,
Be strong, brave, giving, gentle, kind,
Always be the best version of you.

EPILOGUE

CAMERON WALKED along the familiar section of Main Street, wishing he had never led the charge to build this town in the first place.

Like a shiny new penny grown old, over the past twenty-five years since the new town was founded, Mason had quickly grown from a place where families could find an affordable home and still enjoy all of the camaraderie and amenities of an old-fashioned community with shops, cafés, a movie theater, and a park to a run-down, grimy place where drug addicts and hookers lingered on the street corners, businesses were boarded up, and many homes were abandoned, their formerly manicured lawns overgrown with weeds, their windows cracked and broken. All one could feel walking down the street was fear.

Cameron's son Mason had grown up into a hard, young man full of anger and spite and had ultimately landed in prison for killing another young man over a drug deal gone awry. Mason's attorney had argued in court that his client had acted in self-defense, that the victim had attacked him with his fists when he wasn't able to fulfill the transaction they had agreed upon, and Mason had happened to have a small gun, legal of course, on him which he used to shoot and kill his alleged assailant.

The jury had found Mason guilty, not of first-degree murder but of a lesser charge of involuntary manslaughter, and he was sentenced to a year in Rikers Island Correctional Center. He had managed to stay out of prison since, but lost all contact with his family, and the last they heard, lived a hard life dealing drugs in New York City.

Meanwhile, Cameron's younger son Kyle had left home young, as soon as he turned eighteen, walking away from college to become a welder with his dad's construction company. But he never quite fit in with his coworkers, preferring to be alone on lunch breaks, not joining anyone who went to the bars after work, an isolated man who was fearful of the world because all he had learned growing up was how to best steer clear of his abusive big brother.

Cameron and Ivy had tried to move when they saw the town growing seedier by the year. At first, Cameron knew it wouldn't look good since he had headed up the construction of it and didn't want to bail on his own project. He had even joined a crime watch committee with local government officials and other community leaders to try to stop the bleeding, both figuratively and literally. It all started when police authorities responded to an incident in which a young, white college girl, a junior at New York University, was home visiting her family in Mason during summer vacation and was brutally raped and nearly killed by two teenage Iranian illegal immigrants who, it was discovered, were members of an illegal Islamic terrorist cell.

The incident caused several families to move, and the committee pledged to conduct an investigation into finding out whether there were more terrorist elements in Mason, yet they were allegedly never able to uncover any evidence.

A year later, a young, black man was walking home from work at a local restaurant when he was jumped by three gang members, robbed of the cash he was carrying, beaten with an aluminum baseball bat, and left for dead. He managed to survive for three days in the hospital before dying of internal hemorrhaging. The FBI joined forces with the NYPD, but the case was never solved and the suspects never apprehended, which meant they were possibly still at large in Mason.

The word spread that terrorists and criminals were still afoot in the community and no one was safe, police or no police, committee or no committee, and families started moving out by the dozens, leaving Mason, New York a ghost town.

By then, when Cameron agreed with his pleading wife that they should move, it was too late. They couldn't recapture even a third of their mortgage in selling their home.

Cameron redoubled his efforts on the committee, working over sixty hours a week and then spending another twenty or more on correspondence, in town hall meetings, following up with local and state legislators, and as a liaison with town authorities to try to change the sanctuary status of the town and allay the people's fears.

But with another liberal president and Congress in office, the process was painstakingly slow, and Cameron soon learned, futile.

Cameron and Ivy had tried their best to shield their sons from all of this, but as teenagers do, Mason and Kyle started hanging out with various groups of friends. One group in particular was a gang that dealt drugs, which Mason joined. Kyle was rejected and never did quite get over it, and the two brothers rarely spoke after that.

ELIZA'S HEART broke every time she talked to Cameron, but always Alex implored her not to visit, not to get involved or "sucked in" by his drama, and to detach from their son's whole family and focus on their own new one.

Sometimes Eliza felt like she was choosing Stephen over Cameron and her grandchildren, showing favoritism like she and Alex had done with Austin.

But she also knew she couldn't "fix" her son or his family, and her husband and youngest son needed her.

Stephen, meanwhile, had grown into a handsome young man who had a musical streak like his brothers but just played piano for fun, had graduated with honors from the University of Arizona, and worked as an aerospace engineer for The Armstrong Flight Research Center, NASA's premier site for aeronautical research located inside Edwards Air Force Base in southern California.

He had married his college sweetheart, Holly, and together they had one son named Nicholas who was already three-years-old and was Eliza's newest pride and joy.

Eliza and Alex moved to Flagstaff once they both retired. The heat of Phoenix got to be too much for them, and Eliza wanted to live closer to her father now that they had reunited. Even if they had been asked to move back, they had decided not to live in the Navajo Nation since they had become accustomed to living outside of it.

But it was nice being near some of their family members. Stephen, unlike his brothers before him, had gotten to know his remaining three grandparents before they all passed away.

ELIZA WAS BABYSITTING Nicholas that snowy December morning in their home in Flagstaff. Alex was sleeping in due to a cold he had contracted.

Stephen had dropped Nicholas off to his grandparents to head east for business, but he was also hoping to visit with his brother Cameron and his family. He was traveling with Holly. His wife was a petite, young blonde with robin egg blue eyes whom Eliza had come to love as the daughter she never had.

Nicholas had inherited his mother's fair looks and lay blissfully sleeping in his travel crib in Eliza's large family room.

Eliza looked at her grandson, his soft blonde curls laying in ringlets at the base of his neck and suddenly, inexplicably, her heart ached for all of her losses—of Austin, Cameron, Mason, Kyle—and she prayed:

"Dear God, please let this child of yours grow healthy and strong. Keep him close to Your heart and in Your loving care. Let him be a new start for our family, for generations to come, A leader showing others hope and faith in You. Amen."

She didn't hear Alex come up behind her, gently laying his hand on her shoulder and nuzzling her neck with his scruffy chin.

"I hope God hears you, honey."

"I'm sure He does."

"We've been through so much, but I really believe this little guy is going to bring us a lot of joy," Alex said softly.

Nicholas stirred, rolled over onto his back, yawned, opened his wide blue eyes, and smiled. "Nana and Pop-pop," he said in his sweet little voice.

Alex turned to his wife and grinned, and Eliza felt the shadow of grief she had just been feeling slip away. Everything was going to be all right.

ABOUT THE AUTHOR

Michele Chynoweth's novels bring stories in the Bible to life for today's readers with contemporary characters and plots so they can better understand and relate to God's messages of faith and hope. Michele's universally appealing inspirational novels are filled with suspense, drama, and romance, and also include *The Faithful One* based on the Book of Job, *The Peace Maker* based on the story of David and Abigail in the First Book of Samuel, and *The Runaway Prophet* based on the Book of Jonah

Michele believes that while the Old Testament stories in the Bible are compelling, they are often difficult to read and comprehend, so she hopes that re-imagining them in contemporary times with fiction that's fast-paced and entertaining will help readers appreciate God's messages and hopefully bring people back to the Bible itself. Her stories will not only grip you, taking you for a wild ride that will leave you hanging on until the end but they will also inspire you to search your own heart for God's will in your life and find a deeper faith in God's plan.

In addition to being an author, Michele is an inspirational speaker, book coach, and college instructor of writing, publishing, and marketing fiction. A graduate of the University of Notre Dame, Michele and her husband have a blended family of five children and several grandchildren, and live in North East, Maryland. For more information, visit Michele's website, www.michelechynoweth.com

ALSO FROM MANTLE ROCK PUBLISHING

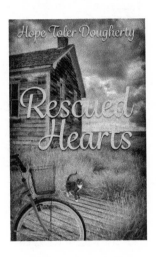

Mary Wade Kimball's soft spot for animals leads to a hostage situation when she spots a briar-entangled kitten in front of an abandoned house. Beaten, bound, and gagged, Mary Wade loses hope for escape. Discovering the kidnapped woman ratchets the complications for undercover agent Brett Davis. Weighing the difference of ruining his three months' investigation against the woman's safety, Brett forsakes his mission and helps her escape the bent-on-revenge brutes following behind. When Mary Wade's safety is threatened once more, Brett rescues her again. This time, her personal safety isn't the only thing in jeopardy. Her heart is endangered as well.

Rescued Hearts by Hope Tyler Dougherty.

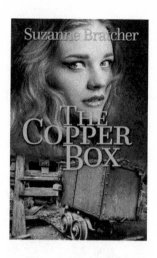

The lives of antiques expert Marty Greenlaw and historian Paul Russell become intertwined when an old lady dies on a long staircase in a vintage Victorian house. As Marty and Paul search the house for a small copper box Marty believes will unlock the mystery, accidents begin to happen. Someone else wants the copper box—someone willing to commit murder to get it. As Marty and Paul face the shadows in the house and in their lives, they must learn to put the past behind them and run the race God is calling them to.

The Copper Box by Suzanne J. Bratcher

Stay up-to-date on your favorite books and authors with our free e-newsletters.

mantlerockpublishingllc.com

facebook.com/mantlerockpbulishing

CPSIA information can be obtained
at www.ICGtesting.com
Printed in the USA
FSHW011208080519
57956FS